A Twist of Fate

BELINDA BENNA

Vinci Books

vinci-books.com

Published by Vinci Books Ltd in 2026

1

A CIP catalogue record for this book is available from the British Library.
Paperback ISBN: 9781036727369
The EU GPSR authorised representative is Logos Europe, 9 rue Nicolas Poussion, 17000 La Rochelle, France contact@logoseurope.eu

By Belinda Benna

Halifax Harbor Hospital

A Glimmer of Hope

A Twist of Fate

Miracle Glow

Love and Other Dreams

The Dreams We Share

The Sky We Seek

The Colors We Desire

The Dance We Remember

The Stars We Chase

Marie & Lukas

Promise Me

Show me the Stars

By Belinda Benna

All I Need

Every Step I Take

Foreword

I researched the medical aspects of this story with care and diligence; numerous specific details have been reviewed by medical professionals.

That said, we're all human, and despite best efforts it's conceivable that some inaccuracies remain or have been unintentionally left in. If you find any, I'd be happy to hear from you so I can correct them.

I wish you many gripping, moving and heart-felt hours of reading at the Halifax Harbor Hospital!

Yours,

Belinda

Trigger Warning

A Twist of Fate contains potentially triggering content. Readers are advised that some scenes may be considered disturbing.

Prologue

SONORA

I always knew that the rug I'd swept my past under might one day lift in the winds of fate. But that it would happen here, of all places—in Halifax Harbor Hospital—I never would have believed.

My chest tightens. I don't want to do it. I don't want to see the shards I've so carefully buried.

But there they are.

Right before my mind's eye.

In them, I see myself—and I know that telling the truth is my only chance to shake Ethan awake. It will save him. But at the same time, it will take away everything he's ever held dear.

He'll never forgive me for it.

You're going to lose him, Mom whispers inside me, heavy with meaning.

"Yes," I say tonelessly, my eyes fixed on the door he just walked through, because I know it's true. "No matter what I do, I'm going to lose Ethan."

Thick tears well up in my eyes, tracing cold, wet paths

down my cheeks before falling from my jaw like they're dropping off a cliff into nothingness.

I'd rather jump into the darkness with you than stand in the sunlight without you. Those were Ethan's words, back when neither of us knew that we would never have either one.

And suddenly, it's no longer about whether we can keep our jobs or save our love from falling apart. Because both are utterly impossible.

There's only one thing left I can do right: I can save Ethan's life—and that's exactly what I should do. Even if it means each of us will leap into our own darkness. Because that thing we were searching for together, that one destiny shining for both of us—it doesn't exist.

Chapter One

SONORA

Three and a half weeks earlier

When life deals you a bad hand, you have two options: you either surrender to your fate and fold before the game even begins, or you bluff until you win.

I've been bluffing for years—because stopping would mean ending up right back where it all started.

That can never happen.

Not even now, as the carefree laughter of my roommates June and Nyla drifts from the living room behind me while I step into the hallway, my heart pounding. The smell of the spinach pizza, which I had deliberately smeared into the ends of my hair just to have an excuse to leave the room, clings to my nose. Five minutes ago, it was delicious—now it makes me nauseous.

Lips pressed tightly together, I glance around at the chaos of moving boxes, a jumble of mismatched shoes, and half-assembled furniture.

Where did Nyla just say she left the mail?

There. On the box labelled *Kitchen*.

My nausea worsens as I reach for the mail.

Before I can go through the stack, the front door of our newly established shared apartment swings open. Olive—whom the four of us cheekily call our Glamour Lady—sweeps in on high heels. A delicate fragrance, as subtly elegant as she is herself, surrounds her.

"Oh dear," she says, eyeing my pizza hair and setting her shopping bags down on one of the boxes.

Dior. Gucci. Valentino. At the sight of the logos on Olive's shopping bags, a flurry of numbers instantly adds up in my head to a dizzying total. Still, I flash her a cheeky grin.

"Don't you think the green of the spinach goes perfectly with the dark brown of my hair?" I strike a model pose, then gesture toward the bathroom door behind her. "I'll clean it up real quick. The others are in the living room." Or rather, in our future living room, because at the moment, "construction site" is probably the more fitting term.

"Alright, see you in a bit." She smooths out her already wrinkle-free Marlene Dietrich trousers and turns to leave, then pauses. "Did we already get mail?"

My heart skips a beat. "Just ads."

"Let me see, maybe there's something interesting in there."

"Don't tell me you secretly shop at discount stores," I reply, hoping to distract her, and raise an eyebrow suggestively.

"Hey, Olive, we're in the living room!" I suddenly hear Nyla call out.

Olive furrows her brow in confusion. I point to her high heels. "You're kind of hard to miss," I say with a mischievous smile and disappear into the bathroom with the mail before she can ask me again.

Relieved, I close the door behind me and listen outside. A few clicks of high heels. Cheerful greetings. Laughter.

Thank God.

I exhale all the air that had built up inside me over the past few seconds. Then I turn to the mail.

Needlessly, my fingers tremble as I reach for the flyer on top. Even if the letter is in there today, it's not a big deal at all.

Beneath the flyer, I find a fashion magazine that Olive definitely subscribed to. Followed by…

There it is.

Fuck.

I just needed two more weeks—nothing more—they could've given me that.

But the fact that they sent the letter isn't even the biggest problem, because the envelope doesn't just bear my bank's logo—across the address field, the words Final Notice are emblazoned in oversized capital letters.

For a moment, I close my eyes. "Dear God, please let Nyla not have seen this letter when she picked up the mail," I whisper pleadingly, because that would make something I totally have under control and that's absolutely unimportant look like the exact opposite.

If my roommates find out I'm broke, they'll start asking questions. And even if I stay quiet, they'll look at me in that certain way. The one I swore I'd never have to see on anyone's face again.

I tuck the chemistry textbook under my arm and grab my bag. There's no need to check the time—I already know I have to hurry.

"Hey, Sonora, wait up," Chris calls after me.

"Gotta run," I reply, striding toward the classroom door, one hand protectively holding the dangerously torn strap of my bag.

He catches up to me. "There's a party at the pier later. It'd be cool if you..." He lowers his gaze awkwardly, his fingers fidgeting nervously. "It's a Valentine's Day party for... um..."

"Couples," I finish his sentence and immediately bite my tongue.

He's been trying to ask me out all school year, and every time it breaks my heart to turn him down—even though I think he's sweet.

He nods hopefully. "I thought maybe we could... only if you want to, of course..."

Hurting him is the last thing I want. Still, I shake my head. "I can't today," I say, trying to keep my voice light.

His disappointment is written all over his face. He tugs at his Burlington sweater. "Okay, maybe another time then."

I wish it were possible, but that day will never come.

"Mhm," I say, pointing to the oversized clock on the wall. "I have to go, sorry."

I wave to him and make my way as quickly as possible to my rusty VW van, which I parked today a few blocks from the high school in front of a hardware store.

It doesn't have central locking, so I fish the key out of my jeans pocket and insert it into the lock of the sliding door behind the driver's seat. Just to be safe, I glance around before opening it.

No one's watching me. That's good.

In a flash, I slip into the van, close the door, and switch on the small lamp, since barely any light makes it through the cardboard I've taped over the windows.

My waitress uniform lies on the mattress, next to a stack of medical textbooks from the library and the bag where I collect my dirty laundry. I change at record speed, tie my hair into a ponytail, and grab the bright pink cap.

As I slide the van door open with a flourish, I suddenly spot Chris.

He's standing less than two meters in front of me. With my scarf in hand, he peers over my shoulder into the van.

Great. "What are you doing here?"

"You forgot this," he says, handing me the scarf without looking at me. Instead, his eyes are fixed on my van.

I wish I were tall enough to stand in front of the bus and hide all its flaws. The rusty spots, the chipped paint, the dents.

Seconds of silence pass.

"So, uh…" he says, nervously running a hand through his hair.

"Yeah, I live in that bus," I say with a casual shrug, trying to make the situation easier for him. "It's a pretty awesome life, so full of freedom." The nights aren't cold at all and it's really no problem to find a new parking spot every few days, preferably close to the last one so I don't waste too much gas getting there. "A boring apartment wouldn't be for me." With electricity, running water, a fridge, and parents. Who needs all that anyway?

I watch as his body slowly tenses up. "Do you have a bathroom in there?"

"Of course," I lie, even though I know it wouldn't make a difference if he found out I shower at the gym. It's going to happen anyway.

Yeah, it's starting.

He looks down at the ground.

And now his gaze starts at my shoes and slowly travels upward.

He sees the holes in my sneakers—maybe he's really noticing them for the first time. Just like the frayed hem of my uniform. The faded T-shirt. Now he realizes I'm not wearing any jewelry. Not on my fingers, not on my wrists, not around my neck.

He wonders why he never noticed before. How he couldn't see that I'm not the princess he thought I was, but a damn Cinderella.

And now he's relieved I kept turning him down, so he doesn't have to be ashamed of his penniless girlfriend.

I take a deep breath to brace myself for what's about to happen next.

Here we go.

He looks at me. With that pitying expression people give a stray cat limping down the street, looking for something to eat.

That's exactly how he's looking at me. Even though the beat-up VW van behind me is just the tip of the iceberg.

Time to shut this down before he gets any ideas about asking uncomfortable questions.

"I'd really love to treat you to an espresso from my Black Luk," I say as smoothly as if I actually had the most expensive coffee machine in the world in my van. "But I've got to run. Rain check, okay?"

He looks away, embarrassed. "Okay."

I hadn't thought about that in ages—and even now, I shouldn't be, as I continue to stare at the bank letter in the bathroom of our shared apartment.

Chris never asked me out again, nor did he mention the espresso I'd promised him. Instead, from that day on, he and his friends looked at me with that one particular expression. Just like everyone else in my life who knew more about me than they should have.

As if poverty were all I was. As if I had no goals, no hopes, no dreams.

"Bullshit," I mutter bitterly. I *am* more than that, and I *have* more than that. So much more.

Determined, I fold the letter and slip it into the back pocket of my overalls. Then I tug down the neckline of my T-shirt and look in the mirror.

The tips of the butterfly's wings on my sternum peek out. I trace the lines of the tattoo with my index finger.

"We'll get through this together, Sonnygirl," I hear Mom whisper. *No, I'll get through this. On my own*, I answer silently, because that's the way it is.

"Pull yourself together," I tell the woman with the dark eyes, whose thick lashes finally stop fluttering. "You're a surgeon, you're starting your new job at Halifax Harbor Hospital tomorrow night, and in two weeks you'll be able to make your loan payments again."

She nods with resolve and lifts the corners of her mouth.

This is so much better than before. This woman is me.

I rinse the pizza crumbs out of the ends of my hair and step into the living room a little later. Autumn is home by now. She's just stuffing something that looks like an employment contract into her overflowing book bag. Her long red hair falls into her face.

"I think I've had enough pizza for today," I say, pressing both hands to my stomach as if pizza were the only thing weighing on it.

Nyla's gaze flicks to me, and I immediately try to read her brown doe eyes to see if she noticed the warning about my student loan from the bank when she dropped the mail off in the hallway earlier. Is that pity in her expression? Does she look at me a second too long?

Even if I don't know for sure, I want to believe that my secret is still safe as I settle onto one of the moving boxes I'd already used as a stool earlier. Autumn makes herself comfortable on the not-so-clean floor, sitting cross-legged. Nyla studies the food options, absentmindedly playing with her oversized earrings. Olive pushes aside the clear plastic cover on the couch and pats the seat cushion before sitting down. June, the fifth member of the group, smirks as she lets down her ponytail, making her look even more like Barbie than she already does.

None of my four roommates really know me. None of them will ever find out who I truly am or what I've done. For a split second, I wonder if the others are hiding something too. If they also have a rug under which a past lies buried—one they'd never uncover at any cost.

I quickly shake off these unnecessarily complicated thoughts. Everything is perfectly fine.

The five of us are not only going to crush this shared apartment life, but also our new jobs, which we're starting tomorrow at Halifax Harbor Hospital. Each of us will be working in a different department, but we all have one thing in common: we'll be doing it with the same wide grin on our faces.

"You know what?" June, who managed to snag a trial contract for the highly coveted specialist position in the diagnostics department, lets her gaze wander around the room.

"Wha?" Autumn asks with her mouth full.

A warm smile spreads across June's face. "I think this is going to be amazing," she says, voicing exactly what I'm thinking too.

Chapter Two

ETHAN

When a heart stops beating, the body is flooded with a cocktail of endorphins, serotonin, and dopamine, which means that every person leaves this world in a state of absolute bliss.

But when a heart is *only* emotionally wounded—deeply, but still beating—it's a completely different story.

That's not a guess.

I know it from personal experience.

The engine of my Harley vibrates against my thighs, the wind brushing across my neck. Dense forests rush past me at breakneck speed, and the skyline of Halifax emerges on the horizon. I lean into the curve, breathe in the sensation of weightlessness, feel life pumping through my veins from my broken heart.

Feel my wound.

The sound of waves.

I let it rise inside me, want it to consume me as I focus intently on the road ahead. I keep accelerating until I reach the city gates. Hear the tide. Breathe in the pain.

Salt on my tongue. Sand between my toes.

Traffic grows heavier, and I weave my way through it, but soon have to stop at a traffic light. Impatiently, I rev the engine while staring at the red light, feeling the memory pulsing through my veins.

The light turns green, and I shoot forward, heading straight for the harbor, next to which stands the Halifax Harbor Hospital. I force myself to look at the water as I pass the docks. Force myself to notice the rocking of the waves.

A piercing scream.

The way the screams in my head grow louder and louder—that's exactly right. That's how it has to feel.

But when I reach the hospital parking lot, they fall silent. I turn off the engine. My jaw clenches as I pull off my helmet, shrug off my leather jacket, and smooth the blazer I'm wearing underneath.

The rescue siren.

I lift my gaze to the clinic's glass façade, check my tie knot first, then my cufflinks. I'm finally here. Brimming with anticipation, I walk toward the entrance.

Bitter sobbing.

The spacious lobby is a whirlwind of activity. Patients, doctors, and nurses scurry across the gleaming tile floor. Carts rattle. Phones ring. All of it blends with the turmoil churning inside me.

Next to a lounge furnished with red chairs stands Dr. Roberts, the hospital's chief physician. Everything about him reminds me of a brown bear: the burly build, the full beard, even the lumbering way he approaches me. "Dr. Stone, welcome," he says, extending his hand. Laugh lines form around his eyes, and his expression is warm.

I return his firm handshake. "I'm happy to be here." All

my life, I've never wanted to work anywhere but this hospital. Here, where—on that day more than twenty years ago—my dream of becoming a doctor first began.

We need a doctor, quick!

"The pleasure's all ours." He nods toward the elevators. "Shall we?"

On the way to the second floor, I check my hair, even though the short cut doesn't allow a single strand to be out of place.

Dr. Roberts gives me a smile. "We'll start with a brief introduction. The staff is already waiting for you. But I should warn you."

I raise my eyebrows. "Afraid of what?"

"Well, you're joining a tightly knit team." He clears his throat. "Some might have trouble adjusting to new input."

"As long as they do their job, there won't be any problems." Whether they like me or not is irrelevant. Our work matters. It's the only thing that truly counts.

My boss pats me on the shoulder. "That's exactly what I wanted to hear."

No sooner has he spoken the words than the elevator stops. The doors slide open, and I follow my boss into the surgical ward, where a large group of staff has gathered.

In my team's faces, I see guardedness, skepticism, and rejection.

Dr. Roberts claps his hands to get everyone's attention. "Ladies and gentlemen, I'm very pleased to introduce your new department head and senior physician: Dr. Ethan Stone."

Obligatory applause follows. The nurse with the messy bun twists her lips into an annoyed pout. A blonde woman in jeans and a T-shirt stares at me provocatively with piercing blue eyes.

"We're thrilled to welcome a top surgeon to our team. A rare talent you won't find anywhere else in Canada," my new boss continues.

As he sings my praises—my excellent degree, my rapid career progression, and my outstanding expertise in cardiac surgery—the pain returns, hot and all-consuming.

A piercing scream.

It echoes inside me, filling even the darkest corners of my being.

This is how it's meant to be. This is how I can be the best version of myself.

"Dr. Stone, if you would, please." With a sweeping gesture, the boss beckons me over.

"Gladly." I step forward and lift my chin. Unfazed by the wall of coldness radiating from my team, I smile. "I'm excited to be here and to turn this surgical department into a flagship unit together with all of you."

The woman with the piercing blue eyes lets out a sigh, another glances at her watch.

The memory pulses inside me.

An engine roars. Blue lights flash.

"To make that possible, I expect top performance from each and every one of you," I continue, and immediately hear someone gasp. I lock eyes with the nurse wearing the messy bun, most likely the culprit, because this is no game. "Mistakes are something I cannot and will not tolerate."

Suddenly, everything goes dead silent.

"I don't care in the slightest what you think of me. I'm not here to win anyone over." I pause, letting my words sink in. "I'm here to save lives."

That is my mission.

That's all I want.

"And if I get the impression that any one of you isn't

here at Halifax Harbor Hospital every day for that same reason, I won't tolerate it." Yes, it's harsh. But that's life. It doesn't offer second chances—we all have to give our best every single moment. "This is a hospital. What we do determines life or death."

Some staff members nod, others exchange conspiratorial glances. I shove my hands into the pockets of my suit pants and start pacing in front of the team.

"When I expect top performance from you, it's not about racking up accolades for the department, and certainly not for you—or, God forbid, for me," I say firmly. "It's about our patients." I look each employee directly in the eyes. "I won't tolerate anyone going rogue. Every surgery is to be discussed with me, every treatment approved by me in advance."

"How is that supposed to work?" someone suddenly calls out from the crowd, though I can't tell who it was.

"By being reachable for you at all times through the on-call senior physician's phone," I reply calmly. "And when I say at all times, I mean twenty-four hours a day, seven days a week, fifty-two weeks a year."

A murmur spreads through the room. "Does he even have a private life?" I hear a woman whisper.

I don't. And I don't need one. "My work is my life," I answer, even though the question wasn't directed at me.

They didn't see that coming. They probably thought I'd expect top performance from them while I spent my weekends leisurely playing golf.

I'm not that kind of senior physician.

And I never will be.

"Any more questions?" I raise my eyebrows. "Go ahead," I add when no one responds, and suddenly I'm met with nothing but lowered eyes.

Some pretend to study the files in their hands, others seem to be inspecting the floor for stains. Even the blonde, who had been locked in a tense staring contest with me until now, suddenly has to pluck a loose thread from her shirt.

Dr. Roberts nods approvingly.

"My door is always open if you have questions or need help. You'll find my address and all my phone numbers on the bulletin board in the doctors' lounge." I don't know if they believe me or if they actually understood what I just told them. But soon they will—I'm sure of it.

A nurse clutches a patient file to her chest; the colleague beside her fiddles with the box of rubber gloves.

"Good. Then let's get to work," I say to the group. "We've got a lot to do."

Chapter Three

SONORA

Wearing blue scrubs, I'm crouched on the low bench in the center of the locker room. Supposedly, someone was supposed to pick me up for my first shift, but I've been waiting for half an hour now.

I lower my gaze to my bright white sneakers and wiggle my toes inside the leather.

They cost me thirty-five dollars, but I had no choice. The old ones were just too beat up. Still, the guilt gnaws at me. Mostly because I didn't manage to speak with my bank advisor today to request a deferral on my loan payments. I had no choice but to open an account at another bank and max it out immediately, just to make at least one payment.

Now I'm in debt to two banks. But at least I no longer have a student loan that's come due and requires a new creditor. And in two weeks, I'll get my first paycheck. Things will start looking up from there.

The door swings open and a colleague rushes toward me. She looks older than I am, maybe in her early forties. Her cheeks are flushed bright red, her chin-length blonde hair is a mess, and her piercing blue eyes are glowing. She looks like she just ran a marathon.

"You must be Sonora. Hi, I'm Claire, deputy head of surgery. Sorry I'm late—an acute appendicitis case came in… which turned out not to be one after all." She shakes her head, baffled. "Really strange, the appendix was perfectly fine, even though all the symptoms… Well, anyway, I hope you'll forgive me."

I wave it off. "No problem."

"Alright, let's get started." She puts her hands in the pockets of her lab coat and nods toward the exit.

We leave the locker room. "What's first on the agenda?"

"Post-operative monitoring." She gestures for me to follow her. As we walk down the hallway lit by fluorescent lights, she explains where everything is and who the key contacts on the ward are.

"You'll find the patient files here at the nurses' station," she says, stepping up to the semicircular counter to pick up a few charts. With the folders tucked under her arm, she gives me a probing look. "I'm sure you know how to talk to the nursing staff, right?"

"Everyone on the ward does an important job—no one's better or worse," I reply, catching myself wishing that were just as true outside these walls.

Claire nods approvingly and hands me some of the files. "Basically true, but…" She lowers her voice. "That doesn't apply to our new boss. Be careful around him."

That doesn't sound good. "What about him?"

She immediately rolls her eyes. "The chief physician and the board made a huge mystery out of the new guy, so naturally I was curious. So curious, in fact, that I came in this morning during my time off just to watch his inaugural speech."

"Okay…" I have a feeling this is heading nowhere good.

"You should've seen him standing there. In his tailored suit, perfectly styled hair, and that disgustingly flawless toothpaste smile. Like he's a model, not a doctor. And he's only thirty-seven—way too young to be a senior physician," she continues. "He's a total ego pig, it's so obvious."

Ego pig? Great. "And then?"

Her expression turns disgusted. "Once you meet him, you'll know exactly what I mean. During his speech today, he really showed his true colors." Holding the medical files, she quickens her pace. A nurse approaches us from the opposite direction; we greet each other with a nod. "When he said he wouldn't tolerate mistakes and expected top performance, it was all clear."

And what happens if someone makes a mistake? That's the question that immediately pushes to the surface, but I'm definitely not going to ask it. It would make me seem worried—weak, somehow—and that's not an option. So I just snort in disdain as we pass through a deserted area with plastic chairs and a floor-to-ceiling window, next to which stands a rubber plant.

"Then he just claimed the on-call senior physician's phone for himself—and permanently, even when he's not at the hospital." Bitterness laces her words. "As if he's the only one capable of doing a good job, as if he were God himself."

Ugh.

"Anyway, our Dr. Perfect will learn soon enough that things work differently at Halifax Harbor Hospital."

"And how do things work here?" I ask—after all, I need to get everything right.

"Collegially," she replies. "Since I started here fourteen

years ago, we've always stuck together. We're a team—we protect and support each other."

"Got it." I smile at her, relieved. Maybe our boss is an asshole, but as long as the team stands strong, he's fighting a losing battle and my job is safe. Hopefully.

To steer my thoughts in a more pleasant direction, I glance around. "Which patient are we starting with?"

Claire opens the top patient file from her stack. "P010324-049, Room 208, bilateral hernioplasty."

That's what we should focus on. I take the file from her with determination. "When did the inguinal surgery take place?"

"This afternoon, no complications."

I look up to find the door. "Good, then we'll check the dressing and the wound, and make sure the pain medication is dosed correctly."

My enthusiasm earns me a wrinkled nose from Claire. "If you keep this up, you'll be Dr. Perfect's favorite in no time," she comments in a tone that tells me she'd hate me for it.

Whether I'm his favorite or not doesn't matter to me. I just want to keep this job. I laugh like she's made a really good joke, then nudge her. "Come on, the patient's waiting."

Before we reach the door to Room 208, Claire's pager beeps. She pulls it from the waistband of her pants. "Code blue."

"A missing person?" I glance around—the hallway seems calm.

Claire hurries off. "Code blue means surgical emergency."

Oh. At my last job, it meant something else. I should've known the Halifax Harbor Hospital has its own codes.

"Understood." As I pass by, I toss my patient files onto the nurses' station counter and hurry with Claire into the stairwell.

Not two minutes later, we dive into the chaos of the emergency room, where even at night the phones are ringing off the hook and the waiting room is packed with patients. I gasp for air as Claire, on the way to intake, grabs two disposable gowns and hands me one. She moves so effortlessly that I'm once again reminded of my poor physical condition.

"What's going on?" she calls to the tall man with the headset, who seems to be coordinating everything, while I tear open the plastic wrapping of my gown.

He gestures toward the wide double doors leading outside. "Acute abdomen. Arrival in…" His eyes flick to the clock, and a split second later I hear the siren wail. Blue lights flash behind the door's glass panels. "…one minute."

"Got it," Claire and I say in unison. My disposable gown nearly tears as I pull it on in a rush.

This is my first case. My first chance to prove what I'm capable of.

The siren grows louder, the blue lights brighter.

I fumble two rubber gloves from the wall-mounted box, put on my safety goggles, and run with Claire to the door. We take our positions on either side, and I slip the gloves on.

Brakes screech.

Blue light flickers across the white wall.

Hurried instructions.

Metallic scraping.

Footsteps.

Claire nods at me.

I mirror her gesture.

The door bursts open, and along with the cool night air, my first case at Halifax Harbor Hospital sweeps in.

Chapter Four

ETHAN

I wedge the phone between my ear and shoulder. "Ethan Stone, how can I help you?" I greet the unknown caller and walk toward my cabin. The lamp above the front door switches on, casting a soft glow over the night. The many maple trees sway in the wind, and the pebbles in front of the porch glisten dully.

"Dr. Wells here," says a woman's voice.

"Who?" I fish my house key out of my pocket. The light jingling drowns out the ever-present chirping of crickets.

The caller clears her throat. "Dr. Sonora Wells. I'm part of your team, currently assigned to the night shift, and I need your approval."

Direct. Clear. Confident. And apparently a team member I haven't met before.

"What have you got?" I lower my hand without unlocking the door. My full attention is on Dr. Wells.

"Male, thirty-seven, with severe abdominal pain," she replies matter-of-factly. "Diagnosis: perforated gastric ulcer."

"CT scan?" I lean against the door.

"In your inbox."

Wow.

For a split second, I'm so surprised that I'm at a loss for words. Either she was given a stern warning about me, or she's simply professional—which can't be said for her colleagues, as my first day on the job made abundantly clear.

"Good," I say, taking the phone from my ear and switching to speaker mode. "I'll take a look right away."

I quickly open my email program. It takes a moment to find her message in the overflowing inbox.

"Are you in the woods or something?" my colleague suddenly asks.

"No," I reply reflexively and tap on the message. The call of an owl echoes in the distance.

"Mhm," Dr. Wells comments knowingly, and I could swear I hear her chuckle.

Which, of course, is impossible. Confused, I shake my head and take a closer look at the CT scan. "We need to close this perforation." No doubt about it.

She confirms my assessment, and we go over the details of the surgery. Our exchange is so smooth and natural that I'm almost disappointed when the conversation starts winding down shortly afterward.

"Keep me updated, especially if any unforeseen complications arise."

"Okay, Dr. Stone, will do," she replies cheekily. "Good night."

I say goodbye and slip the phone back into my jacket pocket.

"Dr. Sonora Wells…," I murmur, still impressed by the energy she had just radiated.

Mhm, she now adds in my thoughts, just to top it all off, and once again I imagine I can hear her chuckling.

"No, you don't." I touch my temples, knowing it's just the exhaustion from my far too long workday playing tricks on me. Yawning, I unlock the door and step into my cabin.

Darkness envelops me.

And silence.

Silence.

It's the kind of silence that marks the end of everything. The silence after which nothing is ever the same again.

It suffocates me.

I quickly turn on the light and walk through the loft-like space that combines the living room, dining room, and kitchen. My destination is the old record player. I switch on the turntable and place the needle on the record.

"Is this the real life?" comes the four-part harmony from the speakers. "Is this just fantasy?" I sing along and close my eyes. Then, just before the piano melody takes over, I turn up the volume knob.

Bohemian Rhapsody by Queen floods my cabin, the bass vibrating in my chest. With a deep breath, I lift my far-too-heavy eyelids and look at the photo wall behind the record player.

I smile at my favorite picture of Liam—the one where he's sticking out his tongue and making a silly face. Next to it hangs the photo of him with his surfboard.

In an instant, my thoughts are back there.

At that beach.

On that one day that changed my life forever.

Waves crashing.

"You coming, Ethan?" Liam's voice sounds far away.

I don't look over, too busy getting lost in the eyes of the blonde girl who's seductively licking her popsicle.

"Ethan! The waves are perfect. Come on."

God, she's hot. "So, what brings you here?" I ask her.

She lets her gaze wander across the beach, the increasingly stormy wind tugging at the beach towel we're sitting on. "I'm into surfers," she replies.

"Is that so." I give a pointed tap on my new surfboard lying beside me in the sand. "And what else are you into?"

"Ethan!" my brother yells again.

The girl tosses her hair back. "I think you should go to him."

No way. "He can manage without me."

Right on cue, Liam calls out to me again. Out of the corner of my eye, I see him trudging through the sand toward us, his sun-yellow surfboard tucked firmly under his arm, wet hair clinging to his face.

The girl grins. "Your brother's hot," she says, and I can't help but grin too—after all, Liam and I are identical twins.

I lean in toward her. "Is he now?"

She moistens her lips. "Totally."

"Come on already." Liam sounds damn close.

Damn, I can't go. If the blonde disappears while Liam and I are in the water, I can't risk it. Not before she at least gives me her number.

I turn to face my brother. Leaning on his board, he shifts impatiently from one foot to the other.

"Go on ahead, I'll catch up." My expression tells him I've got something seriously important going on here.

Chewing on his lower lip, he lets his gaze wander back and forth between me and the blonde. Next to the sun-yellow of his board, he looks like a raincloud. "Ooooookay," he says at last, and thankfully takes off.

I try not to hear the disappointment in his voice. And not to think about the fact that this afternoon was supposed to be for both of us. We got our new boards yesterday for our sixteenth birthday and couldn't wait to try them out.

But now, well, now thanks to the blonde girl, I feel like it can wait a little longer.

"So, you're into surfers," I pick up the conversation from earlier and give her a crooked smile.

"Hot surfers," she corrects me with a look that makes my hormones go absolutely insane.

The wind picks up, and I move closer to her. "Are you cold?"

"A little." She's lying—I can see it in her eyes.

But I don't care. She's welcome to lie to me if it means I get to sit this close and wrap my arm around her.

Damn, this woman smells amazing…

Dazed, I close my eyes. Everything feels so far away. The beach. The sea. The sound of the waves. The screams.

"Will you tell me your name?" I gently stroke her upper arm.

She lets her head sink onto my shoulder, her hair brushing against my neck. "You have to guess."

I barely register the commotion stirring around us. "Kristin?"

The blonde giggles. "You think I look like a Kristin?"

"I think you look like the next Mrs. Stone," I reply, without thinking twice.

Her laughter blends with a piercing scream. I feel warm and cold at the same time.

"What was that?" I tear my eyes away from her and see people rushing toward the shore, a lifeguard diving into the water with his rescue buoy.

Something has happened.

I get up, scanning the horizon for whatever it is everyone else seems to see. "What the hell…"

There's nothing.

Only the waves breaking out on the sandbar and rolling forcefully toward the beach, a few surfers lying on their boards and—wait a second—they're all paddling toward the same spot.

The same spot the lifeguard is heading for.

Instinctively, my eyes dart between the surfers. Around me, hushed murmurs begin to rise.

"Where's Liam?" A cold shiver runs down my spine, followed by another as I reach the last surfer without spotting him. "Where is he?"

The next wave rises, crashes—and tosses a surfboard into the air.

It's sunshine yellow.

Suddenly, my heart stops.

Silence.

I can hear, all too clearly, the sound of my breath leaving my open mouth. Panic fills the silence.

Then I start running, screaming.

My own screams echo inside me as I continue staring at Liam's photo.

"Nothing really matters to me," Freddie Mercury sings in the background. The piano music fades, growing softer until it disappears completely.

Silence.

There is no pain. No guilt.

I don't feel a thing—and I hate it.

"I'm so sorry," I whisper, trying to fill the silence inside me with the darkness that keeps my heart beating. As the intro of the next song begins to play, I turn away. I channel the torment flaring up in me once again into what matters most: work.

With a cappuccino from my Black-Luk coffee machine, I settle into the wingback chair next to the bookshelf and open my work bag.

There was simply too much chaos at the clinic today, so I brought the staff files home to continue familiarizing myself. I haven't met some of the employees in person yet. Dr. Jake Avens, for example, but his file doesn't interest me at the moment. What I'm far more eager to learn about is this Dr. Wells from earlier. I sift through the stack until I find her documents.

"Dr. Sonora Wells, there you are." With a mix of curiosity and tension, I open her file.

From the photo, a confident woman with an impressive mane of curls smiles back at me. The picture was taken in sunshine, yet something tells me this Dr. Wells would shine even if she were standing in the middle of a downpour.

My gaze lingers on the photo a little too long. I'm not exactly sure what it is that fascinates me in such a strange way. Maybe the dimples in her cheeks. Maybe the naturalness—she's wearing no makeup, no jewelry. Or is it her dark eyes, carrying something unfathomable within them?

Lost in thought, I take a sip of my coffee.

Is that ambition in her expression?

Mhm, she hums knowingly again in my mind. Accompanied by Freddie Mercury's voice, pleading intensely for somebody to love, I immerse myself in the file.

She's new, started today at Halifax Harbor along with me, and apparently volunteered for the night shift right away—that's unusual.

My gaze flicks back to her photo.

"Why the night shift?" I ask her.

Find out, her eyes reply, a mix of quick wit and amusement.

"I will."

The chair creaks as I shift my weight. I turn the page and studied her résumé. Unlike many others on the team, she hasn't studied in the U.S. She went to Dalhousie University, a fantastic school here in Halifax. Instinctively, I search her documents for her transcripts.

"Not bad, Miss Sunshine," I murmur, impressed by her perfect grades.

Lost in thought, I turn back to her résumé as the next song on the record begins to play.

After university, she must have spent some time abroad, and upon returning, worked at the Queen Elizabeth II Health Sciences Centre. And before college?

My gaze drifts downward.

She attended Halifax Grammar School in South End—a prestigious high school with an excellent reputation.

Interesting. She's clearly intelligent and went to an outstanding school. At the same time, something doesn't add up. If she's that smart, why didn't she end up where the elite study—at Harvard?

Did she perform poorly in high school?

I search her file for the relevant transcripts, but I can't find them. They probably got lost in the HR department.

I can't resist the urge to study her photo again. In this moment, I'm certain I can decipher the expression in her eyes: an unwavering kind of confidence and determination.

Even if her résumé leaves some questions unanswered, my gut tells me this woman could be the best on my team. I definitely need to keep an eye on her.

A smile creeps across my face as I continue to look at hers. "This is going to be interesting," I say, deciding to meet her in person as soon as possible. Then I close the file.

Only now do I notice that the music has long since stopped. I jump up to play the record again and get back to work.

Chapter Five

SONORA

I've never performed so many surgeries at night as I have at Halifax Harbor Hospital. This is my third shift, and once again, Claire and I have a complex case on the table. But I'll handle this one too—just like the perforated stomach ulcer on the first night shift and the appendix on the verge of bursting on the second.

I'm here to give it my best, and with every successful operation, I get one step closer to my goal.

Accompanied by the steady beeping of the heart monitor, I place the final screw that should stabilize the bone fragments of Autumn's young patient once and for all. The ventilator hisses, the valves click into place, and the next breathing cycle begins.

"Fluoroscopic check, please," I say, prompting an assistant to position the X-ray machine over the girl's fractured shinbone. I set the instruments aside. Together, we leave the OR while the imaging is in progress.

The images appear on the monitor. "That looks good. We'll check once more for bleeding, then close up."

I glance briefly at Claire, who nods in agreement and clearly yawns beneath her surgical mask. The hour hand on the clock behind her is approaching the big four.

"We should send the images to Dr. Stone for approval as well," I suggest, because after everything I've heard about him, that would probably be the wisest course.

"Right. Let's see if he's reachable this early in the morning." She signals to a nurse to make the call. "Put it on speaker."

The dial tone sounds.

Once. Twice…

"Ethan Stone."

Claire takes the call while I'm still wondering. How did he pick up so quickly? Is he still awake—or already awake again? He answered my call three days ago just as fast, even though it was shortly after midnight.

When does this man actually sleep?

"Check for bleeding and close up," Dr. Stone's voice booms through my thoughts, sounding so alert that I'm certain he hasn't slept.

I wonder what he's been doing instead?

"On it," Claire chirps, overly cheerful. "Thanks for the green light, boss."

"Of course. Feel free to call anytime if there are any issues," he replies obligingly and ends the call.

"Good thing he reminded us to check for bleeding, otherwise we might've totally forgotten," Claire says, rolling her eyes at me.

I nod. Whatever is behind his behavior, it's definitely not normal. "Then let's not disappoint him," I reply, focusing once more on the girl's broken leg.

An hour later, I sink into one of the chairs in the doctors' lounge and place today's patient files on the table just as my colleague Jake enters the room in surgical scrubs.

He tilts his head to the side, his brown hair falling over his forehead, where faint lines are beginning to show. "Coffee?"

"A ten-shot would be great," I reply with a yawn. This night shift was intense—good thing it's almost over.

The coffee machine hums to life, and the bitter aroma drifts across the room toward me.

Jake joins me with two cups in hand. His gaze flicks between me and my files. "Want some help? If Dr. Perfect finds mistakes in your notes, that could end badly for you."

There he is again, Dr. Perfect, who seems to haunt every corner without ever showing himself. It's slowly driving me crazy that I haven't met him yet. But that's about to change. I was supposed to be on the night shift again next week, but at the start of today's shift, I found out that—for whatever reason—tonight is my last one for now.

"Just a tip—he hates it when someone has illegible handwriting." Jake gives me a crooked grin.

I raise my eyebrows questioningly. "Seriously?"

"Didn't you hear he had a nurse fired yesterday?" Jake asks, fishing for drama.

No. And I don't even want to know that, let alone how quickly people get fired around here.

Oh God, I hope he didn't call me into the day shift just to fire me too! A control freak like him might've looked through my application documents and…

I feel sick.

Jake doesn't seem to notice how my stomach is tightening. "And she hadn't even broken a single hospital rule. It was just because he couldn't read her handwriting, which he claimed endangered patient safety."

This Dr. Perfect really does seem completely insane. "That's awful," I reply, opening the patient file with deliberate emphasis. "I should probably get started. Wouldn't want to get kicked out for making late entries." I make it sound like a joke, even though it's anything but.

If I lose this job too, I'm completely ruined.

"Sure." Jake smiles. "Let me know if you need any help."

"Thanks." Glad to focus on something other than Dr. Perfect, I turn my attention to the surgical report from the procedure I just performed. Out of the corner of my eye, I see Jake wander over to the sofa with his coffee and reach for the remote of the small TV.

As I note in my best handwriting that no further complications occurred during suturing, the wail of sirens and the thudding of helicopter rotors suddenly fill the doctors' lounge.

"Now to a breaking news report from downtown Halifax." A woman's voice echoes from the speaker.

Instinctively, I look up.

Images of a wild car chase flicker across the screen. A dark limousine swerves through the street in the helicopter's spotlight, slamming into parked cars, racing over the sidewalk. The anchorwoman, with short black hair, looks seriously into the camera. "Police are pursuing a fleeing jewel thief down Robie Street, heading out of the city. His rampage has already claimed at least five lives."

I'm instantly wide awake. I jump up from my chair and rush to the TV.

"Damn," Jake mutters in shock, leaning forward on the couch.

Mesmerized, I stare at the screen. My breath catches for a second as the police car clips the fugitive's vehicle from the side. The limousine's rear end skids out, and before I can make sense of what's happening, the car flips over with a loud crash. Ambulances and fire trucks race to the scene, the helicopter descends lower.

"The suspect appears to have been apprehended, ladies and gentlemen." The anchorwoman smiles in relief at the camera, then places a finger on the small earpiece through which she's apparently receiving live updates. Behind her, firefighters begin cutting open the driver's door of the wrecked car.

Eyes wide, the anchorwoman gasps and removes her finger from her ear. "It's just been confirmed that the jewel thief is Peter Blake!" Her voice rises.

"What?" Jake shakes his head. "The guy's worth millions and he robs a jewelry store? What the hell is wrong with him?"

"Hm," I murmur, puzzled, because I don't understand it either. But I know all too well that many people carry secrets inside them. Things that must never come to light. Wounds they wish more than anything had never existed.

"Always the rich—they're never satisfied," Jake growled.

At that moment, the paramedics pull the accident victim from the car. The man in the suit appears unconscious; one of the medics loosens his tie and immediately begins chest compressions.

"Wouldn't be a shame if he didn't make it," Jake mutters.

"Wouldn't be a shame if she didn't make it," echoes a deep voice from my past inside my head—one that has no business being here.

Shaking my head, I focus on the television.

"We've just learned that Mr. Blake is being transferred to Halifax Harbor Hospital." The anchor seems to regain her composure; at least her expression is once again cool and professional.

"Great," Jake snorts, clearly annoyed.

Not a second later, both our pagers go off at the same time. I don't need to look to know what mine sais: Code Blue.

Chapter Six

SONORA

My heart is pounding faster than it should as I lean against the waist-high wall of the rooftop terrace, eating the boiled potatoes I'd brought from home for breakfast.

There is absolutely no reason to be nervous—not the slightest one. And yet, the thought of meeting the boss today makes sweat bead in my palms.

I inhale the salty sea air drifting over from the harbor and tell myself again and again that everything is perfectly fine. Over the years, I've perfected this tactic, and even now I can feel how strong my protective shell is becoming.

I let the fork slide into the Tupperware and close my eyes for a moment. Seagulls screech, and the first rays of sunlight tickle my cheeks.

No matter what happens today. No matter how hard this Dr. Stone tries to make my life. I won't back down—I'll show him what I'm made of.

I force the corners of my mouth up into a smile with practiced ease. One more deep breath to relax and…

A sharp clatter makes me flinch.

My fork!

I quickly open my eyes—and spot a man crouching down in front of me. He's wearing a leather jacket that stretches over broad shoulders, paired with dark dress pants and elegant leather shoes. Now he reaches for my fork, the handle of which is peeking out between the dark gray concrete slabs.

"I've got it," I say quickly, dropping to my knees.

A split second later, we both reach for the fork at the same time. Our fingers touch, and a tiny jolt of electricity sparks at my fingertip.

"Oh," we say in unison, and for a moment, it feels like his voice echoes in my chest along with the electric shock.

I lift my eyelids.

His face is so close to mine that I can see every detail. His hair is the color of Lawrencetown Beach: a warm brown with golden highlights that shimmer in the morning sun. In his green eyes, I notice tiny flecks of brown. His clean-shaven, angular jawline—like his narrow nose—is so symmetrical that I have to look twice to believe this man is real.

"Here you go," he says.

Still dazed from the jolt, I frown. "Hm?"

He nods toward his hand, and my gaze follows. Even his hands are flawless. Perfect fingers holding my fork. I catch myself staring at those fingers—which is still better than staring at his face.

"Um… thanks," I say, taking the fork from him and standing up so fast I get a little dizzy. I quickly snap the Tupperware lid shut before he gets the idea to ask why I'm having plain potatoes for breakfast.

He pushes himself up from his crouch and takes a step back. "Dr. Wells, right?"

How does he know my name? Instinctively, I search for the answer, and the moment I catch a glimpse of a tie knot peeking out from behind the zipper of his leather jacket, the breath catches in my throat.

Perfect face.

Surgeon's hands.

Knows my name.

Shit, this must be Dr. Perfect. And he really lives up to the name. If he walked into my hospital room during rounds, I'd think I had accidentally wandered onto the set of Grey's Anatomy.

"Dr. Stone." I have no idea why, but I smile. Stupidly. It's a stupid smile.

"Someone's done their homework." When he smirks like that, he doesn't seem at all like the asshole he is. "Nice to finally meet you in person."

Should I offer him my hand? No. If he doesn't offer first —which he doesn't—then better not. A confident nod will have to do. "I've been looking forward to it as well," I reply without batting an eye.

He should know right away that I'm here to make something of myself, and that I'm not afraid of him—or anything else, for that matter.

His reaction lasts only a blink of an eye, but I catch it. The amused lift of his eyebrows, the flicker in his eyes.

A knowing "Mhm" escapes my lips. Now that it is out in the open, I have no choice but to meet his gaze while I slip the Tupperware and fork into my shoulder bag.

He looks at me inquisitively and stays silent for a moment, as if I have thrown him off track.

I like that.

A lot, actually.

"There's a meeting in the on-call room before today's

rounds," he says, shoving his hands into the pockets of his suit pants. "Go ahead. I'll be right behind you."

So he doesn't confront me—on the contrary, he seems reserved, his expression lacking the harshness he wis rumored to have.

Strange.

But not bad.

"Mhm." I give him a knowing grin that lingers a heartbeat too long, then head off. When I reach the heavy door to the hallway, I paused.

He has no more business being up here than I do. This isn't an official rooftop terrace, but a secluded spot where I can eat the meals I bring without having to face the inevitable questions that come with them.

How does he know about this place? And why did he come up here this morning?

Lost in thought, I walk down the plain corridor toward the elevators. I lift my chin and pull my shoulders back. Then I cast one last furtive glance at the door leading to the rooftop terrace and step into the elevator.

Once I arrive in the surgical department, I head toward the on-call room, which is already fairly crowded. Among several colleagues, I spot Jake and Claire, who both seem to have switched to the day shift at the same time as I did.

So Dr. Perfect didn't just change my schedule. Whatever that might mean, one thing is certain: the change has nothing to do with me personally, he doesn't want to fire me, and he definitely hasn't found out that my application was a complete lie.

Very good.

"Hi." I wave to Claire, who immediately signals me to come over. "What's this meeting about?" I ask once I reach her.

She rolls her eyes in boredom. "Probably the boss wants to set a minimum walking speed so we can be even more efficient."

Jake laughs and gently nudges Claire with his elbow.

"Good morning, ladies and gentlemen, glad you could make it," I hear Dr. Stone's commanding voice behind me before I can respond.

The room falls instantly silent. I turn around and look at him inquisitively.

The mischievous smirk I saw on the roof just moments ago is gone. He stands like a perfectly formed tree, unshaken by any storm. His suit is flawless, his expression professional down to the tips of his hair.

Slick as oil.

"Before we begin rounds, I'd like to make something clear." His gaze sweeps across the room. "I've heard that some of you have an issue with patient P060424-026, Peter Blake."

Out of the corner of my eye, I see Jake biting his lip. I know how he feels about Mr. Blake—we admitted him together in the early hours yesterday and transferred him to surgery for observation and further evaluation due to his enlarged aorta. Not for a single moment during treatment was Jake able to set aside his hatred. He was so caught up in his emotions that he couldn't make clear decisions.

Dr. Stone clears his throat. "Mr. Blake is a patient like any other. What he did, when, how, or why—it doesn't matter."

"That rich bastard has five deaths on his conscience because he robbed a jeweler for fun." It's Claire, surprisingly, who dares to interrupt the boss. "You have to understand that this affects us. We're only human, after all."

I can't help but study his reaction.

What's your next move, Dr. Perfect?

To my surprise, he smiles at Claire. It's a forced smile, full of coldness. "No, our patients are only human," he replies—and as unbelievable as it is, for a moment my heart skips a beat.

Did he really just say that? Did he take sides with a man who, in everyone else's eyes here, doesn't deserve anyone to speak up for him?

I don't want to, but I can feel all too clearly that I'm staring at him. His gaze flicks toward me, and I could swear he lets out a low "Mhm," even though his expression remains motionless.

Damn. Earlier on the roof, I thought I had impressed him, but now I'm starting to feel like that awkwardness might have been an act.

What kind of game is this man playing, anyway?

Next to me, Claire raises her hands in a calming gesture. "Don't worry, we're professionals. We'll treat Mr. Blake to the best of our knowledge and conscience."

Completely calm and unimpressed by Claire's forced demeanor, Dr. Stone leans against the wall. "That's not enough."

What is that supposed to mean now? Confused, I search his flawless face for clues, but find none.

"I expect more from you than just fulfilling your medical duty. More than just functioning," he continues.

It's fascinating how naturally he chooses his words. How he accepts the murmurs now spreading through the group without batting an eye.

He fixes his gaze intently on Claire. "I expect you not to see Mr. Blake as a patient you have to treat because it's your duty. But as a human being who deserves our help."

Wow.

That's all I can say. I can't believe he's standing up for someone most people would say doesn't deserve it. And even less can I comprehend what it's doing to me.

Dr. Stone raises his eyebrows expectantly. "Do you have any questions about this?"

Everyone stays silent. So do I.

"Very well. Then that's settled." He pushes up his shirt sleeve. "Dr. Avens, Dr. Walters, Dr. Wells, I'll see you promptly at seven o'clock for rounds."

Chapter Seven

ETHAN

Jake and Claire are whispering behind my back as our rounds reach Room 106. I shoot them a warning look over my shoulder; out of the corner of my eye, I notice that only Sonora looks focused. At least that's something.

I step up to the door, knock, and open it.

A police officer jumps up from the visitor's chair and nods at me. "I'll wait outside," he says, squeezing past Sonora, Jake, and Claire toward the door.

My gaze falls on our patient, who lies before me handcuffed to the bed, forcing a smile for us.

"Good morning, Mr. Blake." Many senior physicians don't take the time to greet their patients during rounds. They simply have their staff present the medical facts and make decisions. I never wanted to be that kind of doctor. "How are you feeling today?"

"It's hard to breathe," he replies.

With a gesture, I ask Jake to hand me the medical file and open it. "The wall of your aorta is enlarged near the heart. That's why you're feeling this pressure in your chest," I explain to him. "Has it worsened recently?"

"My heart?" His expression shifts to confusion, as if no one has explained the nature of his injuries to him.

Instinctively, I check the names of the staff who've already been in contact with him. Sonora and Jake handled the initial admission, during which they only suspected the aortic aneurysm. It's understandable—even good—that they didn't want to give a diagnosis without definitive test results. Claire appears to have entered the results of the ordered examination into the file. She should have informed the patient. I'll speak with her afterward, but for now, my focus should be on Mr. Blake.

"The aorta is your largest artery. It carries blood from the heart throughout the body," I explain to him.

Worry lines form on his forehead.

"Your artery is enlarged near the heart, which is why we've admitted you to surgery." I leaf through the medical file as Mr. Blake gives me a nod to show he understands. "Dr. Walters, what complications can arise from an aortic aneurysm?" I ask Claire matter-of-factly.

Claire surely knows the answer. She's not only the most senior and highest-ranking colleague on the round, but also my deputy. She doesn't need to answer check-up questions—that's usually the responsibility of the junior doctors.

Without looking at the patient, she clenches her fists.

Suddenly, Sonora steps forward. "Potential complications include tears or rupture of the aorta."

Assertive. Purposeful. Attentive. I like her. "Go on."

She brushes the wild curls from her pretty face and turns to our patient. "Not every aortic aneurysm requires surgery, but there are situations in which we have to intervene," she explains calmly to him. The fact that she's speaking to him instead of me pleases me even more. Is she doing it to impress me? "That's why Dr. Stone just asked whether the pressure in your chest has increased lately," she continues, while I search in vain for an answer to my question.

I sense that it's time for me to step back. I quietly observe the conversation between Sonora and Mr. Blake. I already suspected she was competent when I read her file. But she also seems to know how to handle patients.

The professional manner in which she encourages Mr. Blake to describe his symptoms in more detail. The ease with which she listens to his heartbeat with the stethoscope. How she closes her eyes to hear better. Her extraordinarily long lashes gently press together. There's a kind of… warmth emanating from her.

It's as if she's doing exactly what I asked everyone to do earlier. She sees our patient as someone who deserves our help, not as a bored millionaire who robs businesses and runs people over for fun.

Is that her true nature or a tactic to impress me? I know there are rumors circulating about me. It's obvious that Sonora has heard them.

Jake clears his throat quietly beside me. Out of the corner of my eye, I see him exchange a glance with Claire, who gives a barely noticeable shake of her head. Something about this brief moment makes me suspicious, but I can't quite put my finger on what it is.

"Thank you very much, Mr. Blake," I hear Sonora say in a soft voice. Carefully, she pulls his hospital gown back down and returns to me. "I suggest another ultrasound to check how the aneurysm has developed." Her eyes tell me she believes it has grown.

I silently let her know I understand and hand her the file. "Go ahead."

As she takes it, she smiles so warmly that dimples form in her cheeks. Charming dimples that, along with the bright sparkle in her eyes, feel strangely like a beam of light piercing through my chest.

I catch myself looking at her longer than necessary. Thinking about what it is that makes her such a... fascinating doctor.

"Do I need surgery?" Mr. Blake's question thankfully puts an end to this crazy moment.

"That's what Dr. Wells will determine," I reply, signaling to my team to follow me out of the room. I'd rather not look Jake and Claire in the face, but I force myself to. They need to understand that their behavior doesn't intimidate me. There's a mix of secrecy and suspicion coming from them—certainly toward our patient, but probably toward me as well.

Whatever Jake and Claire's issue is, they need to get it under control before it affects their work. I raise my eyebrows pointedly, nod toward the door, and take my leave of our patient.

We step into the hallway. Unfortunately, I don't have time to address the issue with Jake and Claire right away—my meeting with Chief Physician Dr. Roberts is about to begin, and I want to present the first results of my work after just under a week.

"Dr. Walters, Dr. Avens, I'd like to speak with both of you as soon as possible. Set up a meeting with my assistant," I say.

I still don't know how to tackle the problem, especially since the two of them make a real effort never to cross any clear boundaries. Still, I need to act before things spiral out of control.

I turn to Sonora. "And you'll inform me as soon as the test results are in."

"The aorta was rattling much more today than it did during initial admission yesterday. I think we should preemptively book an OR," she replies.

"I'll operate with you," I say quickly. That should be pleasant.

She nods, her curls bouncing in rhythm. "All right, I'll let you know."

Finally, someone who knows what really matters here. "Very good. End of rounds."

Claire and Jake exhale at the same time and immediately turn to leave. Sonora disappears in the opposite direction, and for a moment, I'm tempted to watch her go.

No idea how she does it. How she manages to make me so curious about her.

Still, my attention should be on Claire and Jake—they're the bigger issue, after all. So I watch as the two of them walk down the corridor, away from me. The bright light streaming in through the window at the end of the hallway turns them into silhouettes.

"It'll be fine," Jake whispers to his colleague.

Claire lets out a heavy sigh. "Just the way he smells… what kind of cologne is that?"

"Acqua di Giò," Jake replies, then whispers something so quietly I can't make it out.

They both laugh. Suddenly, I see Jake's fingers briefly brush against Claire's. The touch feels familiar, somehow… tender.

No, not that too.

Every muscle in my body tenses, and when I see the two

of them disappear into the doctors' lounge, my stomach twists. The door slams shut. Even though it is several meters away, it feel like a shockwave hit me.

Quick footsteps.

I can't help but follow them. When I reach the doctors' lounge, instead of the moaning I'd half expected, I only hear the hum of the coffee machine. Still, a wave of helplessness washes over me.

And then comes the guilt.

I inhale it, draw it deep into my lungs, let it settle.

Curtains flutter aside. Doors swing open.

In my mind, I see Claire and Jake before me, forgetting everything around them as they tear each other's clothes off.

"We need help in Five. Urgently."

My heartbeat quickens, blood rushes through my veins. I feel dizzy.

"Now!"

The memory takes hold of me—I feel it in every fiber of my being, let it consume me.

A tortured roar.

Pain. Everything is pain. I breathe it, I taste it, I feel it on my skin.

I savor it.

Need it.

Beeeeeeeeep.

The continuous tone pierces straight into my heart. Right where my wound is. That one particular place where I wish for only one thing: that it never stops bleeding. So I never forget what truly matters.

Chapter Eight

SONORA

The operating room is filled with a tense silence as I prepare for the upcoming aortic aneurysm surgery. The results of yesterday afternoon's ultrasound were clear—Peter Blake's aorta has expanded further, making surgery unavoidable.

Heart surgeries are always nerve-racking, but this one is special in a different way: I'm operating with Dr. Perfect, the heart specialist in all of Canada. I can't afford the slightest mistake.

I watch him surreptitiously as he gets the go-ahead from the anesthesiologist and reaches for the scalpel. The harsh lights of the OR lamps cast a sharp glow on the visible part of his flawless face.

"Patient P060424-026, aortic replacement at the ascending section of the aorta, near the aortic root. Beginning the procedure…" His gaze brushes past me as he looks up at the clock behind me.

He looks at me intently.

Nervousness has no place not just in the OR, but in my

entire life—yet I can feel my pulse quicken, simply because he's looking at me.

"Eight-oh-three," he says, placing the scalpel on the sternum. His hands move with practiced precision, his expression is focused. No sooner is the incision made than our eyes meet again. There's something magical in the darkness of his pupils, and as much as I'd like to look away, I can't.

Because in his eyes, I see a kind of devotion I've never seen in another person before. In a strange way, I can feel that his heart beats with all its strength for what we're doing in this moment.

That intensity. All the passion reflected in his expression. It's… confusing, and it doesn't fit with the slick, controlled egomaniac he usually is.

Now his surgical mask moves. "Your part, Dr. Wells. Open the chest."

I quickly follow his instruction. As I position the rib spreader, I can feel Dr. Stone's gaze on me.

I'm afraid he's outright staring at me. No wonder I'm feeling a little dizzy.

No. That's not true. I'm completely clear and calm—everything's fine. I force myself to breathe steadily and concentrate fully as I open access to the patient's beating heart.

I've seen quite a few hearts already, yet it's always fascinating all over again. Technically, the heart is just a muscle that contracts and expands rhythmically—but at the same time, it's so much more.

It's what keeps us alive. The thing that always fights for us, no matter how little we do for it. It's the place where we imagine our deepest feelings reside. Our longings. Our pain.

It's the part of us that can break in more ways than any one of our bones ever could.

A melancholic smile creeps onto my lips.

It's just a muscle.

Just. A. Muscle.

I don't want to show any weakness, so I lift my head confidently and pretend I hadn't just been lost in my own thoughts.

His eyes are fixed on me.

Questioning.

"Preparation and connection to the heart-lung machine," I say in a professional tone. Whatever he thinks he just saw, he'd better forget it quickly.

He nods and breaks eye contact. "Alright then, let's go."

Hours pass like minutes as we prepare the patient, connect them to the heart-lung machine, and remove the enlarged section of the aorta. The less I look at Dr. Stone, and the more I convince myself he's not watching me either, the better I can focus.

Whatever was going on with me earlier, it's over. Thank God.

In front of the steady beeping of the monitoring screens, my boss finally selects a suitable prosthesis to replace the removed section of the aorta.

Using the forceps, he holds it in the correct position. "You clamp," he says, addressing me.

"All right," I reply, and pick up a clamp from the stainless steel tray beside me with the forceps. Without letting on how much his scrutinizing gaze unsettles me, I place the clamps.

Now I should get Dr. Stone's approval before securing the clamp with the holder, but I can't bring myself to look up at him. If I do, he might see right through me and realize how unnecessarily fast my heart is pounding. I decide to wait a moment. Since he apparently has no objections, I reach for the pliers and fasten the clamp.

Silently, I place one clamp after another. The same big questions that arise during every heart surgery drift unspoken through the room.

Will the patient's heart beat on its own again after the procedure? Will there be complications? And if so, are we prepared for them?

But that's not all.

Not today.

What does Dr. Stone think of me? What does he see when he looks at me? What does he hear when I speak?

I know I can't let any of these questions drive me crazy —or even ask them in the first place. Alongside skill, one of a surgeon's most important traits is keeping a cool head under pressure.

Not allowing myself to get distracted.

Keeping emotions out of it.

Still, I feel Dr. Stone's presence throughout my entire body. I'm under scrutiny and can't help but cross my fingers when, a short while later, we take the patient off the heart-lung machine.

This is a critical moment. Only once the repaired aorta is flowing with blood again will we know whether we've done a good job.

Outwardly, I maintain my poker face, but inside, I send up a silent prayer as Dr. Stone instructs the assistant to shut off the machine.

The hum of the pumps fades, the hiss of the air supply dies away. Silence falls. The EKG emits the expected continuous tone.

I stare at the motionless heart, holding my breath. The

operating room is so quiet, it feels like everyone else is doing the same.

Even Dr. Stone.

His focus is surely on the heart. He's waiting for it to start beating on its own. I should be looking nowhere else either, yet I glance up.

Maybe because I've been avoiding looking at him this whole time. Because I didn't want him to meet my eyes and make me nervous in that strange way. And because I know this is the only moment I can study him without risk.

His eyelids are indeed lowered. He blinks. His surgical mask moves slightly, as if he is chewing on his lips. The muscles in his neck look tense, his shoulders tight. My gaze wanders down to his hands, which are clenched into fists.

Now he draws in a sharp breath.

The monitoring machines begin to beep—the heart is beating. For a split second, he closes his eyes, his shoulders slump forward, and a sigh escapes his mouth.

And again, I can't look away. Can't stop myself from wondering why he is reacting so emotionally, when he usually comes across like a—granted, damn attractive—robot.

Now he studies the organ, which is reflected on the underside of his protective goggles thanks to the surgical lights.

His brows furrow. At the same time, the machines start going haywire.

I immediately know what is happening.

"Damn," Dr. Stone and I say at the same time.

"Code heart," the assistant shouts.

My pulse skyrockets. I check the surgical site and see the blood pouring from the aorta, right where we have implanted the prosthesis.

"You didn't clamp the prosthesis properly," Dr. Stone snaps at me, highly emotional, and for the blink of an eye, he transforms from Dr. Perfect into a man overwhelmed by panic. From a control freak to someone who has lost all control.

I quickly grab the sterile drapes and press them against the aorta. "The clamps were perfectly fine, I checked them multiple times," I reply, because I am certain of that.

He shakes his head. "Then the prosthesis must have shifted while clamping."

Which, in his opinion, is probably my fault too. He's out of his mind!

Indignantly, I remove the drape to see if the area is still bleeding. It is—and heavily. "We need to reconnect the heart-lung machine; we can't see enough like this," I say, locking eyes with Dr. Stone as I speak.

I won't let you make me nervous, I let him know silently. It was entirely possible that over the past few hours—whatever the cause—he has managed to make me a little nervous now and then, but that is over now.

His surgical mask covers too much of his face for me to tell what he is thinking as he studies me.

Out of the corner of my eye, I see the scrub nurse fixate on Dr. Stone, waiting for his instructions.

"Get the heart-lung machine ready as quickly as possible." Dr. Perfect's voice is professional once again, but the area around his eyes twitches as he looks away from me. "What a fucking mess," he mutters so quietly that I barely hear it over the noise in the OR.

Even if I can't be sure what he was thinking, I have to agree. What a fucking mess.

Chapter Nine

ETHAN

I let my gaze drift across the Halifax harbor, bathed in the light of the late afternoon sun. A few workers are unloading smaller boats, fishermen are sorting their nets for the next morning. The choppy sea makes the boats rock violently. I stare at the water, at its impenetrable darkness, and feel the pull—the relentless force it holds within.

I'm back there again.

On that one beach.

On that one stormy day.

The sound of waves.

The sound of the waves blends with the beeping of the monitoring equipment, which, just minutes ago in the OR, sent a cold sweat down my spine.

Damn, that was close.

The scraping of the door interrupts my thoughts. That must be Claire Walters and Jake Avens.

"Come in." Automatically, I adjust the knot of my tie, then turn toward the door.

I let the skepticism and disapproval in their eyes roll off

me and gesture for my colleagues to take a seat on the sofa in the seating area. “Dr. Walters. Dr. Avens, please.”

The two exchange a conspiratorial glance on their way to the leather seating area.

“Is there a problem?” Claire sits down and wipes her hands on her scrubs.

I’d love to say no, but the truth is, there’s more than one problem. “There is.”

Jake lowers his gaze to the light gray laminate floor and runs a hand through his chestnut hair, which immediately falls back into his forehead. Whether he feels guilty or afraid, I don’t know, but it doesn’t matter.

I take a seat on one of the chairs, rest my forearms on my thighs, and lean forward. With a serious expression, I let my gaze move back and forth between the two. Jake’s jaw grinds constantly beneath his five-day stubble.

“We didn’t make any mistakes. Not today, not yesterday, not the day before.” Claire crosses her arms over her chest. “As you requested, we consulted with you before every surgery and every treatment. Besides, all procedures were successful.”

I’m aware of that—I read all the patient records. I also know that since I started just under a week ago, not a single patient has died under the care of the surgical department.

Which is excellent.

Still, we can’t rest on our laurels.

“And I want to thank you for that,” I say first, because I don’t want to take any of it for granted. Besides, this conversation is going to be hard enough as it is.

I’d rather not have it at all.

But I have to.

It’s my damn duty.

A quiet sigh escapes Claire’s lips.

She's trying to provoke me, but I won't play that game. I lean back. "Still, there's something we need to address."

Jake's gaze flicks briefly to me, his brow furrowing.

"Believe me, I don't enjoy having this conversation. It's uncomfortable, but it's necessary, so I'll get straight to the point." I originally intended to address their behavior during rounds, but what I saw afterward was even more troubling. "We're doctors, and as such, we carry responsibility. We have to stay alert, fully focused on the job, and we can't allow ourselves any distractions."

The two of them remain silent.

"I'm sure you're familiar with the most insidious kind of distraction." Because they've experienced it themselves—I can see in Jake's expression that he knows exactly what I mean. "Feelings," I say in a neutral tone.

Claire's eyes widen. "What's that supposed to mean?"

"That he found out about us." Jake's voice is quiet, but so tormented that I feel like an asshole.

I lift my eyelids and look at my two colleagues, who now stand before me more like a cold, impenetrable wall than ever before.

"I'm sure you're familiar with the rules." And those rules are clear. "Dr. Walters, as my deputy, you are Dr. Avens' superior." Technically, I should prohibit their relationship on the spot, but since they already hate me anyway, I try a different approach—a shared one. "I'm sure you understand that I have to ask you to reconsider this relationship."

Claire shakes her head so vigorously that her chin-length blonde hair falls into her face. "That's our private matter, and besides, it hasn't been a problem until now."

"That may be," I reply, since I have no information to the contrary. "Nevertheless, it's my duty to remind you of the rules." There's a serious reason behind them—relationships in a hospital can be dangerous. They can cost lives.

No one knows that better than I do, and even the thought of it sends the pain of memory stabbing into my chest.

Mom slams on the brakes. The tires squeal. She fumbles for her purse and bolts out of the car. I hurry after her, even though she doesn't seem to notice me at all.

We run toward Halifax Harbor Hospital, burst into the emergency room. In the middle of the waiting area, she looks around frantically.

"Liam. Where's Liam?" she shouts.

A toddler clings fearfully to his dad, a man whose hand is wrapped in a dish towel, glances over at us with suspicion.

"Liam!"

The doors swing open, and a rescue team pushes in a stretcher. The paramedic holds up an IV bag, while her colleague kneels on the gurney. With both hands on the patient's chest, he pumps rhythmically.

"Is that Liam? Is that my son?" Mom rushes toward the stretcher. I'm left standing alone, feeling lost in the crowd. "Liam, sweetheart…"

"Please, ma'am, step aside," a man in a red uniform says firmly.

"That's not…" she murmurs, starting to gnaw at her fingernails. "Where is… I…" She spins in a circle, searching. Her gaze lands on me, but she doesn't see me. She looks right through me, doesn't want to see me, can't bear my presence.

I can't blame her.

To make it right, I turn away, set off in search—I have to find Liam. For Mom.

And for me.

The sand crunches beneath my soles as I run down the corridor, scanning for my brother.

"Heavens, what's taking so long?" a nurse with long braids exclaims. "A doctor to Room Five, now!" she calls out.

I keep moving, checking behind every curtain, peering through every door.

Until I find him.

In Room Number Five.

There he is. Soaked from head to toe. Motionless.

A paramedic is kneeling over him.

I have to do something—but what?

"Find a doctor," I tell myself and march off with clenched fists.

On the way, I pass the nurse from earlier. "Who has time for Five?" Her voice now sounds panicked.

I feel sick. So unbearably sick.

I stumble further down the hallway.

There.

Something moved behind the glass pane.

Without thinking, I burst into the room—and find a female doctor locked in a tight embrace with another doctor, his hand down her pants.

This can't be happening. My brother is dying out there while two doctors are fooling around in here?

No. My brother is dying out there because I was fooling around on the beach.

What kind of idiot am I?!

I'm at a loss for words.

With a stunned look, the guy pulls his hand out of her pants, and she runs her fingers through her hair.

"What's going on here?" The assertive nurse storms toward us, eyes locked on me. "You don't belong here," she calls out, but I don't care. When she arrives and spots the two doctors, her face flushes with anger. "We urgently need help in Room Five," she says coldly. "Now."

The doctor lowers her eyes guiltily and squeezes past me out the door, hurrying down the hallway so fast her coat flutters behind her.

While the two doctors were making out, Liam's heart stopped beating forever.

Mine, on the other hand, started beating differently.

Since then, I've had only one task, one single goal. And even though I've learned over the years that the price for it isn't always easy to pay, one day I'll have repaid my debt—and then it will all have been worth it.

I study the two doctors in front of me. Jake presses his lips together, and Claire grips the couch so tightly that the tendons stand out on the backs of her hands.

"You just want me to step down as deputy so you can consolidate all the power for yourself," she snaps at me in a tone no doctor should ever use with their superior.

"No, I want you to take responsibility," I repeat my earlier words, this time with even more emphasis.

I know they understand that. They're doctors—they're aware of what's at stake.

Now it's Jake who speaks, gently placing his hand on Claire's forearm. "Dr. Stone, please. Claire and I know our responsibilities. We don't let our relationship interfere with our work, no matter who we're with."

I wish I could believe that. But in my mind's eye, all I see are the two doctors who should have been there for Liam.

"The rules state that I must terminate your employment if you don't end your relationship," I say, deliberately keeping my tone neutral. "Nevertheless, I chose to have this conversation. To find a solution together." Which is far more accommodating than I need to be. But if I lose even one more doctor, our patients will suffer for it.

"That rule is completely ridiculous. It's like arresting someone innocent just because you think they might commit a crime someday." A wild mix of disbelief, shock, and fury crosses Claire's face.

I won't engage in this pointless argument. "I strongly advise you to accept my offer and consider a solution."

Jake raises his hands. "What if we stop working the same shifts?"

"That would be one possibility," I reply, relieved that at least he's taking my warning seriously.

"So we don't see each other at all anymore?" Claire snaps at Jake, clearly upset. "Then we might as well break up."

"Thanks for your constructive suggestion, Jake," Jake mocks his girlfriend. "Thank you for trying to save our relationship."

Claire rolls her eyes toward the ceiling with a snort. Jake shifts slightly to the side. And I know: if the two of them could see what I am seeing in this moment, they'd understand.

It is already beginning. Their emotions are taking control.

In this very moment.

"Go home, Claire. Get some sleep," I suggest. She needs time and rest to think clearly. Then I turn to Jake. "And I have a question for you."

He looks at me attentively.

"After this conversation, can you walk out of here and dedicate yourself one hundred percent to your work? Not dwell on how Claire just behaved toward you?"

Yes, that might seem unfair, but that's life.

Besides, I've learned that pain exists to be faced head-on. It's the only way to deal with it. The only way to turn it into something good.

Jake chews on his lower lip, his gaze flicking back and forth between Claire and me.

"I expect your answer by the end of the week," I say. "At the latest."

"Understood," he replies absentmindedly.

"Anything else?" Claire asks in a dry tone.

I shake my head. "That was all. Have a good evening."

"Yeah, sure, we definitely will." Claire jumps up from the couch, grabs Jake by the arm, and pulls him toward the door. "Everything was better when your dad was still the boss here," she whispers to him indignantly as they leave my office.

I watch them go, puzzled.

So that's how it is. Jake Avens is the son of my widely admired predecessor. That probably explains why their relationship has been silently tolerated until now.

With a heavy feeling in my chest, I rise from my chair and set off on a ward round. Seeing my patients doing well, being reminded of all the lives we save—that's what I need after this conversation.

Chapter Ten

SONORA

If it were up to my legs, I'd be pacing in front of Dr. Stone's office. Fortunately, my head controls my actions, and it knows it's best to lean casually against the wall and wait for the boss.

Because when he shows up, I don't want him thinking I'm nervous. Or, worse, emotional.

I'm neither of those things.

I'm furious.

With my hands buried in the pockets of my lab coat, I breathe through the memory of his accusatory expression earlier in the OR. Nurses pass by, soles squeaking on the laminate floor, doors click shut behind them. At the far end of the hallway, a janitor is mopping the floor.

To distract myself, I let my thoughts drift to the upcoming meetup with my roommates later at Waterfront Broadway. I won't be able to afford more than a glass of the cheapest wine, but I'm sure the evening will still be nice.

I glance at the clock. Just before seven. If I want to be on time, I'll have to leave in fifteen minutes at the latest.

A door opens, and I look up.

Claire and Jake step out of Dr. Stone's office and walk past me without looking. Their expressions are like stone.

What could that be about?

"Dr. Wells," I hear the boss say.

My eyes findhim. "Dr. Stone," I reply, still leaning casually against the wall, the corners of my mouth lifting.

His jaw clenches. "Do you want to see me?"

I nod toward his office door. "Definitely."

He studies me for a moment, then openes the door and gestures for me to enter.

Glass façade, leather seating area, high-gloss cabinet fronts.

Fits him—this flashy designer office. The furnishings must have cost a fortune.

When my eyes fall on his desk, I automatically frown. The haphazardly scattered patient files, the pens strewn about, and the partially opened medical textbooks piled up on the table don't match Dr. Perfect at all.

"How is Mr. Blake?" I hear him ask behind me.

Deliberately composed, I walk over to the glass façade and look out into the approaching night. "I think we can move him to the ward tomorrow morning."

"Excellent, then…"

"Earlier in the OR, you implied I made a mistake," I cut him off.

His reflection appears in the window. I watch as he runs his hands through his precisely cut hair.

"I absolutely did not—the staples were placed perfectly." I turn toward him with resolve and look directly into his striking green eyes.

He crosses his arms over his chest, his eyelids narrowing. "Ah, so you're that kind of surgeon."

What's that supposed to mean? That kind of surgeon? "One who doesn't want to be wrongly accused, you mean?" I hold his gaze. "Yes, I am that kind of surgeon."

Shit, that was blunt. But it's the truth, and if I don't make my position clear now, he'll start finding fault with everything I do and eventually get rid of me.

He doesn't even think about breaking our staring contest. "A surgeon who only sees what she wants to see, that's what I meant," he replies.

What's that supposed to mean? "I didn't make a mistake!" I blurt out, a little too emotionally.

Now he takes a step toward me. "What are you trying to imply?" His eyes darken, and I feel queasy. This is dangerously thin ice—I shouldn't push any further. But if I back down now, I lose. "Go on, say it," he says, completely calm, and in that moment, I know it was a mistake to come here.

It would've been better to stand out positively in the coming days, to make up for the supposed mistake I didn't even make.

Why did I think a conversation would make him realize he judged me unfairly?

Because of the selfless way he stood up for Peter Blake before rounds today, who might also be wrongly judged by everyone, whispers a voice inside me that has absolutely no place here.

"Well?" Again, he closes the distance between us.

I shouldn't be staring at him—I should be coming up with a proper response as quickly as possible.

The muscles in his neck tense. "You think I made the mistake."

Probably not—after all, cardiac surgery is his specialty. No one comes close to his skill. "Neither you nor I made a mistake. Bleeding can happen even when we do everything perfectly." I raise my hands in a calming gesture.

His vehement headshake doesn't sit well with me. "Don't come at me with that everything-is-fate attitude. Nothing is fate—we're the ones holding the strings during operations."

Excuse me? Who does he think he is? God himself?

"If you can't accept that, if you can't live it, then you have no place in my department." The glint in his eyes tells me just how serious he is.

My pulse quickens, my palms grow damp. Still, I manage to keep looking at him, and I'll be damned if I stop now. I didn't claw my way out of the gutter for years just to lose everything—because of a mistake I didn't make.

"Understood," I reply, bone-dry.

Instead of satisfaction, his face hardens even more. "Those are just words."

"So you want action," I guess, though I make it sound like a certainty to impress him.

He nods. "The upcoming weekend shift is yours. Use the opportunity to prove to me that you have the right mindset for this job."

A weekend shift? Is that supposed to be punishment? "I will. Brace yourself." He won't break me, and I make sure my expression tells him exactly that.

Surprisingly, a flicker of admiration crosses his face. "Mhm," he murmurs so quietly I barely catch it, yet it sends a strangely pleasant shiver down my spine.

Because I won. At least I think I did.

Good thing I stood my ground with him. It's always better to stay strong. If you don't fight for yourself, you automatically lose. I may be many things—a liar, a cheat, yes, a complete fraud—but I'm definitely not a loser.

"Thanks for the talk," I say, leaving the office with my head held high. As if I had the faintest idea how I'm supposed to handle fate this coming weekend.

The truth is: the only fate we truly hold in our hands, the only one we can ever conquer, is our own. We're powerless over anyone else's.

No one can complete every surgery successfully. Just because Dr. Perfect thinks he's a god doesn't mean he actually is one. Sooner or later, he'll have to come down from his high horse and realize there are things he can't control. Then he'll have to admit that I didn't make a mistake today any more than he did—and I'll be there to remind him.

Chapter Eleven

ETHAN

Damn.

Damn. Damn. Damn.

With the incessant, piercing tone of the heart monitor ringing in my ears, I storm out of the OR, tear the surgical mask from my face and rip the cap from my head.

Why? Why did this happen?

You were supposed to save me, Liam screams inside me.

"Dr. Stone, we still need the time of death." The woman's voice behind me sounds so cautious, as if she's afraid I'll punish her just for speaking to me.

I clench my teeth, knowing I can't show any weakness, no matter how furiously the blood pounds through my veins.

When I turn to look at the clock, I avoid the eyes of my team. "Eight fifteen PM," I reply flatly, then march off.

I had already removed the tumor, everything was fine. So why did I still have to watch a father die?

I failed.

A man died today and it's my damn fault—again.

Sound of waves.

Breathless, I race down the hallway, shove open the door to the fire escape, and step out into the night.

I take the stairs two at a time, heading up to the rooftop —because it's the only place in this clinic where I can be alone. Where I can do what I need to do now, before I lose my mind.

Above me, the first stars sparkle in the dusk as I weave past the air vents on the flat roof. When I reach the edge, I brace myself on my fists. The rough surface of the wall presses into my knuckles.

Sand between my toes.

The sound of waves in my head blends with that of the ocean, lying not far in front of me.

I exhale. Do what I have to do, face the pain. I see Liam, hear his laughter.

Salt on my tongue.

The memory burns bright in my chest, and I welcome it.

My guilt.

Liam's death was my damn fault, and just a few days after he was gone, I realized there was only one way to free myself from it.

Lying in bed, I stare at the ceiling. The city lights cast ghostly shadows on the lampshade.

A piercing scream.

It cuts straight through my heart, but there's nothing left there that could still break.

I blink. I see Liam's face before me. Feel his panic as the current pulls him down into the depths. Gasp for air—none comes.

I'm drowning.

I'm drowning in my guilt along with him.

Night after night.

Day after day.

In every goddamn second of my life, the life I'd give for his without a moment's hesitation.

I turn my head, imagining Liam sitting beside me on the bed.

"If only I could turn back time," I say hoarsely, as I always do. "I'd come with you. Stay close to you. Save you."

Instead of answering, he just shrugs like he always does.

Under the blanket, I clench my fists. "Never again will I let a woman blind me to what really matters," I promise him.

He doesn't believe me—I can tell by the weary snort he lets out.

"But that's not all," I go on, sitting up in bed. "I'll find a way to make up for my mistake." It's the least I can do.

His disappointed gaze lands on me. "There are no second chances in life. You should've saved me," he replies, and in that moment, I realize what I have to do.

I look at him with determination, as hope stirs in me for the first time since his death. "There are so many lives out there I can still save." And every single one is a chance to make up for my mistake.

Liam sighs wistfully.

"I'm going to be a doctor. The best doctor the world has ever seen." Even as I speak the words, I know that this is exactly how it has to be, and I know where I'll work. "At Halifax Harbor Hospital."

The place where Liam died—because only there do I have a chance to make up for my mistake. Maybe I'll have to save a hundred lives, maybe a thousand, maybe even more, but it doesn't matter. I'll keep going, stay focused, keep working on myself—until the time comes.

Since that night, I've known my mission. Saving other people is the only thing that will one day free me from my guilt. But today, my guilt feels heavier than ever before.

I lift my gaze to the sky, to the place where millions of stars burn out unnoticed at this very moment.

And I do it again. Just like back then, when my brother was swallowed by the sea because I didn't watch over him.

Because today, for exactly the same reason, another person is gone forever.

I scream my pain into the darkness of the night, startling myself with the tortured sound that escapes from my broken soul—without taking even the tiniest piece of my guilt with it.

Chapter Twelve

SONORA

His scream should bounce off me, but instead it knocks the air from my lungs, tightens around my throat. Now Dr. Stone doubles over, as if his stomach is seizing in pain.

He hasn't noticed me yet. I should get off the rooftop immediately and forget whatever it is I think I'm seeing right now.

But the tormented expression on his face, lit by the moonlight, the bitter sound of his cry, and the way his body twists make it impossible for me to look away. Impossible not to suspect that he's carrying something inside him that's tearing him apart.

Something he shows no one.

His true self, revealed in this moment, in the middle of the night, on the bare rooftop of Halifax Harbor Hospital. Because he believes no one is here to witness it.

And he's absolutely right.

No one is here. No one saw it.

Because this has nothing to do with me. No—more than

that, this kind of pain that surrounds him is something I want no part of.

I quickly pull the lab coat tighter around my chest and lower my eyelids.

His scream dies away, and I exhale, slipping my half-eaten granola bar back into its wrapper and easing myself out from the ledge just far enough to feel my way along the wall toward the door without being noticed.

"Dr. Wells."

Shit.

I lift my gaze and look into his pain-stricken face.

"Dr. Stone." My voice sounds just as shaken as I feel after witnessing his outburst.

Slowly, his expression shifts, becoming composed and disciplined. "What can I do for you?"

Confused, I shake my head. "Nothing."

"Then why are you following me?" His jaw tenses.

"I'm not…"

"A patient just died, and you have nothing better to do than spy on me?"

Oh. "I didn't know that," I say quietly. "I'm sorry."

Nothing is fate; we're the ones holding the threads during surgery. Not even three days have passed since he explained exactly that to me—and made me endlessly furious in the process. Nothing would've pleased me more than to throw his god complex right back in his face the first chance I got.

That chance would be right now.

Still, I stay silent, because even though he's doing everything he can to present the slick Dr. Perfect, I see a storm raging in his eyes that hits far too close to home.

"He's leaving behind two daughters, five and nine years old. Did you know that? That he had a family? A wife who doesn't know how she's supposed to survive even a single day without him?" He shakes his head, guilt written all over his face.

He's a total egotistical bastard. That's what Claire said about him, and I believed her. I thought he was a heartless perfectionist too, trying to pin a mistake on me during the aortic aneurysm surgery so that—no idea what he was trying to achieve with that.

"I..." Damn it, what am I doing here? I tug at my cuticle so hard it tears.

His expression turns intense. "This must never happen."

"No," I reply, as Dr. Perfect suddenly transforms before my eyes into a man who's anything but an egomaniac with a god complex.

What if he doesn't take a single breath for himself? What if his heart truly beats only for our patients?

Damn.

What if we all misjudged him? Even me. Especially me —I should've known better.

I can feel my already fragile defenses starting to crack, dangerously deep.

Everything is just fine, I tell myself, but that doesn't stop a memory from seeping through the cracks.

Sighing, I let my gaze drift over the display stand with the bracelets. The gold one with the heart charm is missing today, and so is the one with the large red stones. Last Monday, there was still one that looked like a string of dice.

My favorite bracelet is still there. The one with the small, colorful stones that look like a rainbow. Instinctively, I reach out to grab it.

"If you touch it, you have to buy it," the shopkeeper's sharp voice booms behind me.

Right. I quickly clasp my hands behind my back and settle for just looking at the rainbow. I don't need to turn around to know the man who owns this kiosk is watching me.

"Trailer trash," he mutters now, disgusted.

My eyes fixed on the bracelet, I force a smile. "I'll be back tomorrow," I whisper to it. I'm still three dollars short—then I'll have the full ten. "Wait for me, okay?"

Out of nowhere, the shop owner suddenly appears beside me and grabs me by the shoulders. His thinning hair trembles, his steel-gray eyes lock onto mine. "How many times do I have to say it? If you're not buying anything, you've got no business here."

I wrench myself free. "I'm already leaving." With my eyes lowered, I head toward the exit.

"Not so fast, young lady," he yells after me.

Now what. Go or stay? He should really make up his mind.

I stop at the doorframe and wait for him to catch up.

"What's that in your pocket?" He points at the front pocket of my jeans.

"Gum," I reply and pull out the pack so he can see I'm not lying.

His forehead wrinkles as he holds out his palm. "Let me see."

If I hand it to him, will he give it back? Uncertain, I turn the pack over in my hand. "I found it outside by the swings."

"Yeah, exactly, by the swings." He grabs my wrist so tightly that I cry out. "You stole them."

What the hell is going on? "No!"

"Don't lie to me." He drags me to the checkout counter and points his crooked index finger at the shelf with the chewing gum. "See? One pack is missing. You owe me a dollar and fifteen cents."

For a moment, I consider running, but I'm so out of shape I wouldn't get far. "How could I have taken the pack? I was up front by the jewelry stand." And he knows that—he hasn't taken his eyes off me for a single second since I walked into the store ten minutes ago.

"Always the same with you trailer trash. Empty my store and lie to my face." His grip on my wrist tightens. I look down at his age-spotted

hand, wondering where he gets all that strength. "But that's over now. I'm calling the police."

Eyes wide, I stare at him. "I didn't…"

"Quiet. I know kids like you. You're all the same. Skip school, steal, and lie through your teeth," he snaps, and I fall silent. Because I know it doesn't matter what I say. To him, I'm a thief. Trailer trash. And nothing I say or do will ever change his mind about me.

It's been twenty-five years since the store owner had the police take me away. Over a pack of chewing gum I didn't steal. It doesn't matter anymore, has nothing to do with the woman I am today.

Still, that past is now everywhere inside me, and I feel far too clearly that when it came to Dr. Stone, I was just as prejudiced as the store owner had been with me.

I look at him. "I'm sorry," I say, even though he can't possibly know what I truly mean by it. But he knows the words come from the heart—that much is clear from the look on his face.

"Unfortunately, that's not enough," he replies, leaning against the wall. With his gaze fixed on the starry sky, he shakes his head. "It will never be enough."

His words carry so much painful truth that part of me wants to run away right then and there. "That's why there's only one way to deal with it," I hear myself say, because another part of me is stronger in this moment. The part that's crazy enough to want to stay.

Chapter Thirteen

ETHAN

Sonora is right—there is a way. "We have to face the truth, no matter how painful it is. Work on ourselves. Get better," I say.

I hear her breathing, uneven, as if she's afraid of something. "No," she finally replies. "We have to leave behind the things we can't change. Look ahead. Keep going."

Still leaning the back of my head against the cool wall, I turn to face her.

She smiles, her dimples appearing. Even though the moon casts only a pale light on her eyes, I see the same thing in them as I did in her photo from the personnel file: determination. And an unwavering kind of confidence.

"Mhm," she hums, nodding.

There it is again, that *mhm* that always vibrates strangely in my chest. Still, she's wrong.

"Leaving something behind means running away from it," I say, my voice rough. It's harsh, but it's true. We have to face it, feel the pain.

"We can't change what happened." She tugs at her sleeves. "So we should look ahead."

If only it were that simple. "If we've made mistakes, we have to do everything we can to make them right." That's how it is—in life and in our work. There's a reason we review the causes of complications that occur during surgery. We have to analyze them, down to the smallest detail, so we can improve.

A soft snort escapes her lips as she lowers her gaze to her sneakers. Her curls fall across her attractive and suddenly so sorrowful face. "No. That's not how it works."

Curious, I study her. "Then how?"

She stays silent for a while, merely nibbling on her lower lip. "Doesn't matter," she finally says, exhales audibly, and lifts her eyelids.

She smiles at me openly again. Once more, I don't understand it. Just a few minutes ago, a heart stopped beating. How can she still be so… I don't know… so positive?

"That's not it," I hear myself say, far too interested. "So, how does it work?" Even though I don't understand why, I want to know. Desperately.

Her breathing becomes shallow, yet she holds my gaze. As if she's forcing herself with all her strength not to look away. "We have to distinguish between the things we can control and those we can't. Some things are simply fate, and dwelling on them doesn't make anything better. On the contrary, it destroys us."

A cool breeze makes me shiver as my heart tightens.

Accepting fate means giving up.

But before I can say exactly that, she raises her hands. "You see, that's why I didn't want to bring it up," she says, as if she can read on my face exactly what I'm thinking.

I can't help but wonder about her again. Who is this

woman, really? How can she accept life and everything it does to us so lightly?

She probably never had to experience something that completely pulled the ground out from under her feet. She doesn't know what it's like to be dead and alive at the same time.

I let my gaze wander across her face, studying it. The high forehead, the dark eyes with impossibly long lashes, the narrow nose with a small scarred spot on the left side. Her cheeks, where dimples are just barely visible in this moment. And her mouth, which now opens.

"I..." she says.

For the first time since I've known her, the defiance in her expression fades. In its place appears something that confuses me even more than her earlier words.

A gentle kind of wistfulness and a warmth I can almost physically feel. It's as if we're somehow connected.

Something is happening here.

Something that must not happen under any circumstances.

I should put an end to this. Just standing this close to each other by the wall, completely alone in the middle of the night, is already inappropriate.

"You should go," I say quickly, startled by this strange feeling stirring inside me. A feeling that begins deep in my chest, right where my wound lies.

I turn away from her hastily and run my hands through my hair. Out of the corner of my eye, I see her spin around on the spot. Her mane flying, she stumbles toward the door, and even though I know there's no reason to watch her go, I do exactly that.

Chapter Fourteen

SONORA

Hours have passed since I left Dr. Stone on the roof of Halifax Harbor Hospital, yet he remains firmly lodged in my thoughts.

How is that even possible?

He—and his words—should have stayed up there.

I open the door to our shared apartment and let my backpack slide silently to the floor. As I slip off my shoes and massage my ankles, swollen from standing so long, I listen into the silence of the flat.

Our shifts are so different that I never know which of my roommates is home. Who's awake and who's asleep. The day has long since begun, but I can only hope that one of them is here to distract me, so my boss doesn't keep haunting my thoughts.

An electric toothbrush buzzes in the bathroom. The door is slightly ajar, and through the gap I can see Autumn's fiery red hair. I step closer and knock. "Hey, I'm back."

She flinches and suddenly presses her free hand to her

chest. "Jesus, you s-c-a-red me," she exclaims with the toothbrush still in her mouth.

"Sorry, I didn't mean to." I automatically take a step back.

She fidgets with the edge of her bathrobe using her fingertips. "Ahm reah-dy now."

"I'll make some tea in the meantime," I say, since Autumn doesn't drink coffee and I shouldn't have any this close to bedtime either. I apologize again and head to the kitchen. June's room is empty, Nyla's and Olive's doors are closed—chances are they're asleep.

When Autumn enters the kitchen a short while later, wearing jeans and a black long-sleeve shirt, I'm just setting two steaming mugs of fruit tea on the table. "Why are you up so early?" I ask.

She slides onto one of the chairs. "Couldn't sleep."

I pull open the cutlery drawer. "What happened?"

"It's not that important," she replies. "Tell me, how was your shift?"

The two spoons clink softly as I pick them up. "Weird," I answer absentmindedly.

"What happened?"

I hand her a spoon and sit down. "Dr. Perfect happened."

Autumn's eyes widen. "So you got to know him better?"

Oh yes, I did—more than I would've liked. "He's really… I don't know… enigmatic."

With a smooth motion, she pulls the sugar dispenser toward her. "My boss says something completely different," she replies with a shy grin, letting sugar cascade into her tea.

"Oh yeah?" I'm not sure I want to know. Honestly, I

don't care at all. I think. Still, I can't stop myself from giving Autumn an expectant look.

My roommate lifts her chin and sucks in her cheeks. "Ethan Stone is the most gorgeous man I've ever seen. An absolute snack. I'm telling you, Dr. Hall, you wouldn't believe it—he'll leave you speechless. Wait, you've already met him? And you didn't tell me?" Her Dr. Abby Parker impression makes me laugh. I briefly met her boss when the girl with the lower leg fracture I operated on last week was transferred to surgery. But that was enough to now clearly recognize her in Autumn's gestures, expressions, and words.

"You should perform that, seriously, it's brilliant," I reply, grateful for the light-hearted feeling that washes over me.

My roommate sips her tea. "She acts like a love-struck teenager. It's honestly embarrassing."

Anyone who only knows Dr. Stone from the outside would probably consider him a total dreamboat—and not without reason. "He's not that hot."

"Well, purely objectively speaking…" she begins, but doesn't finish the sentence. "Whatever. You said he's enigmatic. What do you mean by that?"

If only I could explain it. But what happened on the roof last night—I'd better not tell her. I lean forward and rest my chin in my hands. "I don't know either. He's just so slick and disciplined." Most of the time, at least. Once again, images of his expression from last night flicker in my mind. He was so tangible, so deeply emotional.

"You should go," he whispers in my thoughts, full of longing, and just like in the moment he spoke those words aloud, a shiver runs down my arms.

Absentmindedly, I stir sugar into my tea and watch the liquid swirl in circles.

"You should go." That's what he said, and I wanted to protest. For a split second, all I wanted was to be with him.

Stay. Give him warmth. And hope.

Damn it, I must've had something like a mini stroke. The man isn't just some random guy—he's my boss!

I wrap my fingers around my cup, trying to chase the memory away, but it's too vivid.

"Be glad you have such a professional boss," I hear Autumn say distantly. "At least you don't have to worry, like I do, that he'll want to discuss intimate details with you that you really don't want to know."

If only she knew… Intimate details, the words echo inside me, and part of me is crazy enough to find the idea of him sharing something personal with me again kind of thrilling.

For heaven's sake, that's enough now. The two of us aren't going to share anything, and certainly not any details that are nobody's business.

"Right," I say casually, forcing myself to look up and smile at my roommate.

Although her forehead is mostly hidden by her long bangs, I can see it furrow. "Is something wrong?"

Something? Everything is wrong. Mostly with Dr. Stone. "It's fine, I'm just tired, that's all."

"Go get some sleep. I have to head to work soon anyway," she says with a motherly tone of care.

"I probably should. But I want to finish this one," I reply absentmindedly, sipping my tea. "Tell me what's going on with you. Have you settled in at Halifax Harbor Hospital yet?" Hopefully, that'll help take my mind off things.

"Mhm," she murmurs, looking just as pensive as I was a moment ago. Then she starts talking about a little girl she's currently taking care of, and the girl's father, who apparently hasn't left her thoughts since.

Where's your father? booms the voice of the police officer inside my head—the one who took the pack of gum from me back then, the one I definitely hadn't stolen. It echoes unnecessarily loud.

At work, my own childish voice mumbles, fully aware that it isn't true.

And your mom?

Also, I reply, staring at my shoes to push back the images forming in my mind.

No, no, no.

What's that supposed to be? Get rid of it.

"Let's see what the day has in store for me," Autumn finishes her story a little later.

"Fingers crossed for a quiet day," I say, faking a long yawn before saying goodbye and heading to my room.

"Don't overthink Dr. Perfect," she calls after me. "He can't hurt you."

Exactly. I close the door behind me, let myself sink onto the mattress lying in a corner on the floor, and stare up at the ceiling.

"Everything is perfectly fine," I remind myself, over and over again. Until I believe it.

Fifteen hours later, I feel like I haven't slept a wink—probably because I kept jolting awake and then spent far too long thinking about Dr. Perfect before managing to fall asleep again.

I slip into my work pants, throw on my lab coat, and clip the pager to my waistband.

Once again, I find myself wondering what will happen when Dr. Stone and I run into each other for the first time since the incident on the roof. I've tried to imagine it—ever since we went our separate ways, I haven't done anything else. And even now, I keep asking myself whether he'll look at me with control or agitation. Whether his voice will sound detached or gentle. Whether he'll bring up what happened.

The last thing I want is to obsess over it, and yet I can't shake these questions. I lean against the wall next to my locker, my eyelids threatening to close.

Damn it, I should've slept instead of letting Dr. Stone mess with my head.

Claire pokes her head through the doorway and waves me over. "Consult in the ER. You coming?"

Grateful for the distraction, I shut my locker. "What's it about?"

On the way to the elevator, she tells me about a broken upper arm from a sports accident. We slip into the lift, and Claire presses the button for the ground floor. "Did you hear?" she asks as the elevator starts moving. "Dr. Perfect is keeping a pros and cons list on each of us."

No, no one's told me that, but it's definitely not good. Not good at all. "How do you know?"

The elevator slows down. "A cleaning lady saw it while she was tidying up his desk."

Oh. That's bad. What's he planning to do with that list?

"Jake and I are probably right at the top of his list now that he found out about our relationship," she mutters, clearly annoyed. "No one ever gave a damn about that stupid hospital rule, but it was the perfect excuse for him to screw us over."

Jake and Claire are together? I raise my eyebrows in surprise.

"Oh, you didn't know?" The doors slide open. "Well, who knows how much longer that'll last. Ever since our wonderful boss gave us that completely unnecessary lecture, Jake's been totally off."

Oh no, that doesn't sound good. "I'm sorry to hear that," I say as we step into the hectic bustle of the emergency room.

Claire waves it off. "Jake and I will manage. Right now, work comes first."

"Which room are we going to?" I ask, glancing around.

"Room Two." Claire turns confidently to the right. I follow her, pulling on gloves as we walk, and finally step into the examination room behind her.

We greet the wiry woman on the stretcher. Her upper arm is a deep shade of blue, with a pronounced swelling near the elbow. Nyla stands beside her, holding the patient's chart. Her short hair is even messier than usual, her cheeks flushed.

"Hey, thanks for coming," she says, nodding to me. Claire steps up to the patient with purpose while Nyla presents the facts: accident details, vital signs, previous treatment. Finally, she gestures toward the X-rays displayed on the wall monitor. "Upper arm fracture."

From here, I can make out a distal humerus fracture. As I step closer, the door bursts open.

Of all people, Dr. Stone walks in—radiating competence, with a face far too attractive and a confident stride to match. His gaze brushes over me—but only for a moment, too brief to guess what he might be thinking.

"What do we have?" he asks, turning to Claire after

greeting the patient. With a slightly irritated tone, she repeats what we just learned from Nyla.

A powerful yawn builds up inside me. I suppress it as best I can and blink to fight the burning in my eyes.

"We need to operate, but only once the swelling has gone down a bit," Claire suggests.

Involuntarily, I study Dr. Stone, but his expression gives no indication of what might be going on inside him. Probably nothing at all.

"Your opinion, Dr. Wells?" He fixes his gaze on me.

I quickly look away.

So far, I haven't had enough time to form a clear picture, so I examine the patient's arm first, ask her a few questions, and then study the X-rays in detail. All the while, I can't shake the feeling that Dr. Stone is watching me.

What is he thinking? About me?

Doesn't matter. He can think whatever he wants—it's bound to be wrong anyway.

I clear my throat. "The patient reports a slight tingling sensation; the ulnar nerve may be compromised due to the fracture." The fact that I'm able to deliver my assessment in such a professional manner gives me the courage to turn around and look Dr. Stone directly in the eye.

His intense gaze meets mine. Unlike me, he looks wide awake, and that's proof enough—he hasn't spent a single second thinking about me or our conversation. Instead, he slept soundly without a care in the world. Meanwhile, I, the foolish one, couldn't get a wink of sleep.

"If we wait to operate, we risk permanent nerve damage, which could lead to numbness and muscle weakness. Chronic pain is also a possibility," I say, still completely calm, fighting against the heaviness in my eyelids so Dr.

Stone won't think I lost sleep over what happened on the roof.

He slips his hands into the pockets of his lab coat. "I agree with you."

I smile automatically. "Good."

No.

Not good!

Because the fact that he agrees with me means we'll be operating together. And as tired as I am, I might end up being inattentive despite my best efforts, which he would immediately interpret as a weakness.

Doesn't matter. I can do this. One energy drink and I'll be ready. Maybe two—or better yet, three.

He studies me intently, and it feels like an eternity before he finally opens his mouth. "Dr. Walters, you'll be assisting me in the OR," he suddenly says to Claire.

"Excuse me? He doesn't want me in his OR?"

He can't be serious. I just took the proper medical history—it should be my case. What the hell is this?

Is he seriously trying to punish me because he lost control of his perfect façade last night?

"As you wish," my colleague replies, overly polite.

"No, I should be the one operating," I reply heatedly. Because in this moment, it doesn't matter how tired I am. What matters is that he's trying to bypass me, and I sure as hell won't stand for it.

No surgeon would accept someone else taking over their operation. Not a single one—and especially not me.

"You'll be handling the postoperative care of the ward patients," he says flatly.

Okay, I don't need any more proof. This is punishment.

What kind of messed-up asshole is this guy, anyway?

And I actually wanted to be there for him last night—how stupid of me.

I lift my chin, letting my gaze tell him that I know exactly what's going on here—and that I'll definitely be coming back to this. Then I leave the exam room without another word.

Chapter Fifteen

ETHAN

Claire pulls on her surgical cap. "Why me and not Sonora?"

I activate the touchless sensor on the faucet and hold my arms beneath it. "She was clearly overtired." The dark circles under her eyes, the tired look, the constant yawning she sometimes managed to suppress, sometimes not. "In that state, she shouldn't be operating—she's doing no one any favors." Least of all herself.

Admittedly, I'm not exactly bursting with energy either. What happened on the roof yesterday has been bothering me more than it should. Technically, we just talked, and yet there was something that...

"And I thought..." Claire begins, pulling me out of my thoughts, though she immediately falls silent again.

"What?" I turn to her and lean against the sink. Maybe this is a chance to convince her I'm not the enemy.

She adjusts her cap. "It's not important."

Exciting. So far, she's never been at a loss for words. "Just spit it out."

She lifts one shoulder. "I thought you wanted to operate

with me to evaluate me. After all, you've never seen me at work before and…" She trails off again.

Why would she think I want to evaluate her? That's just another one of those nasty rumors, like the one that I supposedly fired a nurse just because of her handwriting. Who keeps making up these lies?

"I'm afraid I'll have to disappoint you. It's really just a pleasant side effect of Dr. Wells' fatigue," I say kindly, ignoring her insinuation.

With a pained smile, she wets her hands and forearms first with water, then with the antiseptic liquid soap. "Whatever."

"Have you and Jake made a decision yet?" I ask, even though she just brushed me off so coldly—because there won't be a better opportunity than this anytime soon.

"We're working on it," she replies flatly.

That wasn't what I wanted to hear. "I need your answer by tomorrow."

"Of course."

Thoughtfully, I watch her scrub her arms. Foam forms on her skin—tiny, delicate bubbles that continuously appear and burst.

Like soap bubbles.

Like that crazy moment between Sonora and me last night, which passed so suddenly and yet somehow still lingers inside me.

Part of me wanted her to stay.

Because I was curious, couldn't understand her strange views, even though I wasn't actually interested in them.

"Don't you wash yourself?"

That was Claire, raising both her arms. She had apparently already rinsed off the foam.

If she's already finished, I must have been lost in thought for at least five minutes without realizing it.

There's no way I can go into the operating room like this. Just last night I lost a patient, and it was hell. That can't happen today. Not tomorrow, not the day after, and never again.

"I'll be right there." I signal for her to go ahead.

She disappears through the swinging door. I wait a moment, then pull the small black tin from my pants pocket.

Silence spreads through the washroom. That damned silence, which must be filled as quickly as possible by the beeping of the monitors and the hissing of the ventilator.

I quickly open the lid of the container.

Three are still left.

One will have to be enough.

I reach for the yellow pill and pop it into my mouth. Then I step up to the sink, cup my hands, take a sip of water, and splash the rest onto my face to fully bring myself back to the moment.

Chapter Sixteen

SONORA

Out here in the parking lot of Halifax Harbor Hospital, I can't see the ocean, but I can smell it. My fatigue makes me shiver, and though my shift is over, I'm not going home. Instead, I stand yawning beside the pitch-black Harley that supposedly belongs to Dr. Perfect. The rims and trim are definitely chrome. On an aluminum surface, the colors of the sky—from glowing orange to soft pink to deep violet—would never reflect so intensely.

I wonder how much that thing cost.

Fifty thousand? Eighty thousand?

Must be nice to be rich.

Carefully, I let my fingers glide over the leather seat. Just a moment later, I hear a keyring jingle. Footsteps approach.

There he is. Dr. Fucking Perfect. In a leather jacket, one of those retro motorcycle helmets tucked under his arm. Damn, dressed like that in the sunset light, he looks like People Magazine is about to name him the Sexiest Man Alive.

When he spots me, he stops abruptly. I lift my chin and

cross my arms over my chest. A curl falls into my face; I blow it aside.

"Dr. Wells." Well, well, his voice wavers—I can hear it clearly. He knows why I'm waiting for him here, and he knows I have every right to.

He'd better brace himself. "Dr. Stone, how lovely that we still managed to meet."

He kneads his keyring. The jingling it makes is, for a while, the only sound between us. "How can I help you?" he finally asks.

Instead of answering, I raise my eyebrows expectantly.

His brow furrows. "What happened yesterday on the roof…"

I quickly raise my hands. "Nothing happened there," I reply, because it is better not to go down that road at all. "But a lot more happened today at work."

He sets his helmet down on the motorcycle. "Such as?"

Luckily, his gaze drifts off somewhere toward the horizon, where the sun is probably setting behind the high-rises at that very moment.

"This job is my life," I say, fully aware that he can't even begin to grasp the weight of my words. "I want to move forward in my career, achieve something—do you understand?"

He nods. "You're a good doctor."

"I am. And I will find my path." I love saying things like that. It makes me feel strong and deep down, I know it is true. It even gives me the courage to look him straight in the eyes. "But I can only do that if you stop accusing me of mistakes I didn't make and holding me back during surgeries."

The movement of his chest stills, his mouth opens slightly, and an emotion flickers in his eyes that I can't quite place. I step closer, wanting to know what was hiding there.

Admiration?

Fear?

Curiosity?

All of a sudden, the air between us feels thin, as if it carries less oxygen.

"I'm not doing that," he says with such confidence that he even manages to unsettle me.

"Of course you do," I reply nonetheless.

He fiddles with the chin strap of his helmet, looking as if he needs to think. "See you tomorrow," he says then.

"No, we need to talk about this." Not that I'm eager to spend time with him, but I can't let this slide.

A pained expression creeps onto his face. "There's nothing to talk about." The conflict in his voice makes my heart skip a beat.

This is wrong. It might end up like last night. Or worse. But if I back down now, he'll have it out for me forever. "We should clear this up, please, it's important to me." I let him know with my expression, I will not give in.

He doesn't want to—I can see it in his face.

"In your inaugural speech, you supposedly said your door was always open to everyone," I remind him. Claire has ranted about it more than once in the past few days.

He studies me for a moment. "You have five minutes," he says at last, stepping away from his Harley.

"Thank you, that's all I need." With a gesture, I signal for him to follow me. "You need to understand something: one day, I want to become a senior physician, run my own department," I explain, letting my gaze drift across the high-rises where the last light of day is slowly fading from the glass facades.

He buries his hands in his pockets. "Why senior physician?"

I don't want to be the girl from the gutter anymore, the one people look at only with disgust or pity. I want to do something I—and others—can be proud of. That's the truth, but it's none of his business. "Why did you want to become a senior physician?"

A hint of melancholy appears on his face. "I never did."

It's not the first time he's managed to surprise me and throw me off balance. "What did you want instead?" I hear myself ask, even though I have no interest in his private life.

At the end of the street, the sea sparkles—but it's nowhere near as radiant as the light in his eyes. "Professional surfer."

I can't help but laugh—the image of this composed, perfectionist man on a surfboard is just too absurd. "I'm afraid you're not cool enough for that." No sooner have the words left my mouth than I bite my tongue.

That was inappropriate—very inappropriate.

"You're quick to judge," he replies, and although there's no accusation in his voice, I suddenly feel embarrassed.

"Sorry, I didn't mean to." I turn away and head toward the evening bustle at the Halifax Waterfront Boardwalk.

The cafés are busy, the lively jumble of voices drowns out the sound of waves slapping against the pier. The wooden planks spring lightly beneath my shoes, seagulls glide through the darkening sky.

"How's the woman with the upper arm fracture?" I ask, trying to end the awkward moment.

"The surgery was successful, she should make a full recovery." I hear an intense kind of relief and register the joy that overtakes him as he describes the details of the procedure.

Immediately, I think of our encounter on the roof. Of that all-consuming pain he carried within him. Every doctor wants to save lives, but with him, it seems different. More extreme.

"If everything went so perfectly, then it was probably the right call to bring Claire in for the surgery." Instead of me, hangs unspoken between us, but I'm sure he hears it anyway.

"With every procedure, no matter how minor it may seem, lives are at stake." He looks at me seriously. "I could see you were completely exhausted."

Unlike you, of course. Go ahead, twist the knife, asshole. Wrong. There's no wound. Not because of him. "I would never have operated if I hadn't felt up to it."

A breeze blows my hair into my face, but I still see the pain in his eyes. "The risk was too high."

"There was no risk and you know it," I say, because I can't stand the excuses anymore. "I think you didn't want me in the OR because of what happened on the roof."

He tilts his head. "But nothing even happened there."

Yeah, damn it, I know I said that earlier. "Not to me, at least," I counter, a bit too emotionally, and start picking at my fingernails. "But you, you were…"

"A person died." His bewildered gaze meets mine.

"Yes, people die, because we—no matter how badly we want to—can't save everyone. It's hard, but as doctors we have to deal with it." How does he even survive in this job if he lets things get to him like that over and over again? His reaction was completely over the top.

He stays silent. Because he knows it's true. The way he handled it just wasn't normal.

"Listen," I continue in a calming tone, finally getting to the reason I stopped him in the parking lot. "I don't care what happened to you up on that roof. You've got nothing to worry about from me—I won't tell anyone."

Darkness falls around us, yet I can still see his body tense. "That's not the point. If Dr. Walters had been walking around with bags under her eyes, constantly stifling yawns—which, by the way, you didn't even come close to managing—I wouldn't have let her into my OR either. For the patient's safety, and her own."

Shit, he's actually serious. Isn't he? He didn't want to punish me. "So you're not out to get me," I say, making sure it doesn't sound like a question—he shouldn't think he's rattled me.

The surprise in his expression is genuine. "Why would I be?"

Because he's a chameleon. You never know what he's thinking, who he really is deep down. How can I ever be truly sure of anything?

"Well?" he asks again, as if he can hardly wait for my answer.

"Well, some of the things you do don't make any sense," is the first thing that comes to mind, and I instantly regret saying it out loud.

"Oh really?" He looks at me with a mix of surprise and curiosity. "How so?"

Does he actually want to know, or is he just pretending? "For example, the fact that you ride a Harley, even though you're more of a Mercedes type," I reply hesitantly.

Apparently, that makes him smile. "So you like to put people in boxes. Interesting."

Oh no, now it's about him, not me. "And then there's the fact that you're a die-hard perfectionist who dreams of being a professional surfer." In what world does that even make sense?

"Well, there's more to me than meets the eye," he replies, suddenly seeming to enjoy the conversation. "Sound familiar?"

"And: you go up to the rooftop terrace to scream." Which is by far the weirdest thing of all.

"And you? Why are you up there? Because you'd rather eat standing in the cold than sitting in the cozy warmth of the cafeteria?" A challenging glint flashes in his eyes.

"Maybe I don't like people watching me while I eat." Ha, that one landed.

"Maybe you're afraid someone might find it strange that you eat boiled potatoes for breakfast—plain." His expression challenges me.

So he saw it.

Damn.

"Why would I be afraid of that?" I ask, not even flinching, just to make sure he doesn't get the idea that he might be right. "Are you afraid of potatoes or something?" The thought alone makes me laugh. Dr. Perfect, who fears neither man nor beast, afraid of vegetables. "You don't have to be, honestly, they won't hurt you."

Now he laughs too, and I realize it's the very first time I've seen him do it. A sudden warmth spreads through my chest. "So that's what it looks like when you're amused."

God, did I really just say that? Am I losing my mind?

He suddenly seems almost startled too, running a hand over his head and looking down at the floor. "Well, I guess we've covered everything. I should get going."

I fix my gaze on him—this man who was just so amusing and now has turned back into Dr. Perfect—and I simply don't get it. "Who the hell are you?" slips out of my mouth.

I don't get an answer, just a stunned expression. "And who are you?"

His question cuts right through me. Not just because he's using the same informal tone as me, but because his tone carries so much emotion. "Sonora," I whisper, knowing full well it's not the answer he was hoping for.

"And then?"

My throat tightens. "I asked first," I reply quickly.

He studies me for a moment, and I watch as he gradually composes his expression. "Okay, what would you like to know?" he asks in his typical Dr. Perfect manner.

Nothing, really.

But at the same time, everything.

Chapter Seventeen

ETHAN

Hesitantly, Sonora taps her chin with her index finger. For a brief moment, she seems unsure, but a blink later, her confident, upbeat expression returns. "Why don't you drive a Mercedes?"

Against my will, I have to laugh. This woman is really odd—which is the only reason I haven't walked away yet. I'm curious, want to know what's behind her behavior.

"Seriously? That's your question?" I study her.

She gives a cheeky shrug, signaling that she's waiting for an answer.

I zip up my leather jacket to keep out the cool night air. "Because I like the roar of the engine in my ears."

Skeptically, she pushes out her lower lip. "You like noise?"

"No, I don't like it. I love it." A curiosity about her reaction stirs inside me.

"No one loves noise," she replies, appalled.

"Once you've experienced how suffocating silence can be, you'll do anything to avoid it." Like back then after

Liam's death, when my parents' house was filled with silence.

"Hmm," she murmurs, and I automatically wonder if she's ever experienced that kind of silence herself.

"You know what that's like too, don't you?" I ask.

She gives an almost imperceptible shake of her head, then the corners of her mouth lift. "I live in a shared apartment with four other doctors. Silence doesn't exist there."

I'm not sure whether to believe that that's really all there is. But before I can ask her, she starts talking about her crazy flat share. For minutes, she chatters away so animatedly that I get the feeling she's trying to distract me. From what, I don't know. Still, I let myself get drawn in, and I notice a carefree smile sneaking onto my lips from time to time.

My chest feels light, and even though I know I shouldn't, I enjoy it—just a little.

"And then there's Olive, an intensive care doctor and total glamour queen." She gives me a conspiratorial grin. "If she finds a stain on her shirt, her whole day is ruined. Absurd, right?"

Definitely.

"She might seem a bit superficial at first glance, maybe even selfish, but in reality, she's anything but, and she can't say no to anyone," she continues cheerfully. "But don't tell anyone."

I mime zipping my lips shut. "Sounds like you all have a lot of fun together."

Her expression turns almost proud. "We do."

The end of the Halifax Waterfront Broadway is already in sight. Earlier, I didn't want to talk to her at all, and now I feel like I can't let this conversation end—even though I know I should. Sonora keeps chatting about her flat share as we leave the Broadway and wander aimlessly into one of the side alleys.

I hardly notice how time passes, too caught up in the carefree conversation and the cool evening air surrounding us. When I tell her that I live in a log cabin on the outskirts of Halifax, she laughs so heartily that I can't help but smile too. I enjoy surprising her, and inevitably I find myself wondering when I last had such a good time, but I can't come up with an answer.

Maybe never.

"Did you never want to live alone?" I ask at some point.

It takes her a moment to respond. "Never," she murmurs, her gaze fixed on something beside me that captures her attention so completely she comes to a stop.

I turn my head and see a rotting wooden fence, with weeds growing between its slats. Greenwood Ave 523, I read on the weathered sign. Behind it hides a small, dilapidated Victorian-style house. The shingles on the steep roof are crooked in places, missing in others. Moonlight glints off the broken windowpanes.

Beside me, I hear Sonora's shallow breathing. I glance over at her, but I can't make sense of the expression on her face.

"If someone renovated it, I bet it would look great," I say, because I can't think of anything better.

She blinks rapidly. "Yeah."

I have a feeling this might be the home of her childhood. The way she looks at it carries a sense of longing. We've passed many houses that were bigger, more beautiful, and newer than this one. There must be something special about it for her.

"This house means a lot to you, doesn't it?" I ask, and

the moment the words leave my mouth, I know I shouldn't have said them. The question is far too personal.

Instead of answering me, she starts picking at her fingernails.

Only now do I realize how little she's told me about herself. I actually know more about her roommates than I do about her. Until now, that distance had felt like safety, and I know I should hold on to it. "Why is that?" I hear myself ask anyway, and I don't understand myself anymore.

The corners of her mouth curve into a wistful smile. "Mom and I always dreamed of buying it someday." She shakes her head, as if the thought were absurd. "We had a lot to do in the area, and every time we passed by this house, we stopped."

"You imagined what it would be like to live here." I can't help but picture Sonora as a child. A little girl with a head full of curls, standing right here where we are now, reaching for her mom's hand.

"See the window at the very top, in the bay?" She points with her index finger in that direction. "That would've been my room."

There's so much unfulfilled hope in her words that my chest tightens painfully. "And there?" I point to the wide window in the basement.

"That was the open-plan kitchen with an island, and of course, a Black Luck coffee machine. We would've replaced the window with a glass door so we could walk straight out onto the porch," she continues with a smile, not noticing that I'm no longer looking at the house, but at her. "Outside, we definitely wanted a porch swing, a little table, maybe even a grill. We imagined a cozy spot from which we could look out over the garden."

Suddenly, I'm overwhelmed by the urge to pull her into

my arms. To tell her that she can still make this dream come true. And I catch myself reaching out to her, but just manage to stop in time.

My God, that would be so wildly inappropriate.

"One day it'll be yours," I say, trying to push away these completely misguided feelings. Besides, I truly believe it. There's so much fight in her, so much passion and such a strong will—more than I've seen in almost anyone.

She nods. "Yes, one day," she confirms.

So this is her why. The reason she's so determined to become a senior physician. She's not fighting for herself, but to buy her mom the house she's dreamed of her entire life. Beneath her fierce poker face hides a tender heart.

A tender, beautiful, lovable heart.

"It's late," I hear her say, as if from far away.

Our eyes meet, her dark eyes glimmering in the light of the streetlamp. And for a moment, I think I see in them the same thing I'm feeling right now, even though I don't quite know what it is.

It's warm. And comforting.

It sits right in the middle of my chest, where there's usually only pain, and for the first time, I don't wish it back—even though it's always supposed to be there with me.

"We should go," she croaks. "Try to get some sleep."

Sleep is probably the last thing I'll find tonight, but I still nod. "We should."

Go.

And right away—that much is painfully clear. Because if we keep standing here, this close to each other, and I don't stop trying to catch a glimpse of her soul through her eyes, it might set something in motion that must never be allowed to happen.

Chapter Eighteen

SONORA

"And who are you?"

My boss. That was my damn boss who asked me that question the day before yesterday, far too emotionally, and looked at me like he desperately wanted to know the answer. The same man I walked through Halifax with at night. The one I showed a part of myself to, just like that—something no one else has ever seen. Without thinking, I opened up to him, and he… he… I don't even know what he did.

He did nothing. It was too dark to make anything out.

Yeah. That's exactly how it is.

And when he brought me home and said goodbye at the entrance to my apartment building, it felt like saying good night to an acquaintance. Nothing more.

"What's next? Stroke? Liver failure? Heart attack? Pulmonary embolism?"

There is no next for Ethan and me.

Someone nudges me. "Hey, Sonora, are you okay?"

"Hm," I murmur automatically, lost deep in those crazy

thoughts that hadn't let go of me, not even in sleep over the past few hours.

"June to Sonora, come in."

June. Right. We're walking to the clinic together. And she was just talking about... no idea what exactly. "What did you say?"

Yawning, she rubs her eyes, the dark circles beneath them clearly visible. When she's well-rested, she looks like Barbie herself, but today she resembles more of a ghost. "Ashton's symptoms are getting more and more puzzling," she replies, sounding desperate.

The way she says his name makes me pause for a moment. "Last week, you still called him your asshole patient, and now suddenly he's *Ashton*?" I raise my eyebrows. Since when does she like that weird guy who made her life hell in high school?

My roommate shakes her head. Her blonde hair falls into her face, but I can still see her cheeks turning pink. "Anyway, I really need to finally diagnose his illness if I..."

If she wants to land the attending position in the diagnostics department, I know. "You've got this," I say with a smile, because I'm sure she won't give up until she gets what she wants.

The glass façade of the Halifax Harbor Hospital appears before us. June glances at the time. "But only if I hurry."

I still have an hour before my shift starts, and June's pace is too fast for me anyway, so I signal for her to go ahead. "I'll see you at home then." Whenever *then* is—I've long since given up trying to keep track of our shift schedules.

She gives me a quick hug. "Take care. And don't let Dr. Perfect get to you."

"Oh, he'll get to know me soon enough," I reply casually, but then bite my tongue right after, realizing that he already has. Just not in the way he should have.

We say goodbye, June takes off running, and I continue strolling toward the driveway. In the parking lot, I spot his Harley—gleaming elegantly in the sunlight. A queasy feeling starts to rise in me, but I push it away. It's ridiculous to feel this way just because I'm about to see Ethan Stone again—my boss. Whose employee I am. Nothing more, nothing less.

Ten minutes later, I step into the locker room where Claire is styling her chin-length blonde hair.

"Who are you getting all dolled up for?" I ask with a wink after greeting her.

She lets out a heavy sigh. "At least not for Jake. He broke up with me last night."

"Oh no." I slide the key into the lock of my locker. "Because of the hospital rule?"

Her jaw clenches. "No, just because of Dr. Perfect. No one else gives a damn about that stupid rule."

My stomach knots instinctively. "I'm sorry."

"If it keeps us from getting fired, then I guess it's worth it for Jake. Although…" She stares at her fingernails and sighs deeply. "We could still fall victim to the red pen."

"What red pen?" I take off my street shoes and push them far enough under the locker so no one will see how worn out they are.

Claire reaches for her lab coat. "I told you about that evaluation list Dr. Perfect keeps."

"What about it?" Alarmed, I grip the locker door.

"I've since found out what it's really about." She draws in a sharp breath. "He plans to replace everyone who falls below some vaguely defined red line with someone from his old hospital, so the department can finally be as perfect as he wants it to be."

My pulse quickens. "That can't be true," I say, mostly to calm myself down.

If that were true, he'd scrutinize every one of us down to the last detail. A single phone call to Halifax Grammar School to request my "accidentally" omitted transcripts, and he'd know I never went there.

He'd know I lied to get this job, and he'd start wondering what else I lied about.

That can never happen.

She shakes her head. "The fact is, he keeps this list, and he doesn't do it for no reason. So either he really wants to fire someone, or he just enjoys tormenting his employees with their mistakes."

Either would be a disaster. I swap my jeans for a pair of scrubs. "Do you really believe that?"

"Welcome to the brave new world of Halifax Harbor Hospital—better get used to it." Her voice suddenly turns bitter. "He's such a damn selfish perfectionist, of course he doesn't want weak team members making him look bad."

"Maybe he really does care about the patients. Maybe he just wants them to get the best possible treatment so they can live healthy, happy lives." No sooner have the words left my mouth than I wish I could take them back.

Damn it, what just came over me? Why am I defending him instead of staying vague and ending this conversation as quickly as possible?

Claire's brows immediately draw together in suspicion. "Don't be so naive. He doesn't give a damn about the patients. He just wants a spotless record, to be the hero, to be admired by everyone." A sad snort escapes her lips.

I swallow hard against the resistance rising inside me.

"You're probably right," I murmur, and absurdly, I feel like a traitor.

"Of course I'm right," my colleague huffs, slamming her locker shut. "Watch out for him, or you'll end up at the top of his hit list."

It takes effort to curl my lips into a smile. "I will, thanks for the tip."

She gives me a satisfied nod. "Gotta go, see you later."

I pull my scrubs out of the locker. "See you."

I let out a relieved breath as she leaves the changing room. Not a second later, my phone buzzes with a new email. I pull it from my pocket. Sender: Shadowbrook Cemetery Administration.

What do they want from me? I open the message, and a split second later, I feel sick.

I know I am behind on the payments—where am I supposed to get $425 after being unemployed for months and moving into a shared apartment? But they can't just terminate the urn plot without notice because of that.

My gaze drops to my work sneakers. I'd spent $35 on them. If I'd found another solution, I'd only be short $390—plus the six hundred for the unpaid credit installment. And of course, everyone at the clinic would've instantly noticed I was wearing busted shoes.

I thought the cemetery administration would send a third reminder, and by then I would've already received my first paycheck.

Damn it, how can they just cancel a burial plot like that without notice? What's supposed to happen to the ashes? Am I supposed to take the urn home and put it on the windowsill? Or are they planning to dispose of it?

I don't know which thought is worse. "It won't come to that." Never. As soon as I can, I'll call the cemetery administration to sort it out. In a few days, the transfer from Halifax Harbor Hospital will arrive—until then, they'll have to grant me an extension. I run the numbers in my head.

It'll be fine—it always is, in the end.

And so I can believe it myself, I quickly slip the phone back into my pocket. Not seeing it anymore, not having the message in front of me, makes it easier to look ahead.

Ahead. That's right here, at Halifax Harbor Hospital. Here, where the very future I've fought for over the years is waiting for me. Where one day, I'll be someone others look at with admiration instead of contempt or—worse—pity.

But that's also where Ethan Stone is. The man I should stay away from. Because if I let him see too much of me, I'll lose everything.

Chapter Nineteen

ETHAN

The Excel spreadsheet blurs before my eyes. Numbers turn into black streaks on a white background. Letters dissolve.

Sighing, I rub the bridge of my nose, then blink to clear my vision.

Sonora Wells is the first name on the employee list on my monitor that catches my eye. Inevitably, I think of her—her fighting spirit, her *why*.

Of the wistful smile with which she told me about her dream house. Of the spark in her eyes and the feeling it planted in my chest.

The feeling I shouldn't even be capable of having.

I close my eyes and summon the sound of waves crashing.

Yes, that's it—the only thing I'm allowed to care about.

My heart tightens, and that's when I know I'm myself again. Whatever Sonora did to me, it's over.

With a deep breath, I look toward the floor-to-ceiling window, beyond which stretches a cloudless sky. Gulls glide lazily through the air, and once again I hear the sound of waves in my head, taste salt on my tongue. Then it hits me, suddenly.

Silence.

Oh God, how I hate it.

I jump up from my desk chair in a hurry and walk to the door.

When I open it, I spot Sonora in the hallway. She's pacing back and forth, tugging frantically at her fingernails and murmuring unintelligibly to herself. Now she's pulling at her hair, which gleams in the incoming daylight.

"Come on, don't be such a baby," she scolds herself.

I shouldn't be watching her, and yet I lean against the doorframe, eyes fixed on her. And I can't stop the flood of questions forming in my mind: Is she here to talk about the day before yesterday? Does it feel to her, too, like we went too far, even though technically nothing happened?

With her back to me, she clenches her fists. "You're going in there now and doing your job."

Before I can grasp what's happening, she spins around and immediately spots me in the doorway. I see her swallow hard.

"Dr. Stone." Her tone is very neutral, highly professional. "I need your approval for a discharge."

"Which patient?" I ask, just as composed. Because it's easier that way—it creates distance, and distance is exactly what I need around her.

I don't miss the fact that she stops picking at her nails. "The woman with chronic cholecystitis in room 224."

"The surgery is scheduled for tomorrow. Why would we discharge her?" For a moment, I wonder if this is just an excuse for her to come here and see me.

Did she miss me?

Oh God, why on earth am I thinking something like that?

She shrugs. "She's decided against having her gallbladder removed."

I stare at her in disbelief. "Did you explain to her that she's risking her life?" Probably not. Because if she had, the patient might have made a different decision.

"Of course I did," she replies indignantly. "She still doesn't want the procedure." She holds my gaze. "We can't remove her gallbladder against her will, so we have no choice but to let her go."

Absolutely not. "Not before we've tried everything." I pull my lab coat from the coat rack. On the way to Room 224, I slip it on while Sonora walks beside me, conspicuously silent.

Does she feel guilty? Because she couldn't convince the patient to be reasonable? Or because she, too, is inappropriately thinking about the day before yesterday. I, at any rate, struggle to bring my thoughts back to the here and now.

Damn it, these crazy feelings need to go away—I don't want them. They jeopardize my mission, make me a bad doctor.

I let the sound of the waves rise up, hear the screams, do everything I can to feel like myself again before we enter the patient's room. The fact that we find the woman not lying in bed but packing her bag does not sit well with me.

"Good afternoon, Ms. Cox, I'm Dr. Stone, Head of Surgery." I nod to our forty-three-year-old patient, whose collarbones protrude noticeably beneath the neckline of her T-shirt.

Her gaze flicks back and forth between Sonora and me. "Is there a problem?" she asks in a husky voice, unzipping her bag.

"Dr. Stone also wanted to speak with you before you're discharged," I hear Sonora say in a calming tone.

I fix her with a serious expression. Why are you giving in so easily? I ask her silently.

She lifts her shoulders, a sorrowful look clouding her dark eyes. I did everything I could, it might mean, though I'm not entirely sure.

The day before yesterday, I thought I was finally beginning to understand her. But right now, I don't understand anything at all.

"If you're done with your staring contest, I'd like to leave." Our patient's voice cuts through the silent exchange between Sonora and me. "Where do I need to sign?"

Nowhere. "Let's sit down for a moment." I gesture toward the visitor's table.

Instead of sitting, she plants her hands on her hips. "As I already explained to your colleague in great detail earlier, I'm not going to change my mind. You're wasting your time here."

Fighting for a human life is never a waste of time. "Why don't you want the surgery?"

"I'd rather treat myself." Our patient stuffs a pair of socks into her bag. "Milk thistle, dandelion, and turmeric. That's all I need. Besides, I'm already feeling much better."

Sonora raises her eyebrows pointedly, and this time her expression leaves no room for interpretation. *Do you believe me now that I tried everything?*, it means.

"Ms. Cox, gallstones are blocking your bile ducts, and even if you're feeling better at the moment, your symptoms will return." And each time, the abdominal pain, nausea, and fever will become more severe. "The next episode alone could have life-threatening consequences." As I speak the words, that overwhelming sense of resistance builds inside me.

Every death is meaningless, but one like this especially so.

"Listen here." She points her bony index finger at me. "I told your colleague, and I'll tell you the same: I won't let you butchers cut me open. End of discussion."

I raise my hands in a calming gesture. "Gallbladder removal is an absolutely routine procedure."

Out of the corner of my eye, I see that Sonora is watching me. The fact that I'm also struggling to reason with the patient probably means I accused her unfairly of giving in too quickly.

"Pff, a routine procedure. Don't make me laugh," says Ms. Cox, snatching her wristwatch from the nightstand. "I know all about your so-called routine procedures."

Aha. We're getting closer. I can't help but let Sonora know with a glance that I'm onto something. In her eyes, I see that she likely got this far too—at the very least.

Still, I won't give up. I stroll over to the visitor's table and take a seat. "Would you tell me about it?" I ask kindly, making another attempt to get her to sit down.

Her shoulders slump forward. "I already did. You doctors don't understand."

"Some of us understand more than you might think," I reply, feeling my own wound in the process. To most of our patients, we are untouchable gods in white coats—as we must be—yet we know grief. We know what fear feels like.

Uncertain, she fidgets with the hem of her shirt. I give her time, knowing she needs it. "My sister," she whispers into the sterile silence of the hospital room after a while.

Sonora presses her hand to her sternum and takes a step

back, as if she doesn't want to hear what the woman has to say again.

As if she were afraid.

But of what?

"She had one of those routine surgeries," Ms. Cox continues in a trembling voice. As she says the words "routine surgeries," she makes air quotes with her fingers. "On her spinal disc."

And it clearly didn't go as hoped. I adjust the chair next to me for her, and at last, she steps closer.

Clutching the backrest of the chair, she looks at me pleadingly. "She hasn't had any feeling in her right leg since."

A damaged nerve, possibly irreversible. A rare but serious complication following a spinal disc operation. "I'm very sorry to hear that."

She sits down, giving me a clear view of Sonora, who's standing directly behind her and suddenly looks terribly pale.

"My sister hasn't been the same since," Ms. Cox begins to say. And as she explains that her sister can neither walk nor work in her job as a florist, I feel more and more of her pain. "She's lost everything," she concludes minutes later. "Even her will to live."

Sonora lowers her eyelids and tugs violently at her cuticles.

I turn to the patient. "I understand your fear." More than she realizes. Because that fear—no, that panic—that something which once pulled the ground out from under your feet might happen again, I once faced that myself, powerless. "But your health problems won't go away if you downplay them or ignore them altogether."

The tips of Sonora's hair begin to tremble. She looks like a wild animal caught in a trap.

I would love to find out what's going on with her. But sitting in front of me is my patient—a life I have to save.

I look at Ms. Cox intently. "If we don't operate, your symptoms will get worse and worse. You'll be in severe pain." That's certainly not the life she wants. "If the inflammation progresses and goes untreated, there's a risk of your gallbladder perforating, which means the wall of your gallbladder could rupture. That would lead to a life-threatening peritonitis."

The last thing I want is to cause panic. But she needs to understand that she can't let fear dictate her life.

My patient exhales shakily.

I smile at her. "You don't have to decide right now. Think it over. Your surgery is scheduled for tomorrow—we're holding the slot for you."

She looks at me hesitantly for a moment. "Hmm," she says thoughtfully.

Thank God!

Relief rushes through me, and my chest feels a little lighter. Ms. Cox is going to live.

"Thank you." I gesture toward Sonora, who's biting her lower lip so hard it's turned deep red. "If you have any further questions, please speak to my colleague. She also knows where to find me if you'd like to go over everything again," I offer, because it's simply too important for her to agree to the surgery.

After that, I say goodbye to the patient. Sonora also murmurs a quiet "Goodbye," then we leave the room. As soon as I've closed the door behind me, I fix my gaze on Sonora.

"What was that just now?" I try not to sound accusatory,

but it's difficult. "You would've left that woman to her fate. You would've..." let her die. I should say it, but the words won't leave my lips.

Sonora gasps. "I tried everything to convince her, but she wouldn't listen." Her expression turns serious. "She's a competent adult—we can't treat her against her will."

"No, we can't. But that doesn't mean we're allowed to give up."

This conversation clearly makes her uncomfortable; she can barely look me in the eye. "You think you just won in there, but you didn't."

Of course I did. "Ms. Cox will think it over, and she'll realize she'd rather have a chance at a healthy life than face certain death." That's how it will go—no doubt about it.

Sonora's eyelids flutter, then she looks up at me. Her expression is sad—sad and hopeless. "People don't change just because we want them to," she whispers tonelessly. "That's not how it works."

I wish I could read in her eyes what she's trying to tell me, because I sense that her words have nothing to do with Ms. Cox. Instead, it becomes clear to me that she, too, carries a wound—just like I do.

"Who?" I hear myself ask, far too emotionally, because deep down, I feel with her.

There is closeness where there should be distance, but there is also connection where there had only been loneliness before.

"Who in your life hasn't changed?" Only after the words leave my mouth do I realize I just used a very informal tone with her—but right now, I couldn't care less.

Her expression hardens, her nostrils flare. "This isn't about me."

Oh, but it is—I feel it in my bones.

She stands in front of me with clenched fists, her muscles tensed to the breaking point. "This is entirely about you. About your obsessive delusion that you have to save every single human life."

"I'm a doctor, for fuck's sake," I snap, more forcefully than I intended. "Saving lives is my job." Unconsciously, I step closer to her and point my index finger at her. I nearly touch her chest, which is rising and falling rapidly. "And it's your job too."

"You can fight as much as you want, but you'll never be able to save someone who doesn't want to be saved," she counters now. She wants to seem strong, but I can see her pain. "The only person you have that kind of power over is yourself."

Shaking my head, I study her. She really believes that, and yet I point toward the door to Room 224. "Tomorrow we're going to operate on Ms. Cox. Then…"

Before I can finish my sentence, the door to Room 224 opens. Sonora and I pull apart as if we've been caught doing something forbidden—which, of course, we haven't. A split second later, I see our patient. In sneakers, jeans, and a thin sweater that flutters around her shoulders like it's hanging on a coat hanger. The bag she packed earlier dangles from her hand.

This can't be happening. My heartbeat quickens, pumping pure adrenaline through my veins.

"Where do I sign?" she asks, addressing Sonora. She doesn't even look at me.

Sonora casts me a sorrowful glance, and I hate it. I hate that she was right in her assessment. I hate the thought of leaving this woman to her fate.

We can't let her go!

"Ms. Cox, please, think abou—"

"No." She raises her hands tensely. "I've made my decision."

Frantically, I search for a way to change her mind. "Your sister needs you," I plead urgently. "How is she supposed to cope without you?"

The skin around her eyes twitches. "That's exactly why."

Oh God, this is so twisted. Sweat forms along my spine as I almost physically feel the situation slipping further and further out of my grasp. I'm losing control—of her and of myself.

Now she turns to Sonora. "Either you give me the forms, or I'll leave without signing them."

"People don't change just because we want them to," Sonora's voice echoes inside me. And even though I watch her and Ms. Cox walk together down the hallway toward the exit, I can't accept it.

In no world could this ever be right. I have to do something. Save her from certain death.

But how?

A feeling of helplessness builds inside me like thunderclouds on a humid summer day. I start to run.

To the stairwell.

Up to the rooftop terrace on the top floor.

Outside.

Then the storm breaks inside me.

Chapter Twenty

SONORA

I've been standing across the street from Shadowbrook Cemetery for half an hour, watching as people are swallowed up by the entrance gate and then, a little while later, spit back out. People mostly dressed in dark clothing, carrying flowers and candles in their hands.

I deliberately put on a bright yellow top to bring a little cheer to all the gray and black around me. That, and a whole lot of positive thoughts—because I'm going to need them. Coming here was the last thing I wanted, but ever since I got the email about Mom's grave, I've been trying—unsuccessfully—to reach someone.

"In quickly, out quickly." That's the plan for today, and it should be easy enough. After all, the cemetery's administrative office is right next to the entrance. I won't even be near her grave, won't have to see her, won't have to talk to her.

Everything is perfectly fine.

Taking a deep breath, I start walking, heading for the

entrance, letting it swallow me up like everyone else before me, and then I turn right.

I glance around, searching. Then, between two older couples and a young woman, I suddenly spot Ethan—no, Dr. Stone. In his dark leather jacket, holding flowers and a candle in his hands.

I freeze instantly. Even if I wanted to, I couldn't tear my eyes away from him. What he's doing here isn't even a question. But who is he visiting?

As if he could feel my gaze, he stops and lifts his head. He's about to see me.

Now.

Even though there must be a hundred meters between us, it feels like he's right here, standing in front of me. So close, I can almost hear him breathing.

My heart skips a beat.

Shit, how does he do that? How does he keep getting so much closer to me than he should, without actually doing anything? Just like yesterday, when we were standing in front of Room 224, talking about Ms. Cox's discharge.

Who?, I hear his gentle voice inside me, just like so many times over the past few hours. *Who in your life hasn't changed?* Again, my throat tightens.

There's no way he could have known that. Impossible. So why did it sound like he was sure? And why did that feel so bittersweet?

Now he's walking toward me. When we're face to face, he clears his throat. "Did something happen? Is there an emergency?"

What a strange question. "Why would you think that?"

He pulls out the clinic phone, glances at the blank screen, and looks at least as confused as I am. "Because I've never seen you here before."

Lowering my gaze in search of words, I look at the flowers in his hand. The blossoms are just as sun-yellow as my shirt. I don't want to ask who they're for. It's better if I don't know. Easier.

"I was actually just about to leave." Yes, that's the only right thing to say.

Suddenly, his expression shifts into the same look he gave me yesterday. There's longing and there's hope, and there's a kind of pain that I feel too.

"Who?" he asks again, instead of simply saying goodbye, and just like yesterday, that one word cuts far too deep under my skin.

I try to shrug it off casually, but my shoulders refuse to cooperate. Just like the corners of my mouth, which won't lift.

"Who?" he repeats, so insistently that his voice echoes in my chest. Right where it hurts. Right where no one has any business being.

I fix my gaze on my index finger, pressing its nail into the cuticle of my thumb. "My mom," I hear myself say, and I don't understand myself anymore. Why am I telling him this?

He stays silent for a while, and my mind seems to have nothing better to do than imagine what might be showing on his face right now.

Pity, probably. That disgusting, stupid, useless pity he can keep to himself. I don't need it—from anyone—and least of all from him.

"It was a long time ago. I'm way past it," I say with forced nonchalance and make myself look at him.

Is that… a wistful, knowing smile on his lips? Why is he doing this? And why does it feel like he understands how I'm doing better than I do myself?

"What happened?" he asks, motioning for me to walk with him for a few steps.

Not many people know about my mom. And none of them have ever heard from me what happened to her. "Does it even matter?" I ask. Honestly, I don't want to go with him—wherever it is he wants to go in this cemetery. And yet, I do. Maybe because I need to hear his answer.

He takes a deep breath. "You tell me," he says, and I don't miss that, just like yesterday in front of Room 224, he switches from formal to informal. I can't ignore the closeness that brings either—this closeness that feels like a hug.

We leave the paved entrance area and turn onto a gravel path. The pebbles crunch beneath our feet as I mull over his words.

"No, it doesn't matter," I decide. That's just how it is, and that will never change.

As we walk, he glances over at me. "And what if it matters to me?"

"Why would it?" slips out before I can stop myself.

Strangely, he smiles now—and strangely, it warms my heart. "Maybe I like sad stories."

"No one likes sad stories." On the contrary, people want to hear the beautiful ones—me included.

A reassuring smile plays on his lips. "Tell me about your mom."

I can't, and I don't want to. What's the point of reopening old wounds that have long since healed? "There's nothing to tell."

"What did she die of?" There is nothing pressing in his tone, just genuine interest.

I look at him, stare deep into his green eyes, and find neither pity nor disgust in them. Instead, there is that same warmth again, spreading through my whole body.

"She was sick." I don't even try to lift the corners of my mouth to pretend the thought doesn't hurt. And maybe that's exactly why something shifts inside me. Something that feels like a door in my heart cracking open just a little.

Out comes a memory I had buried there years ago. A memory that should have long since faded. And yet, it now feels like the exact opposite is true.

With a growling stomach, I open the cupboard under the camping stove. The handle sticks to my fingers, and the musty smell of mold that has settled in the corner hits me full force. Today, I can not only smell it —I can see it too.

A single can stands in the cupboard, the label missing. Could it be beans?

I glance over at my mom, who lays in our bed with her eyelids half open, letting out a pained moan with every breath.

"Mom?" I ask. "We don't have anything to eat."

"We don't? I'm sorry, Sonnygirl." She sounds like even speaking is an effort, and I'm immediately overcome with guilt for sounding so accusatory.

Nausea mixes with my gnawing hunger. Still, I push myself up from my crouch with a smile and turn to her. "I'll go shopping, no problem."

She nods sluggishly, beads of sweat crawling across her forehead. "Do you still have some of your school money?"

I shake my head silently. I shouldn't have spent it all—especially not on that chocolate bar. At seven years old, I should know better by now.

My mom lifts her hand, but it drops right back onto the stained sheet. "In my purse."

I look around. Over there, by the door of our trailer, it's lying on the floor. Two steps, and I'm there.

"Will you do me a favor, Sonnygirl?" she asks as I open the purse and grab her wallet.

Three dollars, five cents.

If I walk the few kilometers to the discount store instead of buying from the kiosk, I might even be able to get three kilograms of potatoes.

"My medicine. It should be in there too," my mom says wearily. "I need it."

"Sure." I tuck the money into the only pocket of my pants that doesn't have holes and open the secret compartment of Mom's handbag.

One of the paper packets is still there. She'll need more soon, but it should be enough for today. I take it out and step over to the bed. Looking at Mom—her pale skin, the shadows under her eyes, her thinning hair—isn't easy. Still, I give her an encouraging smile.

She opens her palm, and I place the packet in it. "Thanks, Sonnygirl."

I pick up a spoon and the lighter that's lying on the cardboard box we use as a nightstand. Her fingers are trembling, so I open the packet for her, letting the white powder fall onto the spoon and mixing it with a few drops of water.

"You'll feel better soon," I say as I flick the lighter on.

The memory spreads inside me like a dark fog, taking hold of me in a way I deeply despise. There's sadness mixed with helplessness, and I don't want to feel either.

"What illness did she have?" I hear Ethan ask.

Answering him is impossible, so I shake my head.

He steps toward me. "It still hurts, doesn't it?"

No. It doesn't—not until he just now conjured those thoughts back up in me. "It's in the past." I can hear how fragile my voice sounds.

Suddenly, I feel his hand on my upper arm. He touches me gently, as if he wants to comfort me. Over something I haven't needed comfort for in a long time. Still, it feels surprisingly good. As if he were standing beside me in the middle of the dark fog, giving me something to hold on to.

"Just because something is in the past doesn't make it any less important," he says knowingly.

But it shouldn't be that way. "The past is needless baggage that keeps us from being happy."

His gaze grows even more intense. "Are you?" he asks. "Are you happy?"

I nudge a few pebbles aside with my foot, imagining at the same time how I'm pushing the memory back to where it belongs. Beneath the carpet of my life. Somewhere it can't hurt me.

"I will be," I answer after a moment, and those words already carry more truth than anything anyone else will ever hear from me.

"I don't doubt that." There's admiration in his voice, not the slightest trace of hesitation.

He believes in me.

Believes I can do it.

All my life, I've been on my own, and that was fine. No, it was more than fine. It was right.

But now, standing in front of Ethan with his hand on my arm, I feel a little less alone. And instead of finding his closeness threatening, I savor it with every breath.

Chapter Twenty-One

ETHAN

Stroking Sonora's arm is far too much and not nearly enough at the same time. It's right and wrong, beautiful and terrifying.

It's everything. She, and what she shows me of herself, is everything. Everything that shouldn't be. What I shouldn't be feeling.

Everything that's still there, despite it all.

Oh God.

"Who are the flowers for?" I hear her ask amidst the turmoil of my emotions.

I look down at the bouquet in my hand. Only now do I realize that she hasn't asked about it until this moment.

Now would be the right moment to let go of her upper arm, and yet I can't. My emotions have taken over, and even though my mind is trying to resist, it's powerless.

I'm lost—and I love and hate it at the same time.

"Come with me, I'll show you," I say, even though I should really be saying goodbye to her right now. "But I have to warn you: it's a sad story."

It takes less than a second for her jaw to tighten.

"But you know what I think? Something good can come out of every sad story." I let my hand glide down along her arm. When our fingers touch, a soft tingling rushes through my body.

It's a warning—to put distance between us here and now. Still, my hand remains on hers as I look at her intently, hoping she'll come with me, so we can be a little less alone together.

Now she nods hesitantly.

And I finally manage to let her go.

To be safe, I bury my free hand in the pocket of my leather jacket as we make our way to Liam's grave. We pass other visitors, glance at the candles whose flames are barely visible in the sunlight and breathe in the fresh air drifting from the trees.

We remain silent. Until we reach Liam's grave. "Here we are," I say quietly.

She crosses her arms over her chest, as if trying to hold herself together, while she reads the inscription on the headstone.

"Your brother?" she asks, her voice as fragile as glass.

I place the flowers next to the ones I brought yesterday and set down the candle. "My twin brother."

I'm sure she's done the math. She knows he was taken from life far too soon—at just sixteen years old.

Her gaze drifts across the grave. "Do you come here often?"

"Every day." And I'd come even more often if work allowed it.

"Why?" She looks at me, confused. "Why are you doing this to yourself?"

Yesterday's candle has burned down; I take it out of the

wrought-iron lantern. "It gives me strength." Out of the corner of my eye, I see her shaking her head vehemently. "It reminds me of what matters most in my life."

Human lives and redemption—that's what my world has to revolve around.

Damn it, what am I even doing here with her?

I hear her footsteps, followed by the rustle of her jeans as she kneels down beside me. "Saving lives," she says knowingly, and I'm certain that in this moment, she's thinking of the night she saw my wound on the rooftop after I lost my patient.

I dig the lighter out of my jacket pocket. "Liam is dead because I wasn't there for him." Even as I speak the words, I feel a sharp, burning pain in my chest. I breathe in the pain, hope it swells, want it to take over and finally wipe out these stupid feelings.

Silently, she reaches for the new candle and adjusts the wick.

"With every life I save, I save him too." I know I'm crossing a line here, telling her things that are far too personal for someone who works for me. Still, I want her to know.

She wraps her hands around the candle and holds it out to me so I can light it. "And with every life you lose, you lose him all over again," she whispers, her voice barely audible, as the flame catches the wick.

"Yes." The scent of warm candle wax fills my nose and mingles with the fragrance of fresh flowers. It smells just like it did back then. On the day everyone gathered here to say goodbye to Liam.

Sonora places the candle inside the lantern, then fixes her gaze on me. "This is madness."

"I can't help it," I admit, fully aware that she won't understand.

No one ever has, and she's even less likely to. Still, more than anything, I wish I could get just that from her: understanding.

I look deep into her eyes. "His death was my fault." Everything inside me is pain. I need it, breathe it, taste it, feel it like needles on my skin.

The sound of waves.

Her brow furrows, she bites her lower lip, and with frantic movements, she plucks fallen leaves from Liam's grave.

"It happened on the beach," I begin to explain, but Sonora raises her hands defensively.

"Were you identical twins?" she asks, completely out of the blue.

"Yes."

"I bet you always wore the same clothes, right?" A bright laugh escapes Sonora's lips.

The memory makes me smile. "For a while, we insisted on having the same haircut." My God, Liam drove the hairdresser crazy. But every time we sat in our chairs after the cut and looked at each other in the mirror, we knew it was just right.

Sonora nudges me. Her eyes sparkle brightly. "Could you even fool your parents?"

I get lost in her gaze, feel the lightness it carries. "Oh, definitely."

The corners of her mouth twitch. "Tell me about it," she says in a way that makes it impossible not to.

I push myself up from my crouch. "So, the game went like this: when Mom or Dad called Liam, I'd answer—and vice versa." We were unbelievably good at it. "Whoever managed to fool them the longest won."

"And what was the prize?" Sonora brushes her curls from her face with a smile and nods toward the wooden bench under the tree next to Liam's grave.

"That was the best part," I reply, following her to the bench. "Teenage Mutant Ninja Turtles."

Sonora sits down and crosses her legs into a lotus position. "Trading cards or action figures?" There's a touch of longing in her voice.

I sink onto the bench beside her. "We were crazy about both." My God, the way he lit up every time he won. "When we lost our baby teeth at different times, it was a huge problem."

"I can imagine." Sonora's expression is full of warmth, and once again, I find myself on the verge of getting lost in it.

"Fortunately, we still had our own language, with which we drove everyone mad: Liethamese," I tell her, and in that moment, I realize that I haven't thought about any of these things in ages. That whenever I think of Liam, I only ever see that one day at the beach. I hear the crashing waves and the screams. I taste the salt.

Feel my guilt.

"What did that language sound like?" she asks.

A leaf drifts down from the birch tree beside us and lands in Sonora's curls.

Almost involuntarily, I reach out my hand for the leaf, and suddenly it feels as if the air between us has stilled.

"Deng bui na dontila," I hear myself say, and it's not just the words, but the way I say them that frightens me.

"What does that mean?" she breathes.

You are the light. The words sit so lightly on my tongue, I can barely keep them in. And yet I know I must.

This is going way too far.

She's still Sonora, my colleague, whose entire life depends on her job, as she explained to me just a few days ago.

And I'm still me—her boss, whose heart is supposed to belong to the job alone.

Everything we're doing right now is wrong.

With a deliberate cough, I lower my hand. "It means: Mom doesn't know about any of this."

Her laughter is so contagious that I feel a little lighter myself. It takes her a while to compose herself.

Giggling, she holds her stomach. "You two must've been quite the pair."

"More than that." Much more. Because what she just learned is only a fraction of what defined Liam and me. "Thank you for reminding me," I say softly, avoiding her gaze because it's far too dangerous. Thank you for being here, my stupid, stupid heart adds.

She swallows. "I still have something to take care of, and there's work waiting," she murmurs, unfolding her legs from the cross-legged position to stand up.

"Yes, I have appointments as well." I can feel the sense of relief Sonora gave me in the past few minutes slowly fading—and it has to.

Chapter Twenty-Two

SONORA

Operating rooms are safe places. Spaces where facts outrank every emotion. Where fractures, inflamed body parts, and defective organs lie on the table instead of people and their personal fates.

As surgeons, we're not just allowed to distance ourselves from our patients—we have to. Because if we let emotions take control of our actions, we couldn't be the best version of ourselves.

In the OR, we're not human. We're doctors. We function.

And that has to be true today as well, even though I'm going to remove the woman's kidney cyst—whose anesthesia the anesthesiologist is currently checking—with Ethan of all people. The fact that he's here mustn't change anything. Not my behavior, not my thoughts.

Still, I catch myself glancing over at him. The surgical mask hides most of his face, which only makes the green of his eyes stand out even more under the bright lights. He's studying the monitor with the vital signs intently.

"Shall we, then?" he asks the anesthesiologist in that smooth Dr. Perfect manner of his.

A few days ago, that would've unsettled me. I would've wondered whether this disciplined man was really him. Today, there's only one thing I wonder: how to get my stupid heart to beat at a normal rhythm in his presence.

"Dr. Wells?"

I blink. Fortunately, it only takes a fraction of a second to regain my focus. Ethan has the scalpel in hand, and the patient's abdomen is already disinfected. "Ready to go," I say quickly, and smile—stupidly, since he can't see it under my mask.

Now he focuses on the surgical area and swiftly makes the incisions in the patient's abdomen, into which I insert the thin tubes for the laparoscopic instruments. Through one of the tubes, Ethan positions the camera, and a few minutes later, its image appears on the monitor.

Everyone watches—except me. Instead, I take the opportunity to observe Ethan. He looks like a statue—so flawless. So untouchable. But in my mind, I hear his laughter—that wonderfully cheerful, carefree laugh he had when he talked about his brother this morning.

Deng bui na dontila, his voice now whispers inside me, and once again, the words feel as if they mean something truly special.

"Here we have the cyst."

Damn it, I shouldn't be staring at him like this, longing for the Ethan he revealed to me today. And my heart definitely shouldn't be racing like this because of it.

"Dr. Wells. The dry electrode, please." Ethan's composed tone helps me snap back to reality.

I hand him the dry electrode and the grasper he also

needs. Our fingers touch—just for a moment, not even a second too long—and yet I want more.

Stop. Feelings have no place in an operating room. Not for the patient's sake, and especially not for the boss, who clearly has no trouble focusing solely on our task. So I force myself to concentrate on the monitor.

Together we remove the cyst, find a shared rhythm, work hand in hand, and finally seal the blood vessels. When he asks me to check the surgical site for bleeding, I look especially closely. Here at Halifax Harbor Hospital, he's still Dr. Perfect, who demands top performance from himself and his team. Both he and the patient deserve nothing less from me.

"Looks good," I say, pleased.

"It does."

I'm grateful there isn't the slightest trace of warmth in his voice. Still, I can feel disappointment spreading inside me.

This has to stop. It's wrong, and in more ways than one.

"Then let's close," I say, carefully removing the instruments from the tubes and placing them into the aluminum tray the scrub nurse is holding.

"You suture." He gestures to the suturing kit. The part of his face I can see appears unreadable.

It helps me perform flawlessly as I stitch the small incisions on the patient's abdomen.

A few minutes later, satisfied, I set the suturing kit aside and declare the procedure complete. As I turn toward the exit, I suddenly notice Claire standing behind the glass panel of the observation room.

Arms crossed over her chest, she fixes her gaze on me. Her expression is… knowing.

Did she notice how I looked at Ethan during the surgery? Did she read from my expression what his presence does to me?

The thought makes me feel hot and cold at the same time, and I know that if I don't push it aside immediately, it'll drive me crazy.

She could have a thousand reasons for looking at me like that. Maybe she wanted to perform the surgery herself, or she's upset because she's been assigned to ward duty. She might just be in a bad mood, feeling down about the breakup with Jake, or, or, or.

Or maybe she senses that my emotions go haywire whenever Ethan's around.

No, she doesn't.

With nothing better to do, I lift the corners of my mouth and wave at her.

She waves back.

Ethan walks past me toward the exit and disappears through the swinging door. I don't watch him go but signal to Claire that I'll talk to her outside in a moment—though she doesn't even notice. Her gaze follows Ethan, and with every second she keeps looking at him, her jaw muscles tighten more.

She hates him. Thinks he's that selfish perfectionist I once believed him to be too.

If she knew what he was really like, she'd be ashamed she never gave him the slightest chance from the start. She'd realize she was wrong to accuse him of not caring about our patients.

That's the only thing he cares about. In a way that might even control him too much.

Will Claire ever understand that one day?

Probably not, I answer my own question silently, refusing to let the memory of Ethan's pain rise any further within me, and trudge toward the door, suddenly overcome by exhaustion.

Chapter Twenty-Three

ETHAN

Without looking at Sonora, I left the OR today. During the procedure, I was focused on my work, but as soon as it was over, I avoided her. It was easier that way.

Safer.

Fortunately, I had to head straight into a complex heart surgery afterward, which kept me occupied until late in the evening and distracted me from everything related to Sonora.

Now I'm lying in bed, surrounded by darkness, waiting—like every night—for the screams. For the sound of waves, for the flatline tone, for the sirens.

For all the things that keep me from sleeping.

It's slowly building inside me, but tonight it doesn't reach my heart. I wait in vain for the pain. Instead, I feel something else, something far worse: longing.

For a little light in my darkness.

For a bit of lightness in my heaviness.

For Sonora.

For her to fill my emptiness with her laughter, my coldness with her warmth. Just like she did this morning at the cemetery.

I run a hand through my hair, trying to push these thoughts away. They're wrong. Not just because they make me forget what I must never forget, but also because I'm Sonora's boss.

Only last week, I called Claire and Jake into my office to remind them of the hospital rules and make it clear how dangerous emotions can be in a hospital. Damn it, no one knows that better than I do—and on top of that, I'm nothing but a damn hypocrite. Jake and Claire ended their relationship while Sonora and I were growing closer.

I'm not that kind of doctor!

I have to put an end to whatever it is between Sonora and me—sooner rather than later. Because if I don't, if I let us get any closer, then…

We would both lose everything.

She would lose her job. I would lose myself and every truth I've ever believed in. I would betray Liam and everything I promised him.

Nothing has happened yet. I can still do the right thing.

I throw back the covers, head into the bathroom, and get dressed. Then I leave my cabin and set off toward Sonora's place, ready to face whatever is between us—and put an end to it once and for all.

Chapter Twenty-Four

SONORA

The potatoes are boiling. I lower the heat and tilt the lid slightly, so the water doesn't boil over. In my mind, I go over my finances. I managed to stall the cemetery administration until the end of the month, which means I can use the paycheck—hopefully deposited in two days—to balance and close the temp account. Then there's next month's rent, $438. I need to set some of that aside, so no one starts asking questions. The insurance policies remain on hold and…

"How long are you planning to keep up this potato diet, anyway?"

Autumn's voice is soft, but I still flinch, as if I've been caught. Luckily, it's only for a moment. Then I turn to my roommate with a grin as she lets her oversized shopping bag drop to the floor. The dull thud is surprisingly loud.

"Wow, are there bricks in there?" I ask, eyeing the bulging bag.

She gives a gentle smile. "Just books."

I know. Still, it was the perfect opportunity to distract

her from her question. And I'd better keep going with that before she brings up the potatoes again. "You look tired. Are you okay?"

"I'm fine," she says, rubbing her eyes. "I just really need to sleep." She sinks into a chair and lays her head on the table. Her red hair glows against the white surface. "I'm starting to see things that aren't even there."

I laugh and slide the lid back onto the pot now that the water has calmed down a bit. "Fairy-tale princes or ghosts?"

"I'll leave that decision up to you." She tries to smile, but the corners of her mouth seem too heavy. "Just now I thought your boss was standing outside the house."

Ethan? He's here? In my mind's eye, I see him standing at the front door—absurdly on horseback, clad in shining armor with a sword in hand.

"Definitely a ghost." I try to sound completely relaxed, though I'm not sure I succeed.

Autumn doesn't seem to notice, but in her state, that's hardly surprising. "Okay, I need to go to bed." Yawning, she hauls herself up from her chair and presses a kiss to my cheek. "And stop with this potato diet. Seriously, you don't need to lose weight," she adds, nodding toward the pot next to me.

"I'll think about it," I reply vaguely, my thoughts still stuck on the question of whether Ethan is actually outside or not. And if he is, why he came.

Because of me?

The thought sends a tingling sensation through my stomach that slowly creeps toward my heart. It's so intense I can hardly ignore it. Not for the first time, I realize I'm in serious trouble.

Autumn's eyelids look heavy, yet she gazes at me seriously. "No. That's it with the dieting. You're perfect just the way you are."

Do I hear a trace of wistfulness in her voice? Probably not—everything's fine. With her, with me, and most of all with Ethan—who is definitely not here.

"We'll talk about it tomorrow." I nod toward the door. "Once you've stopped seeing things that aren't there," I say with a wink. And once I've stopped feeling things that aren't allowed to exist, I add silently to myself.

"That's what we'll do." She sighs, turns away, and shuffles out of the kitchen.

I wait until the bathroom door clicks shut behind her and remind myself how strong I am. That Ethan isn't here, and therefore there is absolutely no reason to go downstairs.

"And if he actually were here, it would be all the more important not to leave this apartment," I tell myself firmly. We've already gotten far too close. One more meeting outside the clinic, one more conversation, one more touch, and… No. None of that can happen.

I grip the kitchen counter, listening to the water simmering in the pot. Autumn turns on the shower.

The last time I saw him at the clinic, he seemed fine. Perfect as always. What could have brought him here? Maybe he wants to tell me I crossed a line earlier in the OR. That the looks I gave him were inappropriate.

Maybe it is something else entirely.

What if he *needs* me?

That would be insane. I'm insane.

Still. Not knowing is driving me mad. All those unanswered questions circling in my head—they won't let me sleep.

"He's not down there." I closed my eyes, breathing against the turmoil inside me. "Everything is fine." Even as

I said the words, I knew they weren't true. Nothing was fine. Not at all.

"Pull yourself together, Sonora. This is ridiculous." I push off the kitchen counter with determination, ready to put an end to the chaos inside me—by seeing with my own eyes that Ethan isn't here.

Needlessly, my heart beats a little faster as I slip out into the hallway and shove on my shoes. With every step down the stairs, my breathing grows heavier. By the time I reach the ground floor and push open the door to the outside, the fluttering in my stomach starts all over again.

I know exactly what this feeling is: hope. That Ethan is out here waiting for me. Which, after everything that's happened in the past few days, is just the next item on my list of insanities. There's really no saving me anymore—especially because another item sneaks onto that list right away: the frantic way I look around.

There he is: Ethan, pacing up and down along the side of the house, his head bowed, running his hands through his hair.

Shit, it's true.

The moment of cardiac arrest that steals my breath now goes right onto my list as well.

"It has to be," he murmurs suddenly, so softly I can barely make it out. "Has to. Has to. Has to."

Turmoil. That's what I hear in his voice. It's the same feeling that's consuming me, and yet I step toward him.

"What are you doing here?" My voice sounds hoarse.

He lifts his eyes, and the sight of him hits me straight in the heart. "I…"

"What happened?" I hear myself ask, even though I can see something is tormenting him and I know he's going to talk about it. I'm aware it's going to hurt—so why the hell do I want to know?

He buries his hands in his pockets, as if he needs to stop them from acting on their own. "I wanted to… I… I'm sorry," he says, turning to leave.

As he passes me, I instinctively reach out and place a hand on his forearm to stop him.

For a moment that feels like an eternity, we look at each other. My hand remains on his arm, unmoving.

His breathing is heavy. "Are our patients all right? Were there any issues?"

"That's why you came?" *To ask me that? I don't believe it.*

He nods.

Nonsense. "We had to adjust the pain medication for the woman with the kidney cyst, otherwise it was quiet," I reply anyway. I should be glad for the change of subject, but somehow it feels wrong not to talk about what's really going on—whatever that is.

He seems to relax. "No emergencies?"

Only the one happening right now, I'd like to say. "No," I say instead. All my life, I've looked past the dark topics toward the sun blazing on the horizon, and now's not the time to stop. Whatever it was he actually wanted from me—if he's not going to say it, it's better not to dig any deeper.

"Okay, thanks." He breaks our eye contact, and I suddenly realize I'm still holding his arm. "Anything else I should know?"

A thousand and one things.

That I can't stop thinking about him, even though I couldn't care less. That I long to hear his laugh, even though I've only heard it once. That he touches something deep inside me, in a place I don't let anyone near—not even myself. That this terrifies me, and yet I can't get enough of it.

But also, that whatever this is—it has no future.

The rules at Halifax Harbor Hospital are crystal clear. He knows that just as well as I do—maybe even better.

So I do what I do best: I shove these inappropriate feelings under my emotional rug, where I can't see them anymore, so I can pretend they don't exist.

"No, everything's perfectly fine." The words leave my mouth barely above a whisper. I pull my hand from his forearm and clasp my fingers together. "See you tomorrow."

"Yeah." A wistful smile spreads across his far-too-handsome face. "See you tomorrow, then."

Every part of me is screaming to stop him.

Still, I just stand there and watch as he turns and walks away. As he glances back one last time, his eyes searching mine, and then disappears into the darkness of the night.

Chapter Twenty-Five

SONORA

The nighttime encounter with Ethan—no, Dr. Stone—still weighs heavily on me. I try to shake it off, to focus on my work, to stop wondering why he really showed up at my door. I've managed quite well over the past few hours, not least because we haven't seen each other.

And that's how it's going to stay, because I've just entered the ER, which requested a surgical consult, placing me far from surgery and his office. Just as I begin to feel safe, I spot Ethan of all people, caught in what appears to be a very heated discussion with Dr. Franks, the head of the emergency department.

"The hospital fund could cover it," says Dr. Franks as I pass the two of them as quickly as possible—of course without looking at my boss.

I don't catch what Ethan replies.

I step up to the reception desk. "Where is the surgical consult needed?"

The tall coordinator, wearing his headset as always, points to Bay Three. "Girl, seven years old, swallowed a foreign object. But Jake's already with her. He happened to be here and took over the case."

"All right, looks like it's back to ward duty for me." As I turn away, I notice that the door to Exam Room One is open. Out of the corner of my eye, I catch sight of a woman curled up on the exam table in pain. A tortured sound reaches my ears.

"Female, forty-five, disoriented. Severe cramping abdominal pain, fluid loss, fever."

That was Nyla's voice, but that's not why I stop and take a closer look. It's more a barely tangible feeling that compels me. And it doesn't mislead me.

"Ms. Cox!" I exclaim in alarm before stepping into the room. I knew I'd see her again, but I didn't expect it to happen so soon.

Today, she looks even thinner than before, her cheeks sunken. A woman on crutches with a worried expression is holding her hand. Even if the two didn't look so much alike that she could only be her sister, it would still be obvious.

"Hey, Sonora." Nyla, who's wearing a paramedic uniform today, administers an injection. "What are you doing here? I didn't request a surgeon." Standing beside her is a muscular man in a paramedic uniform who also looks at me questioningly, along with a colleague from the emergency department and two nurses.

"Actually, I'm here because..."

Before I can finish the sentence, Ethan bursts into the exam room. He's immediately at Ms. Cox's side, greeting her. "What has she had so far?" he then asks, turning to Nyla.

She frowns in confusion and gestures toward her colleague. "Dr. Mayer is the attending physician."

"So am I," he replies, signaling her to finally answer his questions.

"Butylscopolamine intravenously for the cramps and the pain, isotonic saline solution for the dehydration," my roommate replies, handing him the medical file. "She didn't want to come at first, but then briefly lost consciousness. We had her sister's consent to bring her in."

"That was exactly the right thing to do." Ethan's jaw clenches. "Thank you."

Nyla and the paramedic say goodbye and leave the treatment room, while the emergency team continues their work, attending to Ms. Cox. I glance after my roommate for a moment, wondering what seems odd about the scene, but I can't put my finger on it. I should be focusing on the case anyway, even though Ethan is already asking Ms. Cox all the important questions in order. She doesn't respond, but at least the painkillers seem to be taking effect by now.

"I want to go home." She shakes her head stubbornly.

Her sister looks back and forth between Ethan, Dr. Mayer, and me, clearly seeking help. "She's been throwing up constantly since yesterday, clutching her stomach, sweating. She needs help."

"Hi, I'm Dr. Stone." Ethan offers an encouraging smile.

"I'm Martha," she replies.

"Hi, Martha, nice to meet you." A flicker of hope crosses his face. "Your sister is suffering from a recurring gallbladder inflammation caused by blocked bile ducts," he explains gently. "The only way to stop it is to surgically remove the gallbladder."

She nods shakily. "Do it."

"No!" Ms. Cox protests, apparently emboldened by the cocktail of medications in her system.

The emergency doctor fixes his gaze on Ethan. "The

initial treatment is complete. My colleague will take her up to the ward," he says, gestures toward the nurse beside him, and turns to leave.

"I won't allow that." Our patient shakes her head vehemently.

"You need help." Her sister's voice is intense and pleading now. So much so that something happens—something that really shouldn't be possible.

I feel her pain.

Our patient crosses her arms over her chest, and the nurse's expression turns sorrowful.

"I can handle this on my own," our patient grumbles.

I can handle this on my own, my mom snaps at me from within. She doesn't belong here. I push her back, breathe through the memory, and fidget with my fingernails.

Martha reaches for her sister's hand but can't quite grasp it. "You can't, and it's time you finally admitted it."

Yes, Mom, I know that, my own voice echoes in my head.

Please don't. I don't want this.

Out of nowhere, Ethan is suddenly beside me, his questioning gaze meeting mine. I swallow against the nausea rising within me along with the memory.

"You look pale, Dr. Wells," he says, far too concerned.

I wave him off. "I'm fine."

He studies me for the briefest moment, then adjusts a stool for Martha so she can sit down. "She needs this surgery," he urges her earnestly. "Talk to her, do everything you can to convince her."

He still believes he can win. My God, when will he finally understand that there's no hope, no matter how badly he wants it?

"I'm fine, I've got this under control." Ms. Cox's words stab into my heart like a knife.

I'm fine, there's nothing wrong, my mom slurs in my mind, and I realize there's only one way left to get myself to safety. From this situation, but even more so from the memory.

"I'm sorry, I have to go." Gasping for air, I whirl around and flee.

"Dr. Wells!" Ethan calls after me. I know he doesn't understand, but I can't do this. I can't keep watching everyone try to reason with Ms. Cox, knowing it will break them.

Sonnygirl, come on, let's just chill for a bit.

Shut up, Mom.

Just shut up!

I march straight out of the emergency room, but my mom's voice follows me. I can't shake it off like I usually do. I keep running toward the roof, and when I finally reach it, I burst outside.

Leaning on my thighs, I gulp in the fresh air, but it's still not enough—I can't get enough oxygen. The world spins. For what feels like an eternity, I fight against Mom's voice and the memories it drags along.

Everything is perfectly fine.

Everything is perfectly …

"Sonora!"

Ethan. Please no. Not him.

And not now.

He's already beside me, reaching for my arms. "What's going on?"

He shouldn't be here, shouldn't be touching me. Panicked, I slap his hands away and momentarily lose my balance. "Nothing." My voice nearly breaks.

"Ms. Cox agreed to be admitted and was taken to the ward. She promised me she'd think about it seriously. Her sister supports the treatment. She'll come to her senses, I'm sure of it." He nods emphatically. "Everything's going to be fine."

It won't be, no matter how hard he fights for it.

He tilts his head, questioning, and looks at me for a moment. "Why did you run off earlier?" he asks. "What's going on?"

"I'm fine. Everything's great." Even I can hear how much my words sound like an excuse.

Unfazed, his hands find my arms again. He catches my gaze. Concern shimmers in the green of his eyes. "No," he says gently. "Nothing is great."

This is none of his business. Even less than it is anyone else's in my life.

"It's actually the opposite, isn't it? It hurts like hell, doesn't it?" he asks, as if that isn't already too much.

He has to stop. That wound has long since healed. Why should I tear it open again? What good would that do?

I open my mouth but can't say anything. Instead, I feel my lower lip start to tremble violently. My heart is pounding hard against my chest.

"The other day you said you can't save someone who doesn't want to be saved," he continues, just like that, as if he doesn't realize what he's doing to me. "What did you mean by that?"

"Nothing," I force out in a choked voice and try once more to pull away, but he holds me tight.

He holds me as if to protect me from falling into the abyss now opening up inside me. He holds me the way a man holds a woman who means the world to him.

"Who didn't let you save them?"

His question echoes inside me. So loudly that the answer claws its way to the surface as a memory from the depths of my soul.

"Three cheeseburgers, coming right up," I say to the construction workers who eat here every afternoon after their shift and have just placed their order. The place is packed; I've been rushing from one table to the next for hours. My legs feel like they belong to an elephant. Out of breath, I stack the dirty dishes left by the previous guests and carry them to the kitchen. As I set the stack down on the pass-through, I call out the new order loudly enough to make sure the cook at the sizzling grill hears it.

Next up, drinks for tables three and five, table ten wanted the check, and table one asked for a maple pie for dessert.

"Miss?" someone asks behind me.

Gasping for breath, I wipe my hands on the bright pink waitress uniform. "Just a moment." I quickly grab the menus and turn to hand them to the guests. "Feel free to find a seat, I'll be right with you," I say to the two police officers standing in front of me.

Neither of the two reaches for the menus I'm trying to hand them.

"Sonora Wells?" asks the older of the two, running a hand over his salt-and-pepper stubble.

I try to muster a casual smile. "That's me."

The younger one furrows his freckled brow. "Can we talk somewhere in private?"

What do they want from me?

"It's urgent." His expression turns serious.

I nod toward the back exit, signal to my colleague that I'll be gone for a moment, and head out.

"Well?" I ask once we're outside in the March air, instinctively wrapping my arms around my chest.

The older man gives a gentle smile and takes off his cap, while the younger steps back to give us some privacy.

"A woman's body was found this morning."

Mom. She didn't come home last night—again.

"We believe it's your mother. I'm sorry." He clears his throat.

I feel the muscles in my face tighten. "Overdose?" I ask flatly.

"That's what it looks like," he replies.

The younger of the two pulls a pack of tissues from his pocket and tries to hand it to me, but I wave it away.

"I see," I say, hollow inside. I always knew it would end like this. Now that the moment has come, I can't let it shake me.

He fumbles awkwardly with the brim of his cap. "I wish I didn't have to ask you this, but… she needs to be identified."

I look him straight in the eyes as I undo the first five buttons of my waitress blouse. "Does the dead woman have this tattoo?" I ask, pointing to my sternum, where the same butterfly sits as on Mom's.

He nods.

"Then she's identified." There's no hesitation in my voice, not a trace of pain, no disappointment.

"You're underage, a colleague from the…"

"We don't need child services," I cut him off. "I'll call Dad—he'll let me stay with him. I'm always there on weekends anyway." The lie slips so naturally from my lips that, for a moment, I almost believe it myself.

The truth is, I have no idea who my father even is. Not that I need him—exactly twelve months from today, I'll be of age.

"That's good. Is there anything else we can do for you?" the officer asks.

I shake my head. "Thanks for stopping by."

Overcome by a sudden wave of exhaustion, I turn away. I didn't want to believe it for so long, but now I can't deny the truth anymore: the only person you can truly save is yourself—and that's exactly what I'm going to do from now on.

Save myself.

One day, I won't be the girl from the gutter with the drug-addicted mom anymore. I'll be someone who made something of herself. Someone who achieved something—something everyone can see.

That's my future, and on my way back to the café, I can already see it ahead of me. Once behind the counter, I clench my teeth and force a smile, then pour the drinks for tables three and five.

"Who didn't let you save them?" I hear Ethan ask again in the midst of my memory. His hands move from my arms to my neck, gently cradling my head.

His face blurs before my eyes. I inhale sharply, yet I still can't get enough air. "That doesn't matter anymore," I reply, because it's the damn truth.

"You know what I think?" he whispers, yet the words reach my heart without effort. "That's not true." A whimper escapes my lips. "And you know what else I think?" He steps closer. His thumbs brush my cheeks. "That nothing will ever matter more to you than this."

I should shake my head, call him an idiot who doesn't know what he's talking about. Pull my shoulders back, lift my chin, wave it off with exaggerated nonchalance.

That's what I should do.

Instead, something happens that hasn't happened in ages: a tear rolls down my cheek.

Chapter Twenty-Six

ETHAN

I catch her tear with my thumb while keeping my gaze locked on hers. And for the first time since I've known her, I have the unmistakable feeling that I truly see her. See who she is deep down inside.

A broken soul who has pieced her shards back together so carefully that she can convince herself she's whole.

"Who wouldn't let you save them?" I ask for the third time, fully aware of how much it hurts her. But if life has taught me anything, it's that you can't run from your pain. You have to feel it, draw strength from it.

Her eyelids flutter. "My mom."

"Cancer?" I guess, remembering how she told me about her illness at the cemetery. "Did she refuse treatment even though you tried everything to convince her it was the only right thing to do?"

Is that what's been haunting her?

She doesn't answer, but her whole body starts to tremble. Without thinking, I pull her into my arms, stroke her back, rock her gently, and feel her muscles slowly begin to relax.

"Heroin," she whispers against my chest, her voice choked.

Even though it hardly seems possible, I hold her even tighter. "Do you want to tell me about her?"

She lifts her eyelids, looks at me through tear-soaked eyes. "Because you love sad stories so much?"

"Because something good can come out of every sad story," I remind her gently.

"Yeah, if we leave it behind." She harshly wipes the tears from her cheeks. "If you'd grown up with a drug-addicted mom in a trailer park, you'd see it differently."

"Where was your dad?" I ask.

As she tells me that he left her mom before she was even born, how they fought their way through poverty together, and how she always wanted the best for her mother but never managed to get her off drugs, she looks at me as if searching my face for a very specific reaction. I don't know if she finds it—only that, in this moment, I deeply admire her for everything she's achieved despite the worst possible circumstances.

She carries even more strength and courage within her than I'd realized.

She is… incredible.

Confusion flickers across her face, mixed with warmth and a flicker of hope. "If I hadn't left it all behind, if I hadn't started fighting for my future the day I walked away from the trailer park instead of mourning the past, I wouldn't be here today."

I place my hand on hers, wanting to stop her from wiping away her tears. And as our fingers touch gently, I sense that there might be a spark of truth in her words.

That she managed all of this because she didn't look back, only forward. Because she suppressed the pain and focused on building a better future.

"But have you ever truly forgotten where you come from?" The question rises from deep within my soul. From the place where my pain and guilt reside. From the place I force myself to face every single day, no matter how much it hurts, so I can be the doctor I need to be.

She looks at me for a while. "I wish I had," she answers softly. "But the girl from the gutter is still inside me."

She hates it—I can see it in her face. More than anything, she wishes she were someone else, and no one feels that more than I do.

I run my fingers gently over her tear-soaked fingertips. "Your past is part of you—it makes you strong."

Lost in thought, she shakes her head, her curls brushing against the back of my hand. "I don't want my past."

"Neither do I," I admit. Not a day goes by that I don't wish things had turned out differently. Not a day that I don't long to be free. "But we don't get to choose that."

A flicker of defiance flashes across her face. "Yes, we do. That's exactly what we do. And we are—both of us."

There's so much truth in her words that I forget where we are, forget who we are. Only Sonora and I and this shared understanding remain. "We are," I say, my voice thick, "but in different ways."

All my life, I've felt misunderstood. Because no one could grasp what Liam's death did to me, no one could understand why it drives me so much, why nothing else in my life matters. But now there's Sonora, in my arms, so close that her breath brushes against my chin, and I know she feels just as misunderstood as I do. Because she doesn't show anyone—not even herself—what her past has done to her, or how deeply ashamed she is of it.

"You know what I think?" I can't help but move a little closer to her.

Her gaze flickers between my eyes and my lips. "That we're really just made of broken pieces?"

Maybe we are—but that's not all. "Broken pieces that suddenly make sense when they come together." My own words run straight through me, and I see in her face that she feels the same.

"Yes," she breathes.

Our noses touch, I catch the scent of her skin, hear the uneven rhythm of her breathing. There's nothing I want more than to lose myself in this moment. To let her nearness fill the emptiness inside me.

More tears dampen my fingers as they gently stroke her cheek. I slowly turn my head, my lips brushing almost against hers. My hands wander into her hair, and then I do something I never thought myself capable of:

Carefully, I kiss the tears from her cheek.

Nothing has ever felt more real, more powerful, or more intense than this moment, as the salty taste of her sadness spreads across my tongue. Gently, my lips move over her cheeks. With every tear I kiss from her skin, I feel more connected to her, and suddenly I realize it's her tears—of all things—that are beginning to heal my broken heart, just a little.

Chapter Twenty-Seven

SONORA

Although it's been three hours since Ethan followed me up to the roof, my pulse is still racing. Over and over, I think about the feeling his lips left on my skin, the words that slipped from my mouth without restraint—words I never even tried to hold back.

I wanted him to know.

And I wanted him to hold me.

Just thinking about how open I was with him, and how dangerously close we were, makes it hard to breathe. Why didn't I stay silent like I usually do, change the subject, crack a joke?

But that's far from everything, because I can feel that I would've been ready for something else entirely. I would've let him kiss me. If he had pressed his lips to mine, I wouldn't have pushed him away.

Him—my boss!

The one who's walking into the staff room right now, where all the employees were supposed to gather for a meeting. The one who holds my future in his hands—and, as of today, a part of my past as well.

Damn it, how did this happen?

How stupid am I to let him get this close of all people?

"What do you think he wants this time?" I hear Claire mutter beside me amid the chaos of my emotions.

"Probably introducing a maximum limit on bathroom breaks," replies a nurse leaning against the kitchenette counter next to her.

Both of them giggle foolishly. Jake watches them with a stony expression.

I clench my fists.

"Hey, Sonora, have you ever worn a diaper in the OR?" Claire gives me a crooked grin, and the murmuring among the staff falls silent.

Ethan enters. "Good afternoon and thank you all for showing up in such numbers."

I quickly focus on him. He positions himself by the window and looks damn attractive in his lab coat. His expression is professional, and I notice that he's deliberately avoiding eye contact with me.

It doesn't hurt in the slightest, because I know why he's avoiding me—and that he's doing us both a favor. What happened between us earlier is already confusing enough. We absolutely must not complicate it any further.

"I'll keep it brief—your patients shouldn't have to wait unnecessarily." His demeanor exudes nothing but professionalism. Not a trace of what lies beneath his words. "The board will honor us with a routine audit tomorrow and will be taking a close look at our department."

A murmur ripples through the room. The two nurses who've been here for over ten years exchange anxious glances, and the residents' bodies tense up. Only the cleaning staff shrug at the news, as if they don't understand what all the fuss is about.

Claire snorts quietly. "Now he's shitting bricks," she mutters to me.

"Dr. Walters apparently has a question." Ethan gestures toward her. "Please, don't be shy—out with it."

She gives a forced grin and shakes her head.

For a moment, Ethan's jaw tightens. Does he know what is going on here? "I'm asking all of you to give your absolute best, because the outcome of this audit means a lot for this department," he says now.

"Of course it does." That's Claire, and she has spoken the words loudly enough for everyone to hear.

"Exactly." Ethan shoots Claire a sharp look. "We need to present ourselves at our best. Tomorrow, I don't want to see anyone wasting time unnecessarily—no personal conversations or secret breaks," he continues in a serious tone.

Claire pulls her lips into another fake smile. "Don't worry, we'll all be just as perfect as you are, Dr. Stone."

My God, that is so inappropriate. When is she finally going to stop provoking him like that?

I clear my throat. "Would you explain what happens if the audit turns out negative?" I ask, deliberately sounding interested, because that's what Claire should have done. I am sure Ethan isn't asking for our help without good reason.

He looks at me briefly, and my pulse skyrockets. I can feel his kisses on my cheeks, his hands on my fingers, his breath on my skin. I can smell his scent, hear his voice.

Broken pieces that suddenly make sense when put together.

Hell yes, that's exactly how it felt. And that's exactly how it feels again now, even though our eye contact lasts only a heartbeat before he breaks it.

"An excellent question, Dr. Wells." With his hands buried in the pockets of his lab coat, he begins to pace in front of us.

"Yes, Dr. Wells, an excellent question," Claire whispers beside me, mimicking Ethan's words.

"Any misconduct, negligence, unprofessional behavior, or disregard for regulations—all of it will be noted in your personnel file if the board observes it during the audit," Ethan says, fixing Claire with an intense gaze. "That must be avoided at all costs."

Well, there it is. I knew it. That's not just a good reason—it's a very good reason for his demand. I, for one, definitely don't need anything added to my personnel file.

"Oh really?" Claire crosses her arms in front of her chest. "And what exactly is the difference between an entry in the personnel file and the pros and cons list you keep on each of us?"

Some colleagues gasp, others raise their eyebrows. My gaze shifts to Ethan, who remains completely composed despite Claire's attack. It's admirable how easily her hostility seems to bounce off him. He truly doesn't seem to care what others think of him. And that, even though he himself came dangerously close to crossing hospital regulations with me today.

Fascinated, I study his face, behind which something hides that's even more attractive than his appearance.

"Entries in the personnel file put your job at risk," he replies calmly. "Entries in my—what you call—pros and cons list are meant to identify your potential and help you grow."

I notice how stubbornly Claire suppresses a snort. "Of course."

Ethan's smile looks tired. "Any further questions?"

"How many bathroom breaks are allowed per shift?" Claire just can't help herself, apparently. To make matters worse, she now pulls out a notepad and pen, as if she plans to write down the answer so she won't forget it.

"As many as necessary," Ethan replies, still perfectly composed, while I'm already on the verge of losing it.

Can't she just let it go? He's being strict for our own good—he made that clear just now. He doesn't want to lose any of us; that's not something she should treat with such condescension. She should just pull herself together and show her best side tomorrow—then we all win.

Now she lifts her chin challengingly. "And what about breaks on the roof?"

I flinch—so sharply that anyone could have noticed, if they weren't all completely focused on Ethan, who stands before us like a rock in the surf despite Claire's attack.

"You're up there quite often yourself, from what I hear." Her tone grows more accusatory. "During working hours."

In which you're supposed to be taking care of your patients, just as you expect us to, hangs unspoken in the air.

"What exactly do you do up there?" Claire presses on, before Ethan can answer.

He screams the pain from his soul and kisses the tears from my cheeks. He is someone who feels and gives and loves, someone who holds others in such a way that they feel like they're no longer falling.

That's what he does up there.

That's who he is, for crying out loud. Not the asshole she thinks he is, just because she refuses to take a closer look!

"Working," Ethan replies with such confidence that even I would believe him if I didn't know better. "As a senior physician, I have to make numerous decisions. Leaving my office helps me gain a new perspective, so I can do what's best for the people."

Okay, so that's what he's doing up there too. That's probably why he was on the roof when we first met.

Claire grumbles irritably. "For the people, huh."

"Yes, for crying out loud, for the people," I hear myself say, far too emotional, because I just can't take it anymore. She needs to understand that she's wrong about Ethan.

Her poisonous glare hits me. *What the hell was that?*, she asks me silently, and maybe I should be ashamed of my outburst, but I'm not.

I quickly glance at Ethan, who looks at me in surprise. "We'll do our best tomorrow. Thank you for the warning," I say, because it just feels right to stand by him, even if no one else sees it that way.

He nods gratefully. "Good. Our patients are waiting."

A sense of departure fills the room. The cleaning staff stroll toward the door, followed by the residents. Claire bumps into me as she walks past. "You're a great colleague, thanks a lot."

On my first day at Halifax Harbor Hospital, she told me this place was all about unity. Why doesn't she see that she's breaking her own rules by shutting Ethan out like this? Yes, she's hurt, but what else was he supposed to do?

I fix my gaze on her intently. "Sometimes it helps to step out of your comfort zone and give others a chance."

Did I really just say that? Me, of all people—someone who knows that people are the way they are, and that no one ever truly changes?

A look of pity takes over her face. I know that expression; I've seen it far too many times in my life. "You really believe he's one of the good ones, don't you?" The corners of her mouth turn down. "What a dreamer you are."

"I'm not," I reply, "I just want to keep my job," and turn to leave.

The rest of the shift is too quiet to distract me from all the questions that have no answers. My last patient for the day lets out a sharp hiss as I remove the adhesive strip from her bandage, so I lift it as gently as possible now.

Ms. Lee, who had a new hip put in yesterday, gives me a grateful look.

"All done." I give her an encouraging smile and set the old bandage aside to check the wound. "It's healing very nicely—I don't see any signs of infection or bleeding. I'll disinfect the area, then put on a fresh bandage for you."

My patient gestures pleadingly toward her fentanyl drip. "Could we turn it up a bit? Would that be possible?"

"Already working on it." I increase the flow rate and give the painkiller a little time to take effect in my patient's body. As her facial muscles begin to relax, I nod at her. "Ready?"

She exhales in relief. "Okay."

Gently, I clean the wound and re-dress it afterward. All the while, I struggle to keep my thoughts in check—they keep drifting back to Ethan on their own.

I haven't seen him since his speech in the doctors' lounge this afternoon. My shift ends in twenty-five minutes, and I still don't really know what I'm going to do afterward.

Just go home? Catch Ethan outside the hospital after his shift and… I don't know what… make him understand he has to forget everything? Everything that happened, everything he knows about me? Yes, that's what I should do.

"Thank you," my patient says, visibly more relaxed as I secure the last piece of tape on the bandage.

I reach for her medical chart to note both the dressing change and the increase in her pain medication dosage. A quick check tells me her infusion should last for another half hour, but I want to be prepared nonetheless.

"Okay, Ms. Lee, I'll get a new IV bag just to be safe before we check the mobility of your hip." Hip surgeries can cause extensive pain, and both standing up and mobility tests are more than uncomfortable so soon after the operation. Still, they're necessary.

She nods gratefully.

I briefly take her hand and give it a reassuring squeeze. "We've got this, don't worry," I tell her, then head for the door.

I slip out into the hallway and march toward the medication storage. If I don't want to miss Ethan, I have to finish on time. I've got just under twenty minutes left, so I quicken my pace and yank the door to the medication room open a bit too forcefully—only to freeze the moment I step inside.

Ethan is standing in front of the narcotics cabinet, his gaze sweeping critically over the stock of medications.

My heart stumbles harder than ever before.

"Hi," I croak, closing the door behind me with trembling fingers.

Chapter Twenty-Eight

ETHAN

"Hi," I reply, while the image of the two of us on the roof keeps flashing through my mind, just as it has all day.

The way I hold her.

The way I look at her.

The way my lips touch her skin.

Damn, I almost kissed Sonora, and right after that, I demanded something from my team in the meeting that I don't even give myself—even though it's the only thing I should be giving.

How could I have lost myself like that up there?

Sonora leans her back against the door. Our eyes meet.

"Listen…"

"What happened today on the…"

We start speaking at the same time.

Clearing my throat, I raise my hand. "What happened today on the roof was extremely unprofessional of me," I say in the only tone that feels appropriate now: controlled, sober, professional. "I shouldn't have pressured you, and I definitely shouldn't have…"

"Should have held me? Kissed away my tears? Made me feel like there's nothing about me that couldn't be loved?"

Yes. Yes. And yes. "… been allowed to get that close to you," I finish my earlier sentence, because that sounds far less threatening than her words.

I should never have let it go that far. I wanted to end it that night when I went to her. Damn it, to this day I don't understand why I didn't.

She nods knowingly and looks at me with a longing that tears me up inside even more than I already am.

I can't give in—not just because feelings like this are forbidden in the hospital, but also because of the promise I made to Liam: that I'd never let a woman distract me again from what really matters.

So I force myself to take a step back and lean against the opposite wall. "I'm your boss, and you're…"

"I know," she replies quickly before I can go on, raising her hands defensively. "Nothing actually happened, after all." Her voice sounds strained.

Technically, that's true, but we came dangerously close.

"I need this job," she continues.

I know that, and I also know she wouldn't risk it for anything in the world. So I nod.

Her gaze turns intense. "Please just forget what happened. Especially what I told you about my mom. About me. And about my childhood."

What happened between us—I definitely want to forget that. But everything else? "Why?"

"Because it doesn't matter, and you shouldn't know it as my superior." A mix of fear and desperation floods her expression. "Please, Ethan. Promise me you'll forget it, just like everything else that happened between us, and that you'll never talk to anyone about it."

I don't understand. She shouldn't be ashamed of her past. On the contrary, she has every reason to be proud of what she's achieved. "But you are…"

"I'm nothing," she cuts me off firmly. "Just a surgeon who wants to do her job well."

And I'm her boss, who for a moment forgot that his work comes before everything else. For the first time in my life, I just want to leave something behind.

Everything we did and said. Every touch and even the smallest feeling has to disappear. I want to forget it—right now.

She picks at her cuticle. "Good, then we're agreed," she forces out and tugs even harder. "We were never up there, I never told you about my mom, and we didn't…"

Her desperate gaze meets mine, and I'm certain that, in her mind, she's lying in my arms right now. That she feels my lips on her skin. That she longs to feel exactly that again.

I look at her.

I feel the pull she exerts and how helplessly I'm at its mercy.

I know I have to leave this instant.

Quickly, I push myself away from the wall.

"That's exactly right, and now I have an appointment," I force out.

I walk toward the door leading to the hallway, the one she's leaning against, and with every inch I get closer, I feel her pull even more strongly.

Silently, I signal her to step aside so I can leave the room. She lowers her eyelids and makes at least a little space as I place my hand on the door handle.

I hear her breathing. Smell the scent of her hair.

I know I have to leave this instant, yet I pause, my gaze fixed firmly on the door.

"Can this work? Can we just be Dr. Wells and Dr. Stone?" she whispers into the silence between us.

It has to. "It's better this way. For both of us."

Although she should agree, she remains silent.

I turn my head.

Look at her.

I hear her breathing. Smell the scent of her hair.

Know that I should walk away right now…

Suddenly, she's in my arms.

I hear her breathing. Smell the scent of her hair.

Know that I should…

Her lips find mine. Or maybe mine find hers. I don't know—I only know that we're kissing, and it feels like an entire firework show is exploding.

I hear her breathing.

I breathe in the scent of her hair.

I know I'm lost.

That it's wrong.

Damn it, what am I doing here?

I pull away from her, take a step back, dazed and confused, no longer understanding myself.

"Um… well." Sonora tugs at her lab coat.

"This never happened," I hear myself say in desperation.

"Of course not." She hurries to the medication cabinets.

Shit. "Have a good evening, Dr. Wells."

"You as well, Dr. Stone," she replies.

A split second later, I leave the medication room. I don't want to, yet I turn around and meet her gaze in a way I shouldn't—one last time.

In her eyes, I see everything I feel myself: panic and longing, pain and desire, all at once.

With the last of my strength, I force myself to close the door between us.

Shit.

Stifling a yawn, I walk down the hallway toward the operating rooms. After yesterday, when I lost myself with Sonora not once but twice in a way I never should have, I didn't sleep a wink last night.

The guilt inside me is overwhelming; it eats through my chest, my lungs, my heart.

It's with me. Always. And I welcome it, because as long as it stays, at least I'll do the right thing.

I glance around briefly—after all, today's audit by the board has been announced, and the goal is to raise as few questions as possible. In the hallway, I spot only ward staff, so I pull the black container from my pocket, decide to take two pills just to be safe, and swallow them before heading to the washroom.

While I scrub in, I focus on the upcoming procedure, and by the time I enter the OR—where, of all people, Sonora has already prepped our patient—I feel ready.

And I have to be, because lying on my table is a man with acute pancreatitis, whose complex symptoms make the surgery even more difficult. I can't afford a single moment of inattention—let alone feelings like fatigue, confusion, or... longing.

"Vitals?" I ask, deliberately neutral, avoiding looking at Sonora. I still don't know how we're supposed to be nothing more than senior physician and surgeon now. Only that I have to find a way back to where we were a week ago.

"Within normal range," Sonora replies, so professionally that it actually helps me focus.

I summon the sound of waves, feel it pulsing hot through my veins as I reach for the scalpel. "Alright, let's begin. Start of procedure: nine-oh-three."

Out of the corner of my eye, I see Sonora pull her shoulders back and prepare the instruments we'll use to keep the abdominal cavity open during the operation. In her scrubs, protective mask, goggles, and colorful cap, she's almost indistinguishable from the other staff in the room—and that's a good thing.

Because now, only one thing matters: the human life lying on the table in front of me.

I make the incisions carefully, Sonora assists me in opening the abdominal cavity, over which I then lean to assess the extent of the inflammation in the pancreas.

At the same time, Sonora leans forward too, bringing our faces closer together.

That's way too close.

Now our eyes meet.

Far too intense.

I feel unbearably hot.

Her lashes flutter. "Excuse me, Dr. Stone," she murmurs, quickly pulling back. "I didn't mean to…"

"It's fine." I quickly look away from her, ask the OR nurse to wipe my forehead, and focus on our patient's pancreas, which unfortunately looks anything but fine. The inflammation is more extensive than we feared.

Sonora was right when she practically forced me, along with that blonde doctor, to take a look at the patient myself today.

I clear my throat. "We need to remove part of the pancreas." I point with my index finger to the area where the inflammation has already caused too much damage. "Dr. Wells?"

"Should I take care of the blood vessels?" she asks, reminding me of the Sonora I spoke to on the phone after my first day at work.

Assertive. Focused. Attentive.

"Yes, please." I reach for the ultrasound-guided scalpel, which allows me to make precise incisions and preserve as much of the healthy part of the pancreas as possible.

Accompanied by the steady beeping of the monitors, I get to work. Sonora manages the blood vessels I injure while cutting. My focus is entirely on my patient, on the task I must complete. We work hand in hand, functioning seamlessly together.

And yet, that very fact leaves a bitter taste on my tongue. Because I know the reason it works.

Because I deny my own feelings, see Sonora only as a doctor.

I lie to myself, shut my eyes to the truth. Just like Sonora does with her past, claiming it's the only right way to deal with it. Just like I've always believed it was wrong. Just like now, in some twisted way, it seems right for this moment in which I dedicate myself to the patient.

I'm completely focused, able to be the doctor I've always wanted to be.

Minutes later, I glance at the monitoring screens before I tackle the final section.

"That looks good," Sonora comments.

With determination, I make the next incision. Suddenly, the pancreas begins to bleed heavily at the cut site. The monitors erupt in a chaotic cacophony of beeping sounds.

"Blood pressure's dropping," the anesthesiologist shouts.

"Shit." That was Sonora, struggling in vain with the

suction device against the gushing blood, frantically searching for the source of the bleeding.

Damn it, despite all precautions, I must have injured one of the main blood vessels.

"It's the inferior pancreaticoduodenal artery," Sonora confirms my suspicion.

"Clamp it immediately, before we lose the entire pancreas. Prepare for vascular suturing." If blood flow to the organ isn't restored quickly, we might not be able to stop the resulting cell death.

The monitors continue to go haywire.

"Pulse is weak," the assistant informs me.

Sonora hands me the suction device and reaches for the clamp. I clear the view for her; she clamps the injured vessel.

I stare at the surgical site, transfixed, as she skillfully sutures the vessel and then checks her work.

"Vessel is patent, blood flow restored," she says.

Thank God. My knees nearly give out as I exhale in relief.

"There you go, that's more like it," I hear Sonora say happily, little creases forming around her eyes.

"That was teamwork at its finest," confirms the assistant, a smile visible beneath her surgical mask.

Absolutely. The man could have lost his pancreas if we hadn't reacted so perfectly. My gaze flicks to Sonora, who seems to shine brighter than the lights above us. Warmth floods my body, and I sense that I might never stop yearning to be close to her. At the same time, the past few minutes have shown that, despite our feelings, we can function together as doctors—and not just adequately, but exceptionally well.

We continue to work in harmony throughout the rest of

the operation, and when I announce some time later that the procedure has been successfully completed, a flood of questions rises within me:

What if you don't have to focus on just one thing every single second of your life, pushing everything else aside? What if it's more about directing your attention where it's needed, depending on the situation?

What if I can still be a good doctor, even though I have feelings for Sonora? What if my priorities in life can shift without any of them losing their importance?

Confused by all these unanswered questions, I leave the operating room. Even though I don't know what to make of these thoughts just yet, I do feel one thing: they're going to stay with me for a long time.

Chapter Twenty-Nine

SONORA

Together with Ethan—no, Dr. Stone—I leave the operating room and take off my surgical gown. Best if I disappear as quickly as possible and hold on to my heart as tightly as I can. So it comes with me and doesn't, like yesterday when he left the medication room, stay with him. And yet, that's exactly what happens.

Damn it, we worked so well together just now. It was like we were one, like we could read each other's minds.

We were perfect, and it felt so good that now I want him in my life even more than ever before.

Agitated, I storm into the hallway, then head to the locker room to my locker, where I grab my phone and dial June's number. The call is long overdue, and it'll help take my mind off things—which I desperately need.

"Sorry I didn't call sooner," I say after a brief greeting.

Then I tell her about the surgery and even crack a few jokes to distract not only her but also myself. When I end the call, I feel better—at least a little—and as long as I don't think about the mess I've gotten myself into with Ethan, it'll stay that way.

The next surgery, which thankfully starts in just a few minutes, will help with that.

I close my locker, take a deep breath, and lift my chin.

Three hours and an appendectomy later, I walk toward the doctors' lounge with the patient files tucked under my arm. My shift is almost over, but I still want to check in on Ms. Cox, whom we readmitted to the surgical ward two days ago. Probably only until we get the inflammation in her gallbladder under control again and she feels well enough to discharge herself. Unfortunately.

I head toward Room 225, where I find Ms. Cox and her sister Martha. Leaning on crutches, she's just making her way toward the door when I enter. Her expression is tired.

I automatically recall what Ms. Cox told me about her sister—the botched spinal disc surgery that robbed her of all will to live. I can see it's true as I give her a friendly nod.

"Hello," she says distractedly, then turns to her sister. "Should I stay, or do you want to talk to the doctor alone?"

Ms. Cox sits up in her bed. She looks stronger than she did yesterday, and her complexion isn't quite as pale. "It's fine, Martha, go home and get some rest." The look she gives her sister is affectionate and caring.

The two say goodbye to each other. While Martha is leaving the room, I use the time to review Ms. Cox's medical chart.

The door closes with a soft click.

"How are you feeling?" I ask my patient as I flip to the

next page. Her inflammation markers are still significantly elevated.

"Better," she replies.

I point to the IV line on the back of her hand. "You can thank the medication and electrolytes for that."

"I know." The weary tone in her voice makes me take notice.

"Your underlying condition remains unchanged," I remind her, even though the part of me that longs for a dramatic turnaround knows it's pointless. But the doctor in me can't give up. "Without surgery, it's only going to get worse and worse, until one day—likely very soon…"

"I know."

I know, Sonnygirl, I know I need to change something. And I will, I promise, I hear Mom whisper inside me.

For a moment, I look at Ms. Cox. So many things about her remind me of my mom. The thinning hair, the bony shoulders, the sunken cheeks.

My heart tightens painfully.

I clip her medical chart to the bed frame. "But if you know that, then why…"

"May I ask you something?" She lowers her eyelids.

"That's what I'm here for." I step up to her bed, where the visitor's chair stands—the one Martha must have sat in earlier.

"So... just theoretically... if I were to agree to the surgery... what could go wrong?" Her breathing is so shallow I don't need a stethoscope to know how fast her heart is racing.

I sink into the chair and gently explain the possible complications of the surgery.

"And how often does something like that happen?" she

asks after I've explained that there could also be chronic aftereffects that would impair her quality of life.

"About ten to fifteen percent of patients struggle with that, though the severity varies greatly," I answer truthfully.

No sooner have I spoken the words than her whole body tenses. Damn, she's about to ask me when she can finally be discharged.

In three... two... one...

To my surprise, she stays silent, looking as though she's fighting with herself.

As unbelievable as it is, the trailer-girl inside me suddenly thinks it might actually be possible that she'll agree to the surgery after all.

"Ms. Cox," I say gently, leaning forward to look at her intently. "It's frightening, I know."

"You don't know anything," she replies wearily.

"There are things in my life too that scare me so much I have to block them out just to be able to breathe," I hear myself say.

Have I lost my mind?

Why am I telling her this?

As I pick at my cuticles until they bleed, my patient exhales slowly. "Then you understand how I feel."

With every fiber of my being. "Absolutely, I do," I reply. "But just because you don't want to acknowledge something doesn't mean it doesn't exist."

Oh. My. God.

Those could have been Ethan's words coming out of my mouth, and they felt like the absolute truth. It's his belief, his drive—not mine. How is that possible? How can I say something like that and actually mean it?

Ms. Cox looks at me thoughtfully. "You think I should have the surgery."

There's chaos inside me, but this answer is crystal clear. "It's your best chance."

Now she takes my hand. "Would you look after me while I'm on the table?"

Goosebumps rise on my arms. "Of course," I reply, my voice choked—and then the impossible happens.

I'm hoping she'll still agree to the surgery. With everything in me, I wish she would change her mind.

I look at her pleadingly. In my mind's eye, her face merges with my mom's.

Okay, Mom, I'll help you, I hear my own tear-choked voice whisper.

I can do this. Her words make my heart burst. Even now, though that past lies so far behind me it shouldn't be able to touch me anymore.

"All right. Book an OR," Ms. Cox says suddenly, her voice trembling as she squeezes my hand.

It takes a moment before I realize what just happened.

She is the kind of person I thought didn't exist: the kind who can change their mind—no, their deeply held conviction.

Without meaning to, my hand drifts to my sternum. To the spot where my butterfly rests, reminding me since Mom's death that this very thing isn't possible. A split second later, I feel myself sinking into the whirlpool of my own emotions.

Chapter Thirty

ETHAN

Focusing on the CT scan, I run through tomorrow's surgery for what feels like the hundredth time, while my favorite Queen record fills the unbearable silence of my house.

The patient's aneurysm is in the left ventricle. It's been barely a week since I lost a life during a similar heart surgery. I can't afford to fail tomorrow.

The sound of waves.

I'm going to save this woman. I have to. So I go over the same procedure again and again, even though I've already committed it to memory.

"We can't change what happened, so we should look ahead." Those were Sonora's words when she found me and my pain on the rooftop after the failed surgery last week. And now, they're back with me again, along with all the warmth her presence stirs in me.

I feel a wistful smile creeping onto my lips.

Sand between my toes.

The warmth vanishes.

"The past is unnecessary baggage that keeps us from being happy," Sonora whispers, as if trying to counterbalance my memories. Maybe that's true, maybe it's not. Maybe there's something in between, or maybe it really is all or nothing.

I shouldn't be thinking about that right now. I run a hand through my hair, push away from the kitchen table, and walk over to the coat rack, where I pull the black tin from my jacket pocket. Before I can open it, there's a sudden knock at the door.

It's a tentative knock, and if I weren't standing right next to the door, I wouldn't even hear it over the music in the background.

I slide the tin back into my jacket pocket. There's another knock, this time more insistent.

"Coming," I call out, reaching for the doorknob.

Standing on my doorstep is… Sonora. And she's looking at me in a way that takes my breath away.

"She agreed," she whispers soundlessly.

What is she talking about? And why is she trembling all over?

"Ms. Cox. She wants the surgery. She's going to do it." I can see in her face that she doesn't believe it herself. "She…"

I open the door to let her in, rush over to the record player, and turn it off.

She follows me, and when I turn to face her, she fixes her eyes on me intensely. "She changed her mind."

I smile automatically, relief mingling with that overwhelming longing that Sonora's presence always stirs in me. "So people really can change."

She lifts her shoulders. "I… um…" Now her expression softens, almost pleading. "Maybe."

When she looks at me like that, I can barely control what I feel for her. "Maybe you too?"

She exhales shakily, her gaze never leaving mine. "Maybe even us," she breathes, soundless.

Her words echo inside me. They touch the place where my heart broke long ago. The very spot that, thanks to her, sometimes feels as if it might one day heal after all.

"If people can change… if the impossible can become possible…" She steps toward me, and as if in a trance, I move to meet her. "Then maybe there are paths even where we haven't seen any before."

We stop just short of one another, our arms hanging at our sides. Only a few inches separate us.

Without touching, we look into each other's eyes.

"It could be possible." Even as I say the words, I feel certain it has to be true. I already hold part of the answer—today I realized that I might not have to break the promise I made to Liam, even if I allow myself to feel something for Sonora. She hasn't distracted me from what matters in my life. On the contrary, her presence in that OR made me better than I ever could've been without her.

Or is that just what I want to believe?

My gaze drifts to her lips. There's nothing I want more than to kiss her again. To fall with her—not just for a second or a few fleeting minutes.

Suddenly, she reaches out, places her hand on my cheek, gently strokes me. "Do you really believe that?"

With everything in me, I hope there's a way for us. One that could make us both happier than we ever dreamed. And the craziest part is, I'm not afraid of that feeling. The idea that something could make me happier than my work doesn't feel like failure.

Quite the opposite.

It feels beautiful. Full of hope. Like a streak of light on the horizon of a future I've never allowed myself to imagine.

What if I helped her find a new job? Then at least one problem would be off our backs, and I'd have all the time in the world to figure out whether my feelings for Sonora are compatible with the promise I made.

Sonora's fingertips continue to glide over my skin, unchanged. "What if we…"

I step even closer—so close I can't get any nearer without touching her. We breathe in sync, look into each other's eyes, lose ourselves in one another, and in that moment, we're more connected than if we were embracing.

Chapter Thirty-One

SONORA

Ethan's gaze is full of tenderness and caution. It's as if he's afraid something inside me might break if he looks at me too intensely. As though he's silently promising that he'll never hurt me.

I breathe in his nearness and place my hand on his chest. I feel his heartbeat, let my eyelids fall shut, and become aware of the way my own heart is pounding.

It's the same rhythm.

As if we were one.

It feels right. Letting Ethan this close, standing in the middle of his living room, surrounded by silence and intoxicated by all the emotions flooding me.

Nothing seems impossible.

And now, in this moment, I'm even ready to tell him everything. To shine a light into every dark corner within me and let him see what I usually hide—even from myself. Because I know he'll catch me when I fall, just like he did when I told him about Mom.

Tears push out from beneath my closed eyelids. I don't

know where they're coming from—I just feel this deep connection to the man who's really doing nothing more than standing in front of me, yet somehow giving me something I thought I didn't even want.

But now I know I need it. I need him like I need my heartbeat.

"Hey," he murmurs gently, brushing the tears from my cheeks.

I look straight into his eyes and see nothing but warmth in them. "I have to confess something to you," I say, my voice barely audible.

With a puzzled look, he brushes a lock of hair from my face. "Okay," he says, then guides me to the couch.

No sooner have I sat down than my pulse starts to race. "I'm not who you think I am," I say anyway.

His brow furrows. "What do you mean?"

"The job at Halifax Harbor Hospital." I swallow, feeling the weight heavy on my chest. "I only got it because I lied on my application."

He places his hand on mine before I can start picking at my nails and looks at me intently. "In what way?"

For a moment, it feels like my heart stops.

I exhale in short bursts, then I tell him everything.

That I never studied at Dalhousie University, nor did I graduate from Halifax Grammar School. That instead, I went to high school in Spryfield—the school with the worst reputation in all of Halifax—and later studied medicine at a community college because I couldn't afford a prestigious university.

Ethan looks at me, visibly shocked. "You forged your transcripts?"

"How could I have ever studied at Dalhousie when I had nothing my whole life and lost my mom when I was just seventeen?" I ask, feeling all the despair from back then rise up in me again. "I was living in a van, working two jobs just to stay afloat."

No one knows that—not even my roommates. Telling Ethan now feels both painful and healing.

"I had no choice—I had to work with what I had." And that wasn't much. "A small scholarship thanks to my good grades, a cheap university, low living expenses, and a bunch of jobs with lots of night and weekend shifts."

"Shit." He claps his hands over his mouth.

I meet his gaze. "If this comes out, I'll lose my job."

"No, you'll go to prison," he corrects me, clearly overwhelmed by everything he's just learned.

I nod guiltily, my nose starting to swell. "Now you know —I'm the worst kind of fraud."

All my life, I've lied to everyone who's had anything to do with me, pretending I'm not the girl from the gutter with a subpar degree and a mountain of debt. Pretending I'm not as worthless as I've always felt deep down. "After college, I spent months looking for a job—without success. No hospital wanted to hire me, at least not as a doctor." They would've taken me as a nurse, but how was I supposed to pay off my debt on that salary?

"So you were never abroad?" His face grows even paler.

"No, I put it on my application to cover up the long unemployment. But I had no choice. More than once, doctors with degrees from prestigious universities were given preference," I tell Ethan. "If I'd also had gaps in my résumé…"

With a desperate look, he nods. He knows that's exactly how it works in hospitals, and he finds it just as awful as I do.

"I lost my last job because they found out that,

contrary to what I'd claimed, I didn't have a permanent address at the time." Oh God, I can barely breathe, my chest is so tight, but I have to get this out. He needs to know who I am before something happens between us that he'll regret once he finds out. "Still, I lied again on my application to Halifax Harbor Hospital," I force out. "There was no other way—I never would've gotten the job. And I need it."

He understands, I can see it in his expression. He knows I'm right, that they never would have hired me, that I had no real choice but to lie. Still, it takes him a moment to respond.

"You're a fantastic doctor—that's what really matters." There's so much conviction in his voice that I can't help but smile, despite my despair.

"One day it will be," I say, because that's what I want to believe. "Once I've worked at Halifax Harbor Hospital for a few years and built a good reputation, it'll get easier." No one will ever want to see my certificates again. I won't have to lie anymore. I'll finally be able to put my past behind me for good.

"No." His fingers trace across my palm. "It already is."

He can't know how much his words mean to me. And even less what they do to me. Like a protective bandage, they settle over my wound. I blink back the tears rising once again.

"Thank you," I say, my voice thick, allowing myself to believe him—even if it's just for this one moment.

I entwine my fingers with his, even though I shouldn't. I shouldn't be doing any of this, but I can't help myself.

"Still, the certificates are a problem," he says with concern. "Technically, I should report it."

Panic floods me. "That would ruin me."

"I know, oh God, I know." Agitated, he runs his hands through his hair. "I could never do that to you."

His words hit me straight in the heart. The already strong bond between us becomes unbreakable.

"Tell me more about yourself. I need to know who you really are, want to see everything about you," he says, with a look that makes it impossible for me to deny him this wish.

So I do exactly that. All evening, we talk, despair, and hope together, until we finally fall asleep on the couch.

Chapter Thirty-Two

SONORA

A ray of sunshine tickles my nose, birdsong reaches my ears, warmth surrounds me.

I blink, see Ethan's arm around my waist, hear his steady breathing. His legs are tangled with mine as he lies behind me. Out of the corner of my eye, I see that he's deeply lost in his dreams. His expression is so peaceful, so relaxed. The collar of his shirt is rumpled, a damn attractive shadow of stubble lines his cheeks.

Now a contented sigh escapes his lips. I can't help but turn to him and study his face, wondering what he'll do with everything he learned about me tonight.

Tonight.

Oh God, I shouldn't have stayed.

He opens his eyes. "Good morning," he murmurs awkwardly, then frowns for a split second. "What time is it?"

Maybe too late. Even though we didn't kiss. I glance at the clock. "Just before seven."

He exhales slowly.

"Don't worry, I've got a good relationship with my boss

—he'll understand if I'm late," I hear myself joke, because that's what I do when I don't know how to handle a situation. And this situation is… beyond words.

Ethan doesn't laugh. Instead, I feel his body tense up.

"Your boss has to perform surgery in two hours." A mix of concern and guilt clouds his face.

His words, combined with the alarm that starts ringing now, feel like a cold shower. They bring me crashing back to reality. Maybe it didn't matter *what* we were tonight. *Who* we were—that was the only thing that mattered.

We were Ethan and Sonora. Two people who got to know each other on a level that rarely happens.

Who we are now, I don't know. Still Ethan and Sonora? Can we even be them anymore?

"How about this: I'll make breakfast while you go over everything for the surgery again," I suggest, because I'd rather not think about it right now.

"That sounds great." He peels himself off the couch as soon as the words leave his mouth.

I shuffle after him. He turns to the laptop on his kitchen table, and I keep walking toward the counter.

"Which surgery is it?" My eyes linger on his coffee machine. He has a Black Luck.

"An aneurysm in the left ventricle," he replies. "Access will be tricky, and removal too."

I stare at the coffee machine—something only people who've made it in life own. He's one of those people. I'm not.

Not yet.

"I think I'll have to open the sternum." His fingers drum against the kitchen table. "I ruled out the minimally invasive approach—given the size and location of the aneurysm, it could lead to complications."

"Could lead to complications," echoes in my mind as I let my fingers glide over the sleek chrome trim of the coffee machine. Inevitably, I wonder what kind of complications last night might bring and how we should deal with them—especially at the hospital.

Good thing we didn't kiss. That we respected that boundary. We didn't do anything forbidden—technically speaking, at least.

Absentmindedly, I take the box of muesli from the half-open cupboard while Ethan continues to immerse himself in his preparations. But the thought won't leave me all morning. When Ethan closes the laptop after breakfast with a confident expression, I know I should bring it up. Still, I can't get the question past my lips.

Ethan sets his coffee cup in the sink. "Thanks for breakfast."

I wink. "Putting the muesli and milk on the table was really hard work. Not to mention the bowls."

He chuckles, then steps up beside me with a serious look. "We should talk about how we… um… move forward."

"I don't know." Even though it's unclear what we really are to each other after last night, I do know that he means a lot to me. That I'd love to spend every minute with him, make him laugh, and just be myself around him.

His fingers trace the grain of the wooden kitchen counter. "I can't expect my staff to follow hospital rules if I'm breaking them myself."

"We're not," I reply firmly. "We don't have a relationship." The words burn hot in my chest. "And no affair or anything like that either."

What we have is something entirely different. Something there are no words for.

"No, we don't," he replies. "But then what is it?"

I bite my lower lip to hold back the answer: more. It's more than everything I mentioned earlier.

He exhales in short bursts, and I can see how much he's struggling with himself too. "Damn it, how are we supposed to...?"

The clock on the wall behind him tells me we both have to be at the clinic in fifty minutes. Our patients are waiting, and I haven't even showered yet.

"I've got the day off the day after tomorrow. We could spend it together and think everything through calmly," I suggest, because right now we clearly don't have the time.

Since he started at Halifax Harbor Hospital nearly three weeks ago, he hasn't had a single day off—and probably barely a quiet night either. Letting go and clearing his head won't just do him good, it's probably the only way we'll find a solution.

"I don't know..."

"Everyone needs a break sometimes," I gently remind him before he can finish his sentence. "Even Dr. Perfect."

Lost in thought, he packs his laptop into his bag. "I'll think about it."

"Okay." I give him a warm smile. "Mind if I use your bathroom before I head out?"

"Sure, the towels are on the shelf."

Smiling, I slip into the bathroom to take a shower. A few minutes later, I'm standing in front of the sink, wrapped in an unbelievably soft towel.

"Do you happen to have a spare toothbrush?" I call out, but get no response, so I open the cabinet next to the sink. No toothbrush.

"Ethan?" I try the drawer in the vanity, but all I find are

shaving supplies. That leaves only the mirrored medicine cabinet, which I open next.

A bottle of Acqua di Giò, nail clippers, face cream, and a white container that looks like a pill bottle. I pick it up and unscrew the lid. Sure enough, they're pills. Small yellow ones I've never seen before. What are they for?

The bottle is about a third full. I tilt it slightly, and the pills slide to one side with a soft rattle.

Will you do me a favor, Sonnygirl?, I hear my mom whisper hoarsely. *My medicine. I need it.*

My chest tightens, even though the pills in my hand have absolutely nothing to do with my mom. The fact that I'm even thinking about her right now is ridiculous.

Suddenly, there's a knock at the door. I flinch so hard that I almost drop the bottle.

"Did you call me?" Ethan's voice comes through the door, muffled.

With a pounding heart, I put the can back. "No, thanks. I'm good." I shake my head at myself and my wild imaginings. "Almost done."

With no other choice, I brush my teeth with my finger. I'll stop by the apartment before my shift anyway—it's better that way, after all. Ethan and I shouldn't show up at Halifax Harbor Hospital at the same time or together.

When I leave the bathroom, Ethan greets me with the same pensive expression. I know he hasn't made up his mind yet, but I'm really hoping he gives himself the chance to take a day off to think things through.

"I have to go—got a few things to take care of before my shift," I say, raising my hand. "See you later, Dr. Stone."

He smirks. "Dr. Wells," he replies in the same disciplined manner he's often used with me at work.

I know it has to be done, but it's still hard to bring myself to leave.

Chapter Thirty-Three

ETHAN

"Suction, please."

I wait until Claire, who's assisting me today with the removal of the aneurysm in our patient's heart, clears my view of the surgical area.

I'm wide awake, intensely focused, and fully immersed in the task. Not least because I slept better last night than I have in ages. Holding Sonora in my arms seems to be the best therapy for my insomnia.

I feel a warm smile creep onto my lips at the mere thought of her. At the same time, a wave of worry washes over me. The idea of finding Sonora a different job evaporated overnight.

There's no clinic in Halifax where she could still work. The Dartmouth General Hospital is the closest facility with a surgical department, but whether they'd hire Sonora with her medical degree is questionable. And I can't recommend someone with a forged university diploma.

"Dr. Stone?" someone asks.

My gaze finds Claire, who's eyeing me skeptically. "Yes?"

She gestures toward our patient. "Um… You can proceed."

Right.

"Thank you." I quickly lower my eyelids, check that the removal of the aneurysm hasn't caused any damage, and finally nod with satisfaction. "That looks good, let's close."

I hadn't dared to hope that this operation would go so smoothly. Even though we had to take a few detours to expose the aneurysm, the heart remained unharmed and there were no complications at all. To be sure, I check the monitor readings—vital signs still look consistently good. As I turn away, I notice Claire watching me with that same accusatory look she so often wears.

Until now, I thought it was blind hatred, but now I suspect that I might be the blind one between us. I judged her prematurely, convinced that her relationship with Jake posed a risk to her work, even though they've worked side by side as a couple for years.

Was that a mistake?

"Is there a problem, Dr. Walters?" I ask anyway, even though this is certainly not the right moment for accusations.

She furrows her brows. "Not with me."

"Good, then let's get back to our work." I glance at the clock on the wall, which confirms what I already suspected. I'm running ridiculously late.

"Would you mind finishing up here?" I ask Claire, who immediately lets out a dissatisfied grunt.

"Sure," she replies, then mumbles something so quietly behind her mask that I can't make it out. Might've been "dirty work," but I'm not certain.

"Much appreciated." I nod to her and leave the operating room.

Fifteen minutes later, I adjust my newly tied tie and knock on Dr. Roberts's door.

"Come in." My boss's voice reaches me muffled through the hallway. I enter his spacious corner office whose glass front offers an impressive view of Halifax Harbor. "Dr. Stone, excellent. Come in, there's much to discuss." He waves me over and gestures toward the chair in front of his desk.

"I assume this is about the audit results?" I ask, because I'm quite certain that's why he scheduled this meeting with me.

"That's right." He looks somewhat distracted as he glances around his desk, then grabs a file. "Ah, here it is."

Two days have passed since the board took a close look at the surgical department. I've kept a close eye on the unit the entire time, aside from the hours I spent in the OR for the procedure Sonora talked me into. Everyone behaved impeccably. I know there were no issues, and I also know the board was satisfied with the numbers and facts I presented.

My boss opens the file. "First of all, the board was impressed by your dedication and the efficiency with which you've been running the department—just under three weeks after your start."

"Always the best for our patients," I confirm, enjoying the warm feeling that comes with it. "Our error rate has dropped, and efficiency has increased," I quickly add, because I've worked hard to achieve that.

"You're exceeding our expectations, I have to say, Ethan. Outstanding!" Excitement spreads across his face. "We didn't dare hope we could move on to the next step so quickly."

What's that supposed to mean? Alarmed, I lean forward in my chair.

"Well, you've already accomplished so much for the department in such a short time that the board is confident you could continue doing excellent work even with one less staff member." He nods at me encouragingly.

"Excuse me? I played the strict boss to get my team aligned and ready to show their best during the audit. And now that's the very reason I'm losing a staff member? One less doctor means everyone else has to take on more cases. That will affect the quality of care. That's not an option."

"The budget is tight. Every cent we save helps the clinic," he replies, as if he hasn't really listened to me at all. "You'll figure it out, Ethan. You're a real problem solver, aren't you?"

Anger surges through me.

I can't spare anyone from my team. They all do an outstanding job—they're all essential.

The sound of waves.

I shake my head firmly. "My team members are the problem solvers—every single one of them."

His expression grows intense. "Still, you'll need to give us a name—someone we can remove from the payroll starting the month after next. The sooner, the better."

There's no way I'm doing that! I have to act—I need to find another solution. Because if I don't, if I can't make sure every one of my team stays, people will die.

Salt on my tongue.

"I'll come up with an alternative proposal, something like…"

"Enough." Dr. Roberts slams his hand on the desk so hard that the container of pens rattles. "I thought I made myself clear." His usually kind eyes narrow into slits. "You're supposed to name someone, not come up with alternative suggestions. Why is that so hard for you to understand?"

"Because our patients need us," I reply firmly. He's a doctor too. Even if he no longer treats people, he must understand how important our mission is.

He dismisses my words with a contemptuous wave of his hand. "We're not having this discussion." His stern gaze pins me in place. "If you can't make a decision, I'll make it for you: Dr. Sonora Wells will be leaving the department. She's been here the shortest time, and we can most easily do without her."

Impossible. Never. Not Sonora.

"No!" My objection bursts out far too emotionally, and it takes all my effort to calm myself enough not to seem completely unhinged before I continue. "Dr. Wells is an excellent physician," I add, striving for a more composed tone, though my pulse is still racing.

Unmoved, he studies me. "Well then, name someone else."

"I will," I say, even though I have no idea how I'm going to manage it and rise from my chair. "Anything else?"

He shakes his head. "I expect your final answer by Friday at the latest."

I loosen my tie, but still can't seem to catch my breath. "Understood."

A piercing scream.

"Good." A broad, triumphant smile spreads across his

face. “And once again, congratulations on your fantastic audit result.”

Instead of replying, I give a brief nod, then turn away before I say or do something I can’t take back.

Silence.

I fling the door to the hallway open to fill it. Claire is leaning against the wall opposite Dr. Roberts’ office. Still in her surgical scrubs, one foot casually pressed against the wall, arms crossed.

“Problems?” she asks me coolly. I can see the satisfaction on her face.

“Not that I’m aware of,” I reply curtly.

For a split second, I wish I could just mention her name to Dr. Roberts, but she is far too good a doctor, and our patients don’t deserve to suffer just because she despises me —justifiably so, even. Somehow. Maybe.

My God, I don’t know. Just three weeks ago, I hadn’t doubted my decision for a second, and now my thoughts and feelings are riding a rollercoaster so fast that all the boundaries are starting to blur.

Sonora is right—decisions need to be made urgently, and I can only do that if I find time and peace. The day after tomorrow, I will take the day off. I have to do it before everything slips out of my control.

“Oh, and here I thought you and your curly-haired darling with the pretty button eyes were having trouble,” I hear Claire say amid my thoughts. She raises her eyebrows while I do everything I can to stay as cool as possible, even though her words hit me like poison darts.

Why does she call Sonora my darling?

Does she know something? Has she been watching us? Seen the looks we’ve exchanged lately? Or is it simply because Sonora supported me during the audit meeting?

A sharp throbbing spreads through my temples.

I take a deep breath. "Such accusations are completely inappropriate," I say firmly.

"No, you're the one who's inappropriate," she snaps back angrily. "You and that damn perfect way you run the department, the…" She suddenly falls silent.

"The what?" I search her eyes, trying to figure out what's going on inside her, but all I find is a wild cocktail of far too many emotions.

Her jaw clenches. "Nothing," she mutters through gritted teeth. "I have to go. The patients are waiting."

That's the first reasonable sentence she's said since we started this conversation. "Exactly, our patients. They're the ones who matter most."

"Of course." She forces a smile and pushes herself away from the wall.

We walk off in opposite directions, and with every step that takes us farther apart, I'm increasingly overcome by the feeling that things are in motion here—things I have no clue about. Things that could catch up with me if I don't get them under control as quickly as possible.

Chapter Thirty-Four

SONORA

The salty breeze drifts gently over the dunes of Lawrencetown Beach, carrying the distant sound of the waves to Ethan and me. Sunlight dances on the crests of the waves, where, a few hundred meters from shore, a group of surfers rock on their boards in the water.

I study Ethan, still barely able to believe he has actually taken time off. "Are you sure it was a good idea to come here of all places?" To this one beach, where he lost his brother back then.

He shoves his hands into the pockets of his linen pants, which flutter in the wind, and lets his gaze wander. "I like it here. This place reminds me of what really matters." He looks at me intently. "Have you thought about it?"

Since we said goodbye two days ago, I haven't done anything else. I've been thinking in every spare moment, but again and again, I come to only one solution.

"We could keep it a secret," I suggest, and he immediately stiffens. "No one will find out." I'd make sure of that. I can do it. I've been hiding things from others my whole life

—I am an absolute pro at it. What happened at my last job was an exception, a one-time mistake. I look at him intensely. "Trust me."

He lowers his gaze to the sand. "No way. I can't break the rules I expect others to follow."

"But that rule is stupid," I counter. "You know it—you've experienced it yourself. Whatever this is between us, it doesn't make us worse doctors. On the contrary."

"I can't do this," he repeats, running his hands through his hair. "It's wrong."

"And what's the alternative?"

"I don't know either." With a torn expression, he stares out at the endless expanse of the ocean. "We can't go on like this forever."

His words send a wave of heat and cold rushing through me at the same time. Is that how he feels about us? As if it could last for all eternity? "Forever?" I ask, moved.

His expression remains serious. "Forever."

My knees give way, and I let out a shaky breath, unable to believe what that one word is doing to me—and even more so, that it doesn't scare me.

In that instant, I want to kiss him. Right now.

But it's forbidden.

Not yet, because it doesn't have to stay that way, as I suddenly realize.

"And what if we get rid of the rule? You're in a position to do that, aren't you?" I ask, and in the same moment, it hits me that this might actually be the perfect solution to two problems. "Claire and Jake could be together again, and we could… get to know each other better. See where this leads us."

The idea is brilliant. At work, we'd still have to play our roles for a while so Ethan's move against the rule doesn't look suspicious, but we can handle that easily. Plus, Claire will finally stop hating Ethan and see him for what he really is: a doctor who would sacrifice his life even for a stranger.

"What do you think?" I nudge Ethan, prompting him, but he shakes his head vehemently.

In my mind, I'm suddenly back on the rooftop terrace, where I saw that all-consuming pain in his eyes the night after the failed operation. His guilt, eating him alive. The fact that this man doesn't allow himself to have a life of his own because he believes he has to be there only for others. How this burden he's placed on himself is slowly breaking him.

"Or is it more about the fact that your life is nothing but work?" I ask, even though the topic is so uncomfortable I'd rather avoid it entirely.

He stays silent for a while, then points to a sandy stretch of beach. "Over there, I was sitting and flirting with a girl I'd just met."

I immediately realize this is the beginning of his story. The story I didn't want to hear back at the cemetery, because I thought I wasn't strong enough for his wound. Even now, I could insist he answer my earlier question, just to avoid hearing what really happened with his brother back then. At the same time, I wonder what would happen—between me and him—if I didn't distract Ethan from his thoughts right now.

Maybe I could handle it after all? And maybe, after the pain, there's something more healing than constantly sweeping it under the rug?

Silently, I reach for his hand and squeeze it.

"She was a stranger, and yet I chose her over my brother." His teeth grind together, the muscles in his neck tense. Then he tells me how he sent his brother out surfing alone.

I can sense how this story ends, feel my chest tighten, and I know he feels the same.

With clenched fists, he stares out at the sea. The waves roll in endlessly, breaking near the shore.

Now he raises his hand and points to the sandbank, where a surfer is just now paddling toward a wave. "He was all alone out there. If I'd been with him, I would've pulled him out of the water right away." Guilt and self-loathing flood his expression. "He died because I'd rather flirt with a stranger than surf with him."

Until now I've stayed silent, but I can't anymore. Not when I see how much he hates himself for what happened. "You were a teenager—your hormones were in charge," I say gently. "And besides, there's no way you could've known he was going to get into trouble. He was probably a good surfer, right?"

"That doesn't matter." Looking down, he pushes the sand away beneath his feet.

I make him look at me. "Yes, it does." He shouldn't be so hard on himself. "How long are you going to keep punishing yourself for something that was really just a tragic accident?"

Some things happen for no reason at all. Terrible things. Things we think we'll never survive. Things that make us feel like we'll never be happy again.

I meet his gaze, unwavering. "It was just fate." Just like the circumstances I grew up in. No one's to blame.

"Fate?" Just two weeks ago, he told me he didn't believe in that. Now he stares absentmindedly up at the sky, where seagulls shriek as they fly overhead.

"Yes." Just like the fact that we met each other, I add silently. "And you know what?"

His gaze finds mine.

"I want to believe that fate can be something good," I say, thinking of the two of us and how our paths crossed at Halifax Harbor Hospital. "That it can shine for us—sometimes even brighter than our dreams."

A smile creeps onto his lips. "That's a lovely thought."

"Feels warm in there, doesn't it?" I place my hand on his chest, even though I probably shouldn't.

His hand finds mine, and then I see it in the deep green of his eyes. I see that he feels it. I see that his soul is finding a little peace—right now.

"You're allowed to be happy," I whisper against the sound of the ocean. "Fight the relationship rule."

He rubs the bridge of his nose. "Damn, I…"

Gently, I let my thumb glide across his palm, and I keep going until his expression softens.

"I need to think about it," he says, his voice hoarse. "Give me some time, okay? I don't want to rush things. There's too much at stake."

I can practically feel his inner conflict, along with the incredible burden he believes he has to carry. Every second, every hour, every day. He wants to do right by everyone, wants to get everything right. He demands of himself what no human being could ever achieve.

That ends now.

"Do you still surf?" I ask him.

He shakes his head. "I haven't had time for that in years. What about you?"

"As a kid, I was in the polo club, so I never had time to learn surfing." I wink at him. A bright laugh escapes his lips, and I love it. I love seeing him so relaxed. "Will you show me how it's done?"

His eyes light up. "There's a surfboard rental a few meters down the beach. You're going to love it."

No. I love you. With every beat of my heart. "Absolutely," I murmur, not understanding what's happening to me. All I know is that it feels as if fate has begun to glow inside me in a way I've never known before.

Half an hour later, we're standing at the water's edge in wetsuits, surfboards under our arms. Ethan explains what matters most when surfing. I practice balancing on the board in the sand, and every now and then, I fall into Ethan's arms.

In the distance behind him, the picturesque village of Lawrencetown blends harmoniously into the natural landscape. The charming houses, surrounded by lush greenery, give the place a warm and welcoming atmosphere. Our laughter fills the air, we tease each other, touch each other, lose ourselves in time and space.

Nothing else exists. Not the hospital, not Ethan's guilt, not the girl from the gutter. It's just us. Ethan and Sonora, two people whose souls are free together for a few hours. It's that one feeling I've wished for all my life, and now that I feel it, I want it to last forever.

I know it can, as long as Ethan is with me.

"You ready for your first wave?" He grabs the surfboard stuck in the sand beside him and nods toward the ocean.

I grab my board. "So ready."

Side by side, we wade into the water, lie down on our boards, and paddle out to sea. Farther and farther, toward the low-hanging sun, straight to the spot Ethan pointed out hours ago when he told me about his brother.

When we arrive, we sit up. I glance at Ethan, afraid I'll see that hard expression on his face again. That I'll see the memory in his eyes, along with the guilt that controls him so deeply.

But I find none of that. Only the gentle smile and the shining eyes he gives me. Droplets of water glisten on his skin, and the sun casts his features in a red-golden light.

My longing to kiss him becomes overwhelming. I want to stroke his cheeks, breathe in his skin, lose myself with him.

But I know if I kiss him now, we'll cross a line. If our lips touch, I'll belong to him—with everything I have and everything I am. There'll be no turning back.

He wanted time, and I promised him that. That's all I should be thinking about now.

Our eyes meet as we sway side by side in the water, and I think I can see in his eyes that he's tormented by similar thoughts.

I don't want to see him sad, so I flash a cheeky grin. "Did you know that some fish can change their sex to keep the balance in the school?"

Without breaking eye contact, he suddenly grabs my surfboard and pulls me closer to him.

"Deng bui na dontila," he murmurs hoarsely.

He said that to me once before, back at the cemetery. What did it mean again? Confused, I furrow my brow—then it comes back to me. "Mom doesn't know?"

He shakes his head, his hand finding my cheek. "You are the light."

Suddenly, it feels as if time stands still. As if even the vastness of the ocean around us gets lost in the infinity of this moment.

I let out a shaky breath as he comes closer and closer. I know I have to stop him.

Now.

Right this second.

Still, I move toward him.

Our boards sway in different rhythms, but when our lips finally meet, they find a new, shared rhythm.

Ethan's kiss is full of tenderness and care. It feels as if he were afraid something might break if he kisses me too intensely. As if he were trying to promise me that this—whatever is happening between us—will never hurt. That this, the two of us, can actually turn out well.

More than anything, I want to believe that.

Our lips touch gently, his hand caresses my cheek, I taste the salt on his skin, hear the flow of his breath.

And then I fall. Together with him, I fall and fall and fall, until the sun sinks into the sea beside us.

Chapter Thirty-Five

ETHAN

The waves lap around my legs, the last light of the day tickles my cheek, and the roar of the surf grows louder. But I barely notice any of it, because all my senses are focused entirely on Sonora.

On the taste of her lips, the soft sigh she ggives, the way her breath brushes against my skin. How she intertwines her fingers with mine, as if she wants to wrap me in her light.

And that's exactly how it feels. As if her kiss makes me glow from the inside, and even in the places where my guilt usually swallows any trace of light like a black hole, it becomes just a little brighter.

I open my eyes and notice she is looking at me. When our gazes meet, our kiss deepens. There is nothing I want more than for this moment to never end. For us to stay out here on the sea forever, far away from the obstacles waiting for us beyond the shore. But then the darkness of the approaching night settles over Sonora's face. At night, it can get dangerous out here—we can't stay.

"I think we have to go," I whisper between kisses, but make no move to let her go.

"I know." She covers my cheeks with tiny kisses. "I know," she breathes again as her lips reach my ear.

A pleasant shiver runs down my spine. I bury my face in her hair, inhale her scent. Inhale her, with all her warmth.

"Will you promise me something?" I ask.

"Anything."

I cup her chin, tilt her head up so she would look at me again. Behind her, the first stars sparkle in the sky. "Promise me that this—no matter what happens—will never end." I can't believe I am actually saying it.

A wistful smile creeps onto her face, then her expression turns sad.

"Promise me that no matter what happens, we'll find a solution together," I say, and in that moment, I know I have to talk to Dr. Roberts. There's no other way.

She nods and brushes a kiss against my lips. "Promise," she whispers, her voice trembling.

We sink into another kiss, one that feels like we're sealing our promise.

Only minutes later do I pull away from her with a heavy heart and nod toward the beach. "Ready?"

In the rising moonlight, I can see that her smile is forced. "Ready," she confirms anyway, and we paddle back to shore.

As we trudge toward the surf rental with our boards under our arms, it hits me that we've been out far too long. If the guy we borrowed the boards and wetsuits from earlier is no longer there, we're in serious trouble—after all, we left our valuables with him.

Sonora is unusually quiet, so I take her hand. "We should do this again soon."

"Definitely." She strokes my palm with her thumb.

We approach the surf rental and I spot a light. Even though the owner is anything but friendly, he'll get back what belongs to him, and we'll get back what he held for us.

When he hands me the clinic phone, I see the small white light glowing at the top edge. "Someone called," I say, and a split second later, my chest tightens.

Holding my breath, I unlock the screen.

"Who was it?" I hear Sonora ask, as a darkness falls over me, abruptly extinguishing all the light of the past few hours.

"Claire." She called a total of twenty times, and I didn't pick up.

Waves crashing.

Oh God.

I have no idea if or how Sonora reacts to this information. In the whirlpool of guilt that takes hold of me in that moment, I no longer perceive her.

My body tenses, I turn away without a word and rush out of the cabin. On the way, I tap the first of the five voice messages Claire left me.

"Dr. Stone, please call me. It's urgent."

Not good. This is really not good. I press the next one.

"Mass pile-up on Highway 102—dozens of injured are about to come in."

Salt on my tongue.

I can't breathe anymore, yet I force myself to listen to more messages—fully aware that I deserve the pain they stirr inside me.

"Where the hell are you? Weren't you supposed to be available at all times?"

With each new message, Claire's voice grows more disappointed. When, in the last one, she snaps that she can do without me anyway—and is actually better off without me—I gasp for air, in vain.

A piercing scream.

My pulse speeds up so much I feel my heartbeat everywhere inside me.

My damned heart, still beating. Unlike those who, in the past few hours, have stopped—because I wasn't there for them.

Because I'd forgotten myself out here, had no idea who I was or what the hell really mattered in my life.

Ragged sobbing.

How could I have let this happen?

Suddenly, I feel a hand on my arm. Sonora. She catches my gaze. "What's going on?"

"Hospital. Now. Immediately," I force out.

She nods, worry dominating her expression.

Without thinking, I take Sonora with me on my motorcycle to the clinic. Nothing is more important than getting us both there as quickly as possible, so no more people have to die.

Even before I bring my Harley to a stop, Sonora jumps off the bike and rips the helmet from her head.

"I'm going in first," she shouts over the roar of the engine and takes off at a sprint.

I'm left alone, overwhelmed by guilt and gripped by panic.

From now on, I have to function.

No mistakes.

There can't be any mistakes.

You should have saved me.

As soon as I turn off the engine, I take off my helmet and pull the black tin from the inside pocket of my leather jacket. My fingers tremble as I open it, the pills slipping through them several times before I manage to pop two into my mouth.

Relieved, I close my eyes. Just feeling the tablets on my tongue and knowing they'll turn me into the person I now have to be at all costs gives me a sense of security.

"What are you doing?"

Who was that? I snap my eyes open and see Sonora standing a few meters away. Her motorcycle helmet is tucked under her arm, and her gaze is fixed on the tin, still open in my hand.

"Nothing." I quickly shove the tin back into my jacket pocket and get off the bike. "Why did you come back?"

"The helmet," she replies, confused. "I thought I shouldn't take it into the clinic."

Damn, yeah. She's right. And besides, we shouldn't have shown up here together, as I now realize.

I was careless. Distracted. I lost focus.

But that's over now. "You take the front entrance, I'll go in the back," I say urgently.

She nods. I take off as fast as my legs will carry me and storm through the emergency room entrance into the clinic, where it's surprisingly quiet.

No phones are ringing. Nurses, paramedics, and doctors move routinely through the patients waiting for treatment.

While running, I yank off my jacket and grab a disposable gown. "Where can I help?" I shout to the emergency coordinator as he comes into view. A split second later, I spot Claire standing at the board next to his desk. She turns her head toward me.

"Well, look who finally found the time to grace us with his presence," she says, her face icy.

"I'm here. What needs to be done?" I ask, breathless, ignoring her remark.

What was I supposed to say? That she was absolutely right? That I'm a shitty doctor? A selfish man who takes time off without thinking? Someone who lets down his coworkers and his patients?

Damn it, I should've been on call twenty-four hours a day, seven days a week, just like the past few years.

Claire's expression turns somber. "Nothing. I've already taken care of everything."

Taken care of? "There are no surgical cases open?" I ask, glancing around hastily.

She points to the overview board. "I've postponed all scheduled surgeries that could wait. The staff who were reachable…" She pauses briefly. *Unlike those who only claim to be*, hangs unspoken between us. "…I called in for duty."

"Very good." That was exactly the right call—I wouldn't have done anything differently. I smile at her, relieved. I want her to see how grateful I am. "Thank you, Dr. Walters, that was excellent work."

She frowns for the briefest moment. "You're welcome," she replies distractedly, then slips her hands into her lab coat pockets. "The open femur fracture is already in the OR, as is the ruptured spleen. I reduced the dislocated shoulder and stabilized it for now. I classified a spinal fracture as an emergency—Jake is already on it. There's also another neurosurgical case I've added to the OR schedule."

"Intracranial bleeding?" I ask, since brain hemorrhages are very common after car accidents.

Claire nods. "As soon as the patient with the injured aorta is out of the OR, I'll operate."

"And I'll make sure the cleaning team is ready immediately so the OR can be prepped again quickly," I add.

"Already done." Her disappointed look hits me. *Do you still think I don't know how to do my job?* she asks me silently.

The fact that Claire thought of absolutely everything shouldn't surprise me. She seems to have the situation under control, and yet I still can't relax. "Have we lost any patients?" I ask.

She shakes her head. "Not so far."

Immediately, it feels like I can breathe again—for the first time since I saw her calls.

Nothing bad has happened.

Not yet. And it has to stay that way.

"Alright, I'll take over now. Thank you for your work—I really appreciate it." I nod to her, then focus all my attention on the overview board with the current cases.

"Of course," Claire mutters in frustration. "I'll be in the OR treating the brain hemorrhage."

"I might join you," I say, eyes fixed on the board. The effect of my pills is slowly kicking in. Within less than a minute, I've absorbed every detail, assessed the urgency, and set priorities.

Claire was right. There are no more acute patients; no one seems to be waiting for a surgical consult. My team managed everything without me.

"What are the first responders saying? Are any more patients coming in?" I ask her.

"The accident happened five hours ago," she replies dryly, and again I feel a pang in my chest for not having been here—even though, apparently, my team didn't need me at all.

"I'll assist you with the brain hemorrhage in the OR," I say with all the composure I can muster, and head toward the elevator.

Chapter Thirty-Six

SONORA

He didn't look at me—not even for a fraction of a second.

Like a ghost, he simply vanished, and he didn't show up again for the rest of the evening.

The fact that we were at the clinic so late really upset him, but he only sees one side of the story. He forgets that we both had the day off. We weren't on call, we didn't need to be reachable. He forgets that he's not the only doctor in the world who can save lives. And he forgets that even a doctor has the right to rest. In fact, they have to, in order to do a good job. Even Ethan.

All of this is running through my head, along with the memory of Claire asking me why I responded so late to her emergency call, as I stare into my coffee cup. The pale streaks of milk swirl into the dark liquid as I stir.

Did Claire believe the excuse I gave her? I'm so lost in the question that I barely register Olive and June entering the living room.

"I know someone who's trying to get rid of their tickets.

This is a once-in-a-lifetime chance—we have to jump on it." Olive's voice is practically squealing with excitement.

June lets out a short squeal. "That would be so cool. The five of us on a weekend trip to Sin City, with a Joshua Friedberg concert as the highlight."

Sin is the only one of June's words that doesn't bounce off me. I sink deeper into the soft cushions of the sofa, wishing I could disappear between them and stop wondering what's supposed to happen next.

Does he regret our kiss? Does he think we went too far and is now avoiding me because he doesn't know how to tell me that whatever we had has to be over for good?

For us, it's only black or white. All or nothing. Although all is nothing at the same time—and vice versa.

"Joshua's music is just… sigh." That was Olive again. "We absolutely have to go."

"Hey, Sonora." Someone shakes my arm. At the same time, I force my eyelids and the corners of my mouth upward. June is standing next to the sofa in her running gear, her deep blue eyes sparkling with excitement. "We're doing this, right? Please tell me you're in."

I frown. What were they just talking about? "Um…"

Olive tosses her perfectly blow-dried hair. Her silky blouse shimmers so intensely it almost blinds me. "Girls' weekend trip. Las Vegas. Joshua Friedberg," she summarizes.

The moment she says the words, numbers start tumbling through my head. Flight, hotel, concert tickets, food, drinks, casino, and whatever else the others might want to do. Impossible. That's not going to work.

"When?" I ask anyway, because I can't think of a good reason fast enough to explain why this isn't for me.

"In twelve weeks." June is so jittery that even her high ponytail starts to bounce.

I lift my shoulders in an apologetic shrug. "I'm on duty this weekend." No idea if that's true, but it doesn't matter. The important thing is that they accept I'm not coming along without asking uncomfortable questions.

"What? Your schedule is set that far in advance?" Olive frowns as she picks some lint off the armrest of the sofa.

"That's what happens when your boss is a control freak," I reply, rolling my eyes with practiced ease, as if Ethan annoyed me just as much as he did everyone else in the department.

It's Olive who suddenly curls her perfectly made-up lips into a suggestive smirk. "I've heard about your boss. Supposedly, he's a total hottie."

Oh yes, he definitely is. Just two weeks ago, I would've admitted it and joined the girls in making a few jokes about him. But today, I'd rather keep my distance. "Maybe," I say, brushing it off with a dismissive wave of my hand.

June sinks down onto the coffee table across from me and props her head on her hands. She stares at me. "Aha."

To make matters worse, Olive now plops down next to me, a wide grin on her face. "So there's some truth to the rumors."

What? Rumors? Panic flares inside me, but outwardly I keep my poker face and meet my roommate's gaze. "What rumors?"

"Yeah, what rumors?" June echoes, excited.

Olive's eyes light up. "There's talk in the cafeteria that Sonora and Dr. Hottie Stone are often up on the roof together." She lowers her voice. "Alone."

"Uhhh," June says. "So Autumn wasn't wrong when she saw him outside our building last week?"

"You clearly read way too many gossip magazines," I say to Olive and spring up from the couch—unfortunately a bit too energetically.

"So it's not true?" Olive wants to know. "You weren't on the roof with him?"

I finish my coffee while frantically trying to figure out how to keep Ethan's and my secret. As much as I'd love to share my feelings for him with the girls, what's happening between us can't get out—not to anyone.

"Alright, you caught me. We were up there together and it was insanely romantic," I say with exaggerated swooning. "I said, 'Dr. Stone, I need your approval for an appendectomy.' And do you know what happened next?" I place a hand over my heart with Oscar-worthy drama and let out a longing sigh.

June giggles.

"He replied, 'Do you have the ultrasound image with you?'" I add a sultry tone to my voice to make it even funnier, and it works. Both Olive and June burst out laughing. "He looked at the image and then gazed deep into my eyes. I swear, guys, my heart was pounding like crazy." I pretend my knees are giving out just from the memory and lean against the ridiculously expensive dining table Olive contributed to our apartment. "You won't believe what he said next." I pause dramatically. "He said, 'Okay, the procedure is approved.'"

June wipes tears of laughter from the corners of her eyes. "Divine," she says.

"It was the most romantic thing I've ever experienced," I confirm with a dead-serious expression.

Lately, I've had so many deep conversations with Ethan that I'd almost forgotten how good it feels to just joke about everything. To take life lightly, to ignore the dark parts and strip them of the ridiculous power they hold over us.

I'd love to get in one more jab, but June's expression suddenly turns serious as she glances at her wristwatch.

"It's that late already? I have to go," she says hurriedly, jumps up, and rushes out of the living room. "See you." A few seconds later, I hear the front door slam shut.

Before Olive can circle back to Ethan or this weekend in Las Vegas, I'd better make myself scarce too. "I need to hurry as well—important surgeries today." And the day after tomorrow, I'll be performing Ms. Cox's gallbladder removal, which I still need to prepare for thoroughly. Ever since she decided to go through with the procedure, she hasn't changed her mind.

A small part of me still can't believe it's actually going to happen. But a much bigger part is excited to operate on her and give her a real chance at a healthy life.

"Bathroom's all yours." Olive grabs one of her glossy magazines that are scattered all over the apartment and wedges a pillow behind her back. I turn away and am almost out of the living room when she calls my name. "About Vegas again—I'll check flights and hotel rooms. You ask your boss if you can swap shifts, okay?"

"Okay," I call back, fully aware that there's no way I'm going to do that, and head toward the bathroom.

Chapter Thirty-Seven

ETHAN

After two sleepless nights, I feel like I'm on autopilot as I stop in front of Dr. Roberts' office door. As so often in the past few hours, my thoughts are on the night before last, on the promise I made to Sonora and the feeling I had when I gave it. Once again, I relive the shock that Claire's messages triggered in me shortly afterward—the guilt, the pain, the self-loathing. And ultimately, I return to the moment I realized that no one had been harmed by my absence. To the thought that maybe I'm allowed a bit of life too, that there are other doctors who can cover for me, that perhaps less falls apart without me than I had believed.

I knock.

"Come in."

I suppress a yawn, knowing I can't afford to show weakness right now—no matter how exhausted I am—and open the door. "Good morning."

"Ethan, I wasn't expecting you." My boss places a cup under the spout of his coffee machine. "Would you like one too?"

No matter how strong it is, it won't be enough, but I nod anyway.

He presses a button, and the built-in grinder starts to whir. "What can I do for you?"

The scent of freshly ground beans reaches my nose as I bury my hands in the pockets of my lab coat, trying to appear as relaxed as possible.

"I'd like to propose a change to some of the hospital's policies," I say.

"Is there a problem?" Something in his voice makes me suspect he already knows the answer.

I shouldn't let that rattle me, so I shake my head. "Fortunately not, but there might be some in the future."

The coffee pours into the cup, Dr. Roberts pulls a spoon from the drawer. "What rules are we talking about?"

"Among other things, the ban on visible tattoos. They pose no medical risk, and society has long since accepted them," I say casually, starting the conversation just as I had planned.

"I see. What else?" my boss replies, placing the spoon on the saucer.

"The ban on relationships between employees and supervisors is outdated too," I continue as neutrally as possible.

His eyebrows lift. "Interesting."

What's that supposed to mean? Confused, I take the cup from him as he hands it to me. Fortunately, he turns his back to me then to prepare the second coffee.

"I think we're driving employees away—or worse, scaring off applicants." I take a sip of my espresso. "Highly talented, well-trained doctors will avoid Halifax Harbor Hospital, which in turn makes it harder to provide our patients with top-level care."

And that's just one of many other reasons that are more than understandable.

My boss hums absentmindedly, picks up his freshly filled coffee cup, and signals for me to follow him out onto his office terrace.

His lack of reaction unsettles me. And the fact that, even after we've stepped into the bright morning sunlight, he still says nothing, unsettles me even more.

He just stands next to me at the railing, looking down at the swaying boats in Halifax Harbor and sipping his coffee.

"They hired me to improve this clinic's reputation far beyond the borders of Nova Scotia," I continue, presenting another argument I've prepared over the past two nights. "This is one of my measures."

The wind picks up, yet I hear his quiet snort. Now he turns his head toward me and fixes his gaze on me. "Why this rule in particular?"

I feign surprise. "Happy doctors do better work." That's a fact, and there's another one I came across while preparing for this conversation. "Other clinics have long since recognized that and adjusted their rules."

You should have saved me.

Liam's voice, which I've heard so often over the past few hours, tries to take hold of me again. Of course I know what he wants to tell me. That my damned life and my broken heart should belong to nothing but the job. That I have a debt to repay, and that there's no room for romantic feelings in my life.

"That rule exists for a reason. It was introduced after there were problems with relationships like that." He's still watching me intently. "Favoritism, jealousy, organizational instability."

Distraction, I add silently, thinking of Liam.

Salt on my tongue.

But the two doctors who should have been taking care of him instead of entertaining themselves wouldn't even have been affected by the rule. They were colleagues.

As if my inner self wanted to protest against that thought, a fierce crashing of waves builds inside me, and for the very first time, I want to fight it. I don't want it to control me, don't want to accept what it carries: the message that there's only one thing that's allowed to matter in my life—and the realization that it's not Sonora.

Sand between my toes.

My shoulders feel heavy, just like my head.

Dr. Roberts leans against the railing. "What's really going on here, Ethan?"

"Nothing's going on." The words leave my mouth far too hastily. "I'm just doing my job."

His eyelids narrow. "Are there any secret relationships in your department?"

"Not that I'm aware of." Even as I answer, I hate myself for the lie. When did this even start? When did I go from someone who wanted nothing but the truth to someone whose only way out is lying?

"Are you absolutely sure about that?" Without taking his eyes off me, he sips his coffee. Again, I can't shake the feeling that he suspects something—or thinks he does—and is keeping it from me.

Does he know about Claire and Jake?

Or between Sonora and me? Impossible—after all, we only really kissed for the first time yesterday. Technically speaking, it can't even be called a relationship.

To avoid showing any weakness, I nod firmly. "Eliminating the rule would be an investment in the future. Of course, we still won't tolerate doctors who behave irresponsibly—regardless of the reason." I look at him intently. "If any issues arise, we'll respond immediately." That goes without saying—after all, we're doctors. We bear responsibility, and that will never change.

The sound of waves crashing.

It burns in my soul, hurts in a way I can't endure. It has to stop.

"I understand." Now Dr. Roberts lifts the corners of his mouth. "Thank you for the suggestion."

Thank you and what? Thank you and I'll think about it? Thank you and I'll present your idea to the board? Thank you and now get out of here before I finally figure you out?

"By when will you make a decision?" I avert my gaze and follow a flock of seagulls across the sky streaked with wispy clouds.

"Why are the rules so important to you?" I hear him ask skeptically.

It feels like he's tightening a noose around my neck. "They're not," I reply faster than I can think of the right words.

Damn it. That was the wrong thing to say.

"Then why did you come to me specifically for this?" A dangerously probing undertone colors his voice.

The noose is tightening. "I was nearby and wanted to take care of it right away."

"I see." He places his hand on my back and guides me back into his office. Once inside, he fixes his gaze on me again. "Let me summarize. You believe that at least one of our rules could cost us employees, even though there have never been any resignations because of it."

The noose presses deeper into my skin, making it hard to breathe.

"And even though it doesn't matter to you at all, you came here solely because of it."

Now I can't breathe at all.

He pats my shoulder in a friendly manner. "So, it's neither important nor relevant. How do you think my decision will turn out, then?"

This is the end. I know it—I feel it in every part of me.

This can't be happening.

"I understand," I say, just to get out of here as quickly as possible, and head for the door. "Thank you for your time."

"Gladly," I hear him say behind me as I press down the door handle. "Oh, and Ethan?"

What now?

"Don't forget that I need a name from you by the end of the week—someone we can take off the payroll."

"Of course not," I reply, holding on to the last shred of composure I have left, even as the one future that could have saved Sonora and me fades rapidly within me.

Chapter Thirty-Eight

SONORA

I clip the pager to my waistband and tie my hair up.

Olive's rumors, which I brushed off so casually during our recent conversation, are still gnawing at me. The staff are talking about Ethan and me. Even outside our department. In the cafeteria!

This is bad.

Really bad.

Still, I push the thought aside. There are a good thirty minutes left until Ms. Cox's procedure, and I'm going to do my best. On the way to the scrub room, I'm already focusing on the operation.

When I open the door, I find Ethan. His forehead is pressed against the wall, eyes closed, and he's clenching his fists over and over again.

"Four incisions in the abdominal wall, one centimeter each. Epigastrium, right upper quadrant near the costal arch, left upper quadrant," he mutters to himself, as if trying to cast a spell.

He seems restless, and if I didn't know better, I'd think

he was afraid.

Strange.

As he goes over the steps of the procedure, his breathing grows increasingly rapid. I close the door just enough to keep watching him.

Now he's pulling at his hair. "There can't be any mistakes. No mistakes."

It's slowly becoming clear to me what's going on with him. He did everything he could to convince Ms. Cox to go through with the surgery despite her fear. If he makes a mistake now, if there are complications, if something goes wrong—he wouldn't be able to forgive himself. He can't with any patient, but with her, probably even less so.

My heart tightens because I'm certain he's thinking about his brother now, blaming himself for his death. One look at his desperate face is enough to tell me that the fear of messing things up with Ms. Cox too is consuming him.

"Four incisions in the abdominal wall, each one centimeter," he repeats. His fists slam against the wall beside his head. Then he lets his forehead drop against the tiles, again and again. "No mistakes."

I'm about to go to him, but now he pulls out that black tin I'd already seen in the parking lot after our trip to the beach, from his pocket.

With a jerky motion, he opens the clasp. Yesterday it was too dark, but now I recognize the pills.

They're the same ones I found in his bathroom at home. The unlabeled tin.

His chest rises and falls faster, beads of sweat forming on his forehead. And the look on his face as he grabs four of the pills at once makes me freeze instantly.

I know that look.

That hunger.

That overwhelming urge for release.

What the hell is he taking now—at four times the dose?

"No distractions, no mistakes," he murmurs over and over again, as if his own life depends on the success of this operation.

I stare at him, even though I want to look away, because he is tearing himself apart, and suddenly, a memory I have long forgotten surges up inside me.

"Are you coming over to play today?" I ask my school friend Suzie, stuffing the battered science book into the paper bag I use as a school satchel.

She chews on her lower lip. "Probably not."

"It'll be fun. We'll pretend we're traveling the world in the van." The thought makes me smile. "We'll see the giraffes in Africa and the jungle in Brazil." I look at her, full of anticipation, but hesitation flickers across her face. "Why not?"

She laces her fingers together.

Something's wrong. "What is it?"

"My mom says I'm not allowed to play with you anymore," she whispers tonelessly.

"Why not?" We've been playing together since the start of the school year, and it has always been fine. "We're not doing anything wrong—she doesn't need to worry."

"It's not because of you." With an apologetic look, she pushes her chair in under the table.

"Then what is it?" I set my paper bag down on the floor.

"Because of your mom."

"She's sick," I say quickly. "Sometimes she acts strange, but when she gets her medicine, she's fine." Sometimes she just doesn't have enough money to buy her medicine, and then she gets weird, but that's not her fault. "She already had her medicine today."

Her hands play with the two messy braids that hang down to her stomach. "My mom says your mom isn't sick."

"Of course she is," I counter.

"My mom says your mom doesn't take medicine, she takes drugs. She's a junkie."

A junkie?

"That's not true," I reply firmly. How can she spread such a lie?

Junkies are people who live under bridges and don't work. We have a trailer, and my mom works as a cleaning lady in the nice neighborhoods. She's not a junkie. Never.

"Mom is sick, that's all." I give her a serious look.

She looks at me with a mix of embarrassment and shyness. "But my mom saw her buying heroin."

She definitely did not!

"And then she took it right away." Suzi shrugs. "Through her nose."

"No, my mom doesn't take her medicine through her nose," I explain to Suzi, relieved that it's finally clear this is just a dumb misunderstanding. "You have to give the medicine with a syringe."

Suddenly, my school friend's expression turns sympathetic. "I'm so sorry, Sonora." No sooner has she said the words than she pulls me tightly into her arms. I don't understand what's happening, but her sympathy feels real.

Far too real.

Leaning against the doorframe of the laundry room, lost deep in this memory, I pick at my fingernails.

Today I know that Suzi was right back then, and I still remember exactly how it felt when I finally realized it too—long after everyone else already had.

Mom was a junkie. And I was too blind to see it. Maybe because I was only nine years old and simply too young. Maybe because I preferred to believe her lies rather than face the truth.

Still, one thing has nothing to do with the other.

Come on, Sonora, they're probably just headache pills, I

tell myself. I really shouldn't be seeing ghosts where there aren't any. And of course, he looks relieved now that he's taken the pills. He's probably just happy to be rid of his headache soon.

I glance at him in the laundry room, watching as he gradually relaxes. As his fear gives way to determination. As he shifts from tormented Ethan to Dr. Perfect, and I think about how, back then, a little injection could turn an unbearable woman into my smiling mom.

This is crazy. My mind is connecting two things that have absolutely nothing to do with each other.

I'm just confused, that's all.

I skillfully shove those strange thoughts under my rug. Along with all the other crap rotting there—right where they belong.

Chapter Thirty-Nine

ETHAN

The beeping of the heart monitor feels like needles in my ears, the hiss of the ventilator like an ocean liner. Ms. Cox's disinfected abdomen keeps threatening to blur before my eyes.

I blink to see clearly.

"Dr. Stone, we're ready." Sonora gestures toward our patient, whose lines for the gallbladder removal have already been placed. "Shall I take over?"

"No, I've got it," I say quickly, reaching for the instruments. My gaze shifts to the monitor, heat rising inside me. "Locate the gallbladder." At least, that's what I meant to do, but the small camera we just inserted into Ms. Cox's abdomen is showing a blurry image. "Adjust the camera, please."

Sonora clears her throat. "Um…"

I look at her questioningly. She furrows her brow and gives a slight shake of her head. Her eyes are sparkling. Whatever it is she's trying to tell me, now is not the time.

On our table lies a woman whose life and personal well-being depend on us giving her our full attention.

"Adjust the camera," I repeat, more urgently this time.

"Okay," she says, finally doing what I asked.

The image on the monitor sharpens. I carefully maneuver the instruments to identify the anatomy. I'm fully focused, even though my heart is pounding a bit too hard. Beads of sweat form on my forehead. Why is it suddenly so hot in here?

This operation is wearing me down. So much depends on me doing my job well.

"Dr. Stone. Is everything all right?" asks a strangely distorted voice.

I decide to ignore her and instead focus on the monitor. Only Ms. Cox matters. "The gallbladder is enlarged." Strange how hard it suddenly is to breathe. "Scalpel, please."

Sonora positions it through one of the tubes. When it's time to hand me the scalpel, she doesn't let go. Instead, she looks at me with a questioning expression.

"Do I have to say everything twice today?" I snap at her, a bit too emotionally. Usually, I have better control, but this operation is already demanding enough—Sonora doesn't need to make it harder for me.

"Do you have a fever, Dr. Stone?" she asks meekly.

I shake my head and take the scalpel from her hand. A scrub nurse dabs my forehead dry. "Beginning separation of the gallbladder," I announce, positioning the scalpel.

No sooner have I made the first incision than I can barely see anything on the monitor again. Damn it, how am I supposed to perform surgery under these conditions?

"Shit, this is a mess," Sonora comments now too. "I can hardly see a thing."

I blink, lean my head toward the scrub nurse, and ask her to dry my forehead again. More and more heat rises inside me, my heart is racing. Still, I continue separating the gallbladder—after all, I have a job to do.

Suddenly, the monitors start beeping like crazy.

"Blood pressure's dropping!"

"Pulse is rising!"

I focus on the surgical site. Everything looks fine.

"Tachycardia!"

"Damn it, where did this arrhythmia come from all of a sudden?" That was Sonora's voice, breaking through the chaos of sounds and shouting.

My gaze flicks to her. In her eyes, I see the exact same raw panic I'm feeling in this moment.

Now my left arm starts to cramp. I clench a fist, but Sonora notices. Her eyes dart back and forth between my hand and my face.

"What's going on, Dr. Stone? You look like…"

"She must be bleeding internally," I say quickly. "We need to find it."

"I'll take over." Sonora's tone burns in my ears. She allows no argument, immediately pulling the instruments out of the laparoscopic ports and turning to the assistant. "We're opening the abdominal cavity," she decides, completely disregarding me. "Scalpel, please."

The assistant shoots me a questioning glance. I can't do anything as my pulse continues to race. The operating room begins to spin.

"Scalpel. Now!" someone shouts. Probably Sonora.

My chest feels like it is about to explode, my muscles like I have the worst muscle ache of my life.

"We need the emergency team. And page Dr. Nyla Moore from the ER."

"On it."

Sonora nods, and a split second later, she looks at me in fear. Then her face is suddenly shrouded in mist.

At first it is white, now pale gray.

What the hell…?

Dark gray.

The heat inside me keeps rising—I can't breathe.

Damn it. I know what's happening here! It's …

Black.

Chapter Forty

SONORA

Caught in the chaos of emotions that the past hour has stirred up in me, I leave the OR and pull the cap off my head. I rip the surgical gown from my body, stuff everything into the dirty laundry bin, and storm out into the hallway.

The standby team, always on call for exactly these kinds of unpredictable situations, helped me stabilize Ms. Cox successfully. Now I have to find Ethan. Immediately.

I still can't believe what happened earlier. That Ethan collapsed right in front of me during the operation.

Shit. What the hell was wrong with him?

I shouldn't be showing my emotions so openly, but the worry is eating away at my poker face faster than I can control it. So I rush down the hallway and take the stairs to the emergency room, where I run into Nyla.

"Where's Dr. Stone?" I call out to her, gasping for breath, unable to hide the desperation in my voice.

Holding a clipboard, she gestures behind her. "In Room Three."

"How is he? Is he conscious?" Just a few more steps and I'll be with her.

She nods. "Are you okay? You look like a member of the Addams Family."

That doesn't matter. Ethan matters—he's all that matters. "I need to see him. It's important," I tell her, hoping that's enough to explain my condition. Maybe I shouldn't have run so fast—my body just isn't built for that. "Is he responsive?"

"His cardiovascular system was completely out of whack—heart rate and blood pressure way too high, same with his respiratory rate." Nyla sets the clipboard aside and gives me a scrutinizing look. Then she tells me how she treated him. "I sent five blood samples to the lab for every possible test," she says in conclusion. "Hopefully, they'll find something that explains what caused his issues."

Maybe his collapse was a reaction to all that damn stress he puts on himself, to his unhealthy perfectionism. He really needs to stop neglecting himself like this—it's not doing him any good. "Okay, thanks," I manage to say before turning away to tell him exactly that.

My steps quicken, and by the time I reach the door to Treatment Room Three, my heart is pounding in my throat. I'm gasping for air, even though the walk here was far too short to leave me this winded.

For the past hour, I've been torn between worry and hope. Between love and fear. And now, with Ethan just moments away, I don't know which of these feelings has a tighter grip on me.

I push the door to the treatment room open so forcefully that it slams against the wall. Ethan turns his head and gives me a tired smile.

I walk up to his bed and, without thinking, take his hand. "Hey," I say.

"Hey." He sounds exhausted. "How's Ms. Cox?"

"She's fine. She's going to make a full recovery." I study his face intently.

"Thank God." His eyelids fall shut, and he exhales in relief.

He's so incredibly pale. I bite my lower lip, trying to force out all the terrible thoughts about what might have caused his collapse.

Heart attack. Myocarditis. A problem with the heart valve.

Or maybe it's something neurological. His arm was trembling before he collapsed.

Epilepsy. Brain tumor. Stroke.

"How are you feeling?" I can't help but gently place my hand on his cheek.

"I'm fine, don't worry," he replies, even though he must know I can see that absolutely nothing is fine.

"They took blood samples, we'll know more soon. I'm going to head up to the lab and put some pressure on them. Nyla ordered just about every test there is." Anyone would've done the same—after all, this is Dr. Perfect we're talking about.

His expression freezes. "No."

"No what?" Even as the words leave my mouth, I realize what he's afraid of. "I'll be the picture of calm, don't worry. No one will suspect that you mean anything to me." He shakes his head vigorously, his breathing quickens. "I'll just say: 'You know Dr. Perfect—if he doesn't get what he wants, he loses it.' And then I'll roll my eyes like you're driving me up the wall." I'm good at that—he knows it—but his expression only grows more tense. "What is it?"

For a moment that lasts far too long, he says nothing. "You have to make the samples disappear," he suddenly whispers into the silence between us. "Please, Sonora, they can't analyze them."

"But how are they supposed to figure out what's wrong without the blood…" Something in his expression stops me. Is that… fear?

Does it have something to do with the pills? Maybe they weren't for headaches after all, but…?

"What's going on, Ethan?"

My medicine, Mom's voice whispers inside me.

He looks away, as if he feels guilty.

I need it, Sonnygirl.

She really needs to shut up—there are a thousand possible reasons for Ethan's behavior, after all.

"What would they find in your blood?" I ask, growing more uneasy. "Look at me, Ethan." I gasp for breath. "Look at me and tell me what's going on!"

Our eyes meet. For a while, we just look at each other, and with every beat of my heart, I feel it breaking a little more.

Suddenly, the part of me that still held on to hope for a harmless explanation for Ethan's collapse dies too. My God—maybe he's seriously ill. And not only that: maybe he already knows it!

"What will they find?" I ask again, even though part of me doesn't want to know, and I start picking at my fingernails like crazy.

Leukemia. Hodgkin's lymphoma. Addison's disease.

With every new possibility my mind conjures up, I feel sicker and sicker.

He looks at me hesitantly, and in that moment, I wish I could take my question back. I don't want to know what's wrong with him—not even that there's something wrong at all. Still, I know I can't run away now.

"Whatever it is, we'll get through it together," I say, because that's what I promised him. That what we have—no matter what happens—will never end.

"Amphetamines." The word leaves his mouth without a sound.

No!

"Amphetamines? Are you out of your mind?" My voice nearly cracks, every part of me trembling.

I think of the phone calls he answered wide awake in the middle of the night. How, even after a fourteen-hour day, he seemed so full of energy, like he'd just gotten up. His so-called headache pills.

Oh God.

I don't want to believe that this man—the one who stole my heart, the one I've shown every part of myself to… Fuck!

"You put your own life in danger," I snap at him. "And you made me an accomplice."

Confusion washes over his face. Confusion and so much pain.

"Shit, I watched you before the surgery and convinced myself you were just popping headache pills." How stupid I was, how naive. Just like with my mom back then. So many years have gone by, and I'm still incredibly clueless when it comes to facing a painful truth.

All of a sudden, all my anger vanishes. What's left is a stark emptiness, and from within it, the girl from the gutter with the matted hair and broken shoes looks at me, pleading for help.

"I'll explain everything, but first we have to stop the tests." I feel Ethan grab my hand. "If the lab runs the blood tests, I'll lose my job. My medical license. Everything."

Yes.

That will undoubtedly happen.

His expression turns intense. "I swear to you, what happened today won't happen again."

I hear Mom's whisper inside me, *I know, Sonnygirl, I know I have to change something. And I will, I promise.* Instinctively, I touch my breastbone, the place where my butterfly sits. The one that proves people don't change.

As if Ethan senses what's going on inside me, he shakes his head. "I'm not like your mom."

"You're just as much a junkie as she is," I choke out. "You'll promise me all kinds of things and won't keep a single one."

He's going to disappoint me, again and again. I should leave, get out of here right now, and I should also inform the chief physician about Ethan's addiction—but at the same time, I know I can't.

Because our fates are intertwined.

We both have a secret that could cost us our jobs, and we both know each other's. The only difference between us is that he can free himself from his, while I will always remain the fraud that I am.

Chapter Forty-One

ETHAN

So that's what she thinks? That she can't rely on me?

I can see she wants nothing more than to run, so I hold her back. "This is something completely different."

"How long has this been going on?" she asks flatly, and I know she won't help me unless I give her an answer.

"It all started after Liam died," I begin. "I couldn't sleep anymore, had panic attacks." Back then, I couldn't handle it —I didn't know how to draw strength from them. "The doctors prescribed me sedatives, but they made me unbelievably tired."

She shakes her head. "You didn't take them?"

"I wanted to study medicine." That takes a clear head—Sonora knows how hard it is, how focused you have to be, how much you have to learn. "Being a doctor is my calling. It's what I have to give back to this world." What I have to give back to Liam.

"Saving lives," she murmurs absentmindedly, and in that moment, I know she understands.

She understands how I felt back then, and also that I had no choice but to stop taking the sedatives.

"Exactly that," I confirm, and as she sinks back down onto the bed, I dive into the memory.

What enzyme is directly involved in the replication of DNA?

The question blurs before my eyes, just like the answers. With my head resting in my hands, I try to focus, but everything feels heavy. Even my eyelids, which are trying to close now.

I've already had three energy drinks today, and it's only nine in the morning. Still, my brain refuses to work. But it has to.

Peter, whom I met a few weeks ago here in the prep course for the Medical College Admission Test, pulls the chair next to me back. "Hey, rough night?"

Every night is a rough night. "The entrance exam is tomorrow," I reply, even though that's only one of many reasons I can't sleep properly.

If I don't pass this exam, I can't study medicine. And if I don't become a doctor, I don't know what I'm even still doing here. How I'm ever supposed to find peace again after Liam's death.

"Man, I can't think about anything else." With a sigh, he pulls his biology book out of his backpack and opens it.

I study him, see his alert eyes, the focused expression on his face, and the energetic way he reaches for his pen. "You sure look pretty lively for someone saying that."

A grin creeps across his face, then he leans toward me. "That's thanks to my little pick-me-ups."

"Caffeine pills?" I guess. "Tried those already." They don't help —at least not enough.

Damn it, how am I supposed to ace that entrance exam tomorrow if even those don't help anymore?

"Not quite." He pulls a small, unlabeled tin from his backpack and takes out one of the yellow pills. "Try this—makes you feel like Einstein himself."

I frown. "What is it?"

"Something that'll make the Medical College Admission Test a walk in the park," he replies.

I glance back and forth between his wide-awake face and the pills. "What is it?" I repeat my question.

Instead of answering me, he places one of the pills next to the questionnaire I've been staring at for an hour without being able to answer a single question.

I shake my head. Even though my brain refuses to function properly, I still know this isn't a harmless tablet.

"Take it," he says now, pushing it closer to me. "Then you'll have it as a backup, in case you need it tomorrow."

"The night before the entrance exam for medical school, I stopped taking the sedatives," I tell Sonora in the here and now, as she suddenly looks desperate. "There was no way I could sleep. I was completely wrecked when I took my first Adderall an hour before that all-important test." For the first time since Liam's death, it made me feel like I had the power to take control of my fate.

"How could you?" Sonora asks tonelessly.

"I lost Liam. The only way I can ever make up for that is by saving other lives." One day I'll reach that point—then I'll finally be free.

Now her expression turns anguished. "Don't you see that you're destroying yourself? You're always thinking about everyone else and ignoring what this is doing to you." Her chest rises and falls with emotion. "This madness is tearing you apart, Ethan!"

It's not. I'm a doctor—I've got this under control. "Try to understand." I look pleadingly into her dark eyes. "If I'm not perfect during surgery, if I make mistakes, people die."

"And what just happened in the OR, huh?" she asks, visibly shaken.

Since Liam's death, I've faced every truth head-on, but right now, I sense that this is one truth I couldn't bear. So I stay silent, even though I know exactly what Sonora is implying.

Chapter Forty-Two

SONORA

"You damn well risked your own life!" Is it really worth that little to him?

"Sometimes I sleep badly or I can't concentrate, so I take something to help me work. That's all—there's never been even the slightest problem." He sounds so sincere. "Today I went too far, but I swear to you, it won't happen again."

Our eyes meet, and in his expression I see nothing but honesty—yet I still can't believe him.

"I don't need those pills. I just need you. When you're in my arms, I can sleep." It's true—I saw it myself when I spent the night with him. He slept deeply, peacefully lost in his dreams. "You're all I need."

And he's all I need. But sometimes, that's not enough.

He looks at me pleadingly. "I'm starting the withdrawal today."

I know, Sonnygirl, I know I have to change something. And I will, I promise, I already hear Mom whispering inside me again.

"It was a mistake, I went too far, I realize that now," he

says, and suddenly it hits me how much we resemble each other. Fate turned us both into liars.

I stare at him, see how deeply he believes what he just said, and want nothing more than to believe it too. "You're not in control."

He shakes his head vehemently. "What happened today made it crystal clear that I have to change." There's nothing but conviction on his face. "People can change, you know that. You've seen it yourself," he reminds me.

That's true. It's been less than a week since I realized not everyone is like my mom. That there are people who work on themselves. People who keep their promises. Like Ms. Cox, who found the strength to agree to the surgery and didn't back out.

Still, I can't just let that slide! But how could I turn my back on him now, when he's keeping my secret?

It would ruin his entire career.

I'd be destroying the very man who's stood firmly by my side, even though he knows I lied in my application.

Now he takes my other hand. "I'll never touch that stuff again," he promises me once more, and there's nothing in his eyes to suggest he's lying.

And in that moment, I want just one thing: to give back to him what he gave me—support. Trust. Encouragement.

"You only get one chance." I look at him intently.

"That's all I need."

More than anything, I hope that's true. "I'll keep your secret, and you'll keep mine," I say, just so I can breathe again. It feels wrong, even though I know it's right. That there's no other way for either of us to get out of this. "And as for our shared secret…"

"I spoke to Dr. Roberts—he refuses to scrap the rule

under any circumstances," I hear Ethan say, his voice thick. "But without you…"

I look at him, knowing this secret is yet another reason why there can't be an 'us,' and at the same time feeling that without him, my heart would shatter into a thousand pieces and never heal again.

"What if we don't get it? What if we're running hand in hand toward the edge instead of toward our happiness?" I reply, fighting against the pain that's taking hold of me.

He pulls his lips into a warm smile. "I'd rather jump into the darkness with you than stand in the sunlight without you."

I fight back the tears rising inside me. No one has ever said anything like that to me. Not once in my life has anyone fought for me like this.

"Just the two of us against the rest of the world," I whisper, leaning over him. At least until I've made a name for myself as a doctor in a few years and can apply to another hospital.

He nods. "You and me against the rest of the world."

When I press my lips to his, I feel how true our vow is, and I know we're going to make it.

Together.

No matter what happens.

"Yes," I murmur against his mouth before I tear myself away from him, my heart heavy. "I'll switch your samples."

We nod to each other in silence, then I search the cabinets next to his bed for a blood draw kit and take five vials of blood from myself.

"Thank you," he whispers, full of guilt, and sinks back into his pillow, exhausted, while I walk to the door with the vials in hand. Once there, I throw Ethan one last conspiratorial glance and slip out into the hallway.

I walk quickly to the emergency department's coordination center, doing everything I can to keep my expression under control. I bury my hands in the pockets of my lab coat so no one can see how badly they're shaking. Not even the tall emergency coordinator I'm now approaching.

"Are the blood samples from the past hour still here somewhere?" Did that sound casual enough? Offhand, like I didn't really care about the answer?

Without looking up from his computer screen, he shakes his head. "They were just picked up."

Great. "Thanks," I mutter and take off so fast I almost run into Nyla.

"Hey, what's—?"

"No time, emergency," I shout and dash toward the stairwell, sprinting up to the first floor with my heart pounding. Behind the reception desk sits an elderly lady. The delicate gold chains on her glasses swing back and forth as she talks—of all people—to Claire.

Damn.

Claire mustn't see me under any circumstances, especially not now, when I'm already struggling to keep it together.

I turn on the spot and press myself against the wall next to the doorframe. Beads of sweat trickle down my back, and with every passing minute I wait for the coast to be clear, my breathing grows heavier.

Damn it, what's taking her so long in there? Doesn't she have a surgery scheduled? Doesn't she need to conduct follow-up exams or fill out patient charts?

With every second that ticks by, my chances of switching the blood samples before analysis shrink.

No matter what blood panel Nyla ordered—and I bet it was a full workup, after all, the patient isn't just anyone, but

Dr. Ethan Stone, Head of Surgery—a drug screening is always done routinely. Once the samples are being processed, there's no stopping Ethan's downfall.

I can't wait any longer.

"Okay, Sonora, pull yourself together," I whisper to myself. Lying to others, deceiving and distracting them, is my specialty. Until now, it's always been about me and my fake life. Today it's about Ethan, and he'll lose everything if I fail. Just the thought of it makes my chest tighten.

I take a deep breath in and out. Focus. Put on my poker face. Then I stroll casually into the lab.

Claire is leaning against the counter like it's a bar. "And I'm telling you, I'm this close. I don't need much more," she says, and I immediately know she's plotting something about Ethan. Maybe she's preparing her resignation to throw it in his face. Maybe Jake's too—after all, Claire knows it would hit Ethan hard to lose two doctors at once. "Then he'll finally get what he deserves," she adds in a choked voice. She suddenly seems desperate.

The woman behind the counter looks at her sympathetically. "That must be really hard for you."

"Hey, Claire, is everything okay?" I say, stepping up beside her.

She gives me a forced smile. "Everything's great. What's up?"

"I think Jake's looking for you upstairs in the ward." I try to smile, though I'm not sure if it works. "It seems urgent."

"We just spoke a few minutes ago." Tilting her head, she gives me a probing look. "Are you sure?"

This isn't good.

Not good at all.

My heart is pounding in my throat as I shrug. My shoulders feel stiff—hopefully Claire doesn't notice. "I just heard about it too."

For a moment that feels like an eternity, she scrutinizes me. Out of the corner of my eye, I see a lab technician enter the room through the door behind the counter.

"Where are the samples from the emergency room?" he asks the woman who coordinates everything here.

She points to one of the refrigerators behind her. "There are high-priority samples from our Dr. Perfect in there. Please process those first, or we'll have problems later."

The blood freezes in my veins as Claire continues to study me. She needs to get out of here—now!

"Like I said, I only heard about it, but it sounded pretty urgent. That's all I know," I say quickly.

Meanwhile, the lab technician opens the refrigerator. I hold my breath.

Claire grumbles irritably. "Well, I'll go see what he needs then."

I twist my mouth into a smile, though I'm sure if I manage it.

Go already, I plead silently with Claire as I hear the refrigerator door slam shut.

"Which ones are the priority samples?" the man asks.

"The ones with the red label, Tom, as always," the coordinator replies with a sigh.

Finally, Claire pushes herself away from the counter and turns to leave. With the rack of blood samples tucked under his arm, this Tom trudges toward the lab door. Claire hasn't left the room yet—I should wait—but Ethan's samples will be in the lab in a matter of seconds.

I glance over my shoulder—Claire is still within earshot.

Tom opens the door, steps over the threshold.

"Wait, please," I call out to him, maybe too soon. But once Ethan's blood is in the lab, I won't be able to get it back. "Some of the samples are likely contaminated."

Tom turns to me. "Impossible. We haven't had anything like that in ages."

I hear footsteps behind me. Please don't let it be…

"Contaminated samples?"

…Claire.

Damn.

Now I have to deliver—Oscar-worthy. "Dr. Perfect sent me. He's convinced the injection site wasn't properly disinfected." I roll my eyes demonstratively.

"Control freak," Claire mutters, annoyed.

"Oh yes. He even had me paged just to tell me that," I reply, equally annoyed. "Then he made me take new samples and supervised me like I was a rookie."

The lab coordinator lets out an amused laugh. "Classic Dr. Perfect."

I nod in agreement. "I don't even want to know what happens if you don't switch the samples." I don't have to fake the fear—it's already taken over every inch of my body. "If he has to wait even a second longer than absolutely necessary for his results because the tests have to be redone…"

"Yep, that would definitely be a firing offense for him," Claire confirms, placing a hand on my arm. "Good thing you got here in time. Where are the new samples?"

Her expression is sympathetic—perfect. Not only does she believe me, she actually wants to help. I hand her the new vials, and she signals Tom to come over.

"We don't usually do this," he says hesitantly as he approaches with the blood sample rack.

Claire taps her fingernails on the counter. "Come on,

don't be so uncooperative. Do you really want Sonora to lose her job?"

If Claire knew what I am maneuvering her into right now, she would hate me for it.

My stomach twists in knots, but I can handle it.

For Ethan.

Tom waves his fingers, eyes fixed on the samples. "Hand them over," he says to Claire.

With a satisfied grin, she hands him the five vials. I quickly reach for Ethan's old blood samples.

"Hey, what do you think you're doing?" The lab technician's expression darkens. "I need to dispose of those properly."

Once again, it feels like my heart stopped beating. "I'm supposed to bring them so Dr. Perfect can hold the person who messed up the samples accountable."

Oh God, what am I saying? He doesn't need the samples for that.

"Is he planning to look for germs in the samples himself?" Claire asks jokingly.

With the best innocent look I could muster, I shrug.

"Man, oh man, that guy is seriously nuts." Tom shakes his head, but at least he hands me the old samples.

"Thanks, you're saving my life." I exhale in relief, and as I pretend to wipe sweat from my forehead, I realize my skin is actually damp, which immediately triggers another wave of perspiration. "I'd better get back to the ER," I say hastily and head off.

"That was weird. She's never that panicked," I hear Claire saying to the two lab technicians just as I push through the swing door into the hallway.

Chapter Forty-Three

ETHAN

Sonora did it. That knowledge, along with the memory of the past two nights when we fell asleep wrapped in each other's arms after I discharged myself, dominates my thoughts. She's standing by me, believes in me, and I won't let her down.

Well-rested, I enter my office with a smile on my face and take off my jacket. I feel better than I have in years. Before I even reach my desk, there's a knock at the door.

It's Dr. Nyla Moore, the emergency physician who treated me the day before yesterday. She's holding a medical file in her hand. "Dr. Stone, I have your test results."

"Thank you for coming by." I signal for her to take a seat and hand me the results, trying to appear at ease.

"I expected more, but there's hardly anything unusual," she says as I study the tests and see the same. "The inflammation markers are elevated, nothing else."

I noticed that too. Sonora is probably fighting off a minor infection. "Then I really was just overworked, as suspected." I smile at Dr. Moore.

She nods, her golden earrings jingling. Something about her expression gives me pause. Maybe it's her doe-like eyes, studying me with such curiosity, as if she's trying to uncover something very specific. She's Sonora's roommate—she's probably heard a lot about me, but I'm sure she doesn't know what truly matters.

Now a gentle smile creeps onto her lips. "You should still take it easy. Overlooked infections can lead to serious problems, and what happened was a clear warning from your body—but I'm sure I don't need to tell you that."

"Right," I reply. "Thank you for your efforts, I really appreciate it."

She chuckles. "Anytime." Her gaze lingers on me for a moment, then she rises from her chair. As she leaves the office, she nearly bumps into Dr. Roberts, who was apparently on his way to see me.

I get up from my chair and step toward him. "I'm fine," I say quickly, before he starts to worry unnecessarily. He hasn't been at work the past two days—he probably just found out what happened in the OR.

Hopefully the commotion around the hospital dies down soon—wouldn't want anyone getting the idea to ask uncomfortable questions.

Dr. Roberts steps past Dr. Moore into my office. "Good. We have a lot to discuss."

His expression is so serious that my stomach turns unnecessarily. He can't possibly know—my blood samples were never analyzed. Or did they run a rapid test in the emergency room without telling me?

Hopefully not.

"Have a seat," I say, keeping my tone as calm as possible.

I fumble with my tie knot, trying to get at least a bit of

air. But it doesn't help—especially not now, as he fixes me with an intense stare.

"There's a problem."

My muscles tensed. "Really?"

"You still haven't given me a name to remove from the payroll," he replies, and I struggle not to show how relieved I am that this is all it's about.

"The deadline isn't until tomorrow," I remind him, typing my password into the computer. Last time, he caught me off guard with this topic—today, I'm prepared. "Just a moment, I'll show you what I've already…"

"Don't trouble yourself—the decision's already been made." He leans forward, resting his arms on my desk.

That wasn't the agreement. I immediately take my hands off the keyboard. "Why?" He promised it would be my decision. What made him suddenly break that promise?

"Well, after our conversation, I was worried I wouldn't get a name from you." He picks up a pen and twirls it between his fingers. "So I prepared myself to make the decision on my own if necessary."

If necessary, okay, but that necessity hasn't come up yet. "I still have time," I reply, growing increasingly uneasy. "There's no reason…"

"Oh yes, there is." His bushy eyebrows rise. "Your praise of Dr. Wells got me thinking. You were right—firing Dr. Wells just because she's new wouldn't be fair."

Exactly. That's what I was saying. I exhale at least some of my tension and lean back in the chair.

"So I took a close look at every single person on your team, regardless of how long they've been here," he continues, while I wonder where this is going. Because no matter what name he gives me, it'll be the wrong one.

"Listen, we don't have to fire anyo—"

He raises his hand. "Oh yes, we do." Now his expression turns accusatory. "If you hadn't spent the past few days so focused on finding some kind of alternative solution, you would've realized that by now."

What is he talking about?

"If you had followed my instructions, you would've come to the same conclusion I did." He taps the pen on the table.

My stomach clenches. "And what would that be?" I ask, alarmed.

"Sonora Wells."

Oh God. Please no.

"Her application is a complete lie."

I can practically feel the color draining from my face.

He nods meaningfully. "I noticed her high school transcripts were missing, so I called them. And do you know what I found out?"

Damn it, yes, I know.

"She never attended that high school!" he exclaims, slamming his hand on the table. "Of course, I immediately checked her college degree. And guess what I discovered?"

I struggle not to collapse on the spot. I probably should say something, but I can't—paralyzed by the panic crashing over me like a tidal wave.

He knows.

He knows everything.

And all because I damn well refused to give him a name. If I had named someone, he never would've investigated further!

"The certificate from Dalhousie University is a fake. She never studied there." His face turns bright red. "That woman is not a doctor!"

"Of course she is," I blurt out far too emotionally.

He shakes his head at my resistance. "Oh really? And what makes you so sure?"

Desperately, I search for an explanation I can actually say out loud. "I work with her. She does a fantastic job. Where would she have gotten all that knowledge if she hadn't studied? All that practical expertise? It's impossible."

"We fell for a fraud," he counters. "HR, me—and you too."

"I don't believe that." God, I should be able to say so much more, but the shock and the guilt have me completely in their grip. "There has to be another explanation."

"Maybe so, but that's not all." His voice grows increasingly agitated. "That woman is a ghost. Up until three weeks ago, she didn't even have a permanent address."

Yes, Sonora has only just moved into the shared apartment—that is true.

I raise my hands in a calming gesture. "We shouldn't jump to conclusions."

"Besides, the little fraud claimed she was employed at the Queen Elizabeth II Health Sciences Centre. So I checked there as well," he replies, clenching his fists.

I can't stay seated any longer, so I spring to my feet and walk over to the window. My gaze falls on the water in front of Halifax Harbor.

The sound of waves surrounds me.

Guilt.

Pain.

"The staff there threw her out once it became clear her personal information didn't check out," I hear him rant behind me. "She listed an abandoned and completely derelict house at 523 Greenwood Ave as her home address!"

523 Greenwood Ave? That's the house she and her mom used to dream about.

Oh Sonora, what are you doing? Your secret is eating you alive.

Suddenly, I freeze.

What if my secret ends up eating me alive too? All my life, I've wanted to confront nothing but the truth. To stare fate in its ugly face. To be brave.

And now I'm doing exactly the opposite. I'm ducking away from the truth, hiding in the darkness that I maneuvered myself into together with Sonora.

"The ones at the Queen Elizabeth II Health Sciences Centre uncovered far less than I did and terminated her immediately," Dr. Roberts continues, snapping me out of the whirlpool of thoughts threatening to consume me. "I've already instructed HR to prepare the necessary paperwork."

No. If we fire her, she's finished! "Shouldn't we at least give her a chance to explain?" I ask, beginning to pace in front of the window. If Sonora is telling the truth, Dr. Roberts will surely understand that she maneuvered herself into a terrible dead end she's never been able to escape. "Doesn't she deserve that?"

"She should consider herself lucky if we don't press charges for document forgery," he replies curtly. "That's something I still have to decide."

Not that too.

I bury my hands in the pockets of my suit pants, trying hard to appear completely calm, and look at him intently. "We're clearly rushing this. Please, we can't just fire Sonora without hearing her side of the story." I have no idea if Sonora will go along with it, but what choice do I have? I have nothing to counter the hard facts Dr. Roberts is throwing at me.

Suddenly, more lines form on my boss's forehead than I've ever seen before. "Sonora?"

Did I say Sonora? "Dr. Wells," I quickly correct myself.

With his head tilted slightly to the side, he scrutinizes me. He remains silent for several seconds, while I feel increasingly nauseated. "Then it's true," he murmurs, stunned, and I lose the last bit of control over my facial expression.

I stare at him, unable to breathe, think, or feel. "What's true?" I hear myself ask, even though I suspect his answer will pull the ground out from under my feet.

Chapter Forty-Four

SONORA

I can't stop smiling, and I can't stop thinking about waking up next to Ethan this morning. How tightly he held me, how close we were. The way he looked at me—so full of love and certainty—as he brushed my curls out of my face.

Humming to myself, I slip on my scrubs and reach for the pants.

"Who's the lucky one?"

Did someone say something? I turn my head and spot Claire leaning against the locker next to me. "Hm?" I say.

She grins mischievously. "Come on, admit it—you're in love."

Oh, you bet. "Maybe." I wink at her and start unbuttoning my jeans.

"Tell me everything," she asks me.

A wave of sadness washes over me. But the fact that Ethan and I will have to keep our feelings a secret here at Halifax Harbor Hospital for the next few years is a price I'm willing to pay. Once I've built a solid reputation as a doctor, I'll have a chance at getting a job at another hospital with my real résumé.

I slip into my scrub pants. "So, I met this insanely rich star pianist who instantly fell head over heels for me. At first, I wasn't interested—you know, all the fuss, the journalists, the paparazzi, jealous fans."

Claire bursts out laughing.

"I told him we might be heading straight for disaster. But then, well…" I place my hand over my chest. "Then he said, 'I'd rather jump into the darkness with you than stand in the sunlight without you,' and that was it for me." In my mind, I'm back with Ethan, reliving the moment he said those words. I sigh longingly, wishing I could be with him again right now.

"Yeah, right, as if men like that actually exist," Claire says, shaking her head. Then her expression turns serious. "Now tell me the truth."

"It is the truth," I reply, feigning offense at her distrust as I reach for my coat from the locker.

"Fine, then what's his name?" She pulls her phone from her pocket and unlocks the screen. Her expectant gaze meets mine.

I slip into my coat and move to stand beside her so I can see the screen. "Try looking up Joshua Friedberg," I say, secretly grateful to Olive for coming up with the name a few days ago.

"Pfft," she scoffs, lowering her gaze to the screen. Suddenly, she tilts her head to the side. "What's that in your coat pocket?"

Fuck.

Those must be Ethan's blood samples. They're still in there. Did she see the tubes? No. Or did she?

I hook my thumbs into the pockets of my lab coat and pull it closer to me. "No idea."

"What are you hiding there?" She gestures toward my hands, her expression shifting from skeptical to curious.

"Nothing." Damn it, why didn't I get rid of the samples right away? In my relief at having managed to switch them and my excitement to leave the clinic as quickly as possible to spend the evening with Ethan, I forgot all about them. And yesterday was so warm that I didn't wear a lab coat.

"Let me see," Claire says, holding out her hand expectantly.

Stay cool, Sonora, she didn't see anything. I turn in such a way that there's no chance she can look into my lab coat pocket. "Come on, work's calling."

As I try to walk past her, she blocks my way. "Not so fast."

"What's this about?" I'm not nervous—there's absolutely no reason to be. Still, I can feel my pulse quickening.

"You've got blood samples in there." Claire's gaze turns challenging.

I pretend to pat my lab coat pockets while frantically trying to figure out the right move. The only option is to go on the offensive. She wouldn't let me leave otherwise.

So I feel for the tubes and pull them out with a surprised expression. "Hm," I say. "Where did these come from?"

Before I can process what's happening, she snatches the samples from my hand and examines the labels. "Ha! I knew it. These are Dr. Perfect's samples."

She can't know that. The tubes are labeled with patient numbers, not names. Unless... Has she been snooping around after Ethan?

"Why do you still have them? He was desperate to get

them back." She steps closer and waves the samples in front of my face.

"I had to respond to an emergency, and by the time I got back, he was already gone," I lie, trying to take the tubes back from her. No luck.

Shaking her head, she narrows her eyes. "I don't know anything about an emergency."

"A personal emergency," I counter, feeling rather proud that I came up with that so quickly, even though my head is spinning.

She pulls her mouth into a mocking smile. "A rooftop emergency?"

I hold her gaze. She's not the first person in my life to try and see through me. No one ever has, and she won't either. "What's that supposed to be?"

"You know what's really strange?" she asks, and I immediately realize she's not expecting an answer. "The day before yesterday, you claimed Jake needed me, but he had no idea. Then you were desperate to get the samples, acting like your job depended on it. But not just one, even two whole nights later, you still have them." She taps her chin with her index finger, and my eyes follow her nails. "People have been fired for far less serious things, so why did he spare you, even though you disobeyed his direct order?"

Once again, I get the feeling she's not expecting a response from me. On the contrary, I think she's already come to her own conclusion. A cold shiver runs down my spine, and my heart pounds so hard it feels like it might burst from my chest.

Claire continues to stare at me. "You've always been his favorite." Now she takes another step toward me, so close that we're almost touching. She inhales sharply, and suddenly her eyes widen.

Instinctively, I step back.

Suddenly, she claps her hands over her mouth. "Acqua di Giò," she murmurs in disbelief.

I gasp for air, completely at a loss for what to do or say.

"I knew it." Agitated, she runs her free hand through her hair. "Finally. That's it. The last puzzle piece."

Do something, Sonora, damn it, anything—stop her, distract her, make a joke out of it!, a voice inside me screams, while Claire shoves the blood samples into her coat pocket and turns around in a rush.

"That's it for Dr. Perfect." Her scornful gaze brushes over me.

No sooner has she spoken the words than she takes off running, and in that moment, there are only three things I know for sure: where she's going, what she plans to do there, and that none of it can ever be allowed to happen.

Chapter Forty-Five

ETHAN

What is true?

My earlier question still echoes between Dr. Roberts and me.

My boss lets out a quiet snort. "I didn't want to believe it when Dr. Walters told me about her suspicions."

Claire?

I wave his comment away with what I hope looks like a casual gesture. "Please don't trust her—she's had an issue with me from the start and is doing everything she can to push me out."

He nods. "I've heard that too," he says, thankfully. "And I truly respect that you didn't just put her name on the cut list."

At last, this conversation is heading in the right direction again. I breathe a quiet sigh of relief. "She's an excellent doctor. Whatever personal issues she may have, I'm sure we'll find a way to resolve them." I just need to figure out how—and I won't give up until I do.

Dr. Roberts rises from his chair and joins me by the

window. "I'm afraid I bear some responsibility for her behavior."

"How so?" I ask, studying him curiously.

He gazes out the window, where seagulls are circling in the sky. "She was the internal candidate for your position, and I may have given her hope that she would get the job."

"I see." That must have been devastating for her—no wonder she's so biased against me. "Thank you for your honesty. That helps a lot." Maybe I can try to involve Claire more—after all, she's my deputy. If I give her more responsibility, she might change her opinion of me.

Wait a minute.

Just three weeks ago, I wouldn't have even allowed myself to entertain that thought. Today, I feel like I could—and the idea scares me surprisingly little.

Could I really do that?

Let go, just a little?

Have a life beyond being a doctor?

I listen inwardly, hear the sound of waves crashing, but I don't know what it's trying to tell me.

Dr. Roberts clears his throat. "Well, since we're speaking so openly…" He avoids looking at me. "I have to ask this question—you understand that, I'm sure." His fingers brush over his blazer, and he exhales slowly. "Is there something going on between you and Sonora Wells?"

Involuntarily, I hold my breath. I don't want to lie but breaking my promise to Sonora would be far worse. "No." Hopefully, that sounded convincing.

He places his hand on my shoulder. "You'll receive Ms. Wells' termination letter from HR later today. Make sure she signs it."

I can't do that. But how am I supposed to make that clear to him without…

Suddenly, my office door bursts open with a loud noise. Claire storms in, her face flushed deep red.

“What is the meaning of this?” I ask sternly. “You can’t just—” Sonora appears behind Claire in the doorway, and I fall silent at once. Pure panic is written all over her face, her chest rising and falling rapidly.

Claire runs a gasping hand through her hair. “Dr. Roberts, good, you’re here.” She now pulls the blood samples from her coat. “Here it is.” She gasps for breath. “The proof you wanted. Here it is.”

My gaze flicks to Sonora—she’s as pale as a ghost.

“Blood samples?” Dr. Roberts takes the vials from Claire with a skeptical look. “In what way are these proof?”

“Those are the samples taken from Dr. Stone the day before yesterday,” Claire replies, agitated.

I freeze. Look at Sonora. See her nod, guilt written all over her face.

That’s my blood? Why do the samples even still exist?

Instinctively, I step forward. “Let me see,” I say, addressing the chief, and take the samples, quickly wrapping my fingers around them.

Meanwhile, my boss fixes his gaze on Claire. “I don’t understand—what are Dr. Stone’s blood samples supposed to prove?”

That’s the wrong question. I hurriedly slip the vials into the pocket of my blazer. Maybe because I desperately hope the others will forget about them if they were out of sight. Or maybe, just a little, so I can pretend to myself that they weren’t really here.

“Dr. Stone and Dr. Wells are in cahoots.” Claire’s voice nearly cracks, and as she retracts the path of my blood samples—along with all the inconsistencies that were, damn it, actually true—I feel increasingly nauseous. It feel like she has tied a noose around my neck with her dramatic entrance into my office, and now with every word she is pulling it tighter.

In Sonora's face, I can clearly see that she feels the same. She even sways a little, as if she can't get enough air. Her eyes plead with me to do something.

"And about two weeks ago, the two of them were together on the rooftop terrace. You can imagine what they were doing up there, can't you?" Her venomous gaze lands on me. "A few days earlier, Sonora waited for Dr. Stone out in the parking lot, and they left the hospital grounds together."

"Because I had to set a few things straight!" Sonora shouts. "He excluded me from surgeries—I had to stand up for myself, make it clear to him that he couldn't treat me like that."

Claire shakes her head vigorously. "And what about the meeting before the audit, huh?" she snaps at Sonora, who gasps sharply in response. "Yeah, exactly, you two were already thick as thieves, weren't you? Why else would you have defended him so vehemently?" Tears of despair glisten in her eyes. Sonora remains silent, which only makes everything worse. She's usually so quick-witted, always has a sharp comeback, but this—this is clearly too much even for her.

We've maneuvered ourselves into a dead end, goddammit. How the hell do we get out of this?

A disgusted snort escapes Claire's mouth before she turns to Dr. Roberts. "You must see it too. Countless little things, nothing special on their own. But together… together they make so much sense."

Only now does it dawn on me what's been happening over the past few weeks. She's been watching us the whole time—or rather, she's been watching me. Looking for something she could use to push me out of my position, because she still wants the job.

What she found were my feelings for Sonora.

Oh God.

"Relationships between superiors and subordinates are forbidden." Claire crosses her arms and studies me. "Three weeks ago, you made that very clear." *You fucking asshole*, she adds silently, and I feel exactly like one—because I am.

I understand her. The hatred toward me, the relentless hunt for mistakes she can pin on me—because I gave her every reason. With my need for control, my blindness, my bias.

Now she turns to Dr. Roberts again. "So the rules don't apply to him?"

His gaze flicks briefly to me. "So that's what was behind your visit the other day," he says knowingly.

Claire's shrill voice floods the room before I can react. "Is he getting special treatment because he's oh-so-perfect?"

I'm not. The blood samples in my hand are the best proof of that.

Sonora knows it—I can see it in her eyes. I silently ask her if we shouldn't just lay all the cards on the table, and her answer is a shake of the head.

She wants to keep quiet. Still. At any cost.

And I don't want to lose her, so I stay silent.

Chapter Forty-Six

SONORA

Don't do it, I silently plead with Ethan from across the office. He looks frozen in place, while my chest tightens at the thought of what might happen next.

"The rules apply to everyone." Dr. Roberts's authoritative voice makes me flinch. "But don't worry, Dr. Walters, there's already a solution."

"We don't need a solution," Ethan counters, just as firmly. "Because there isn't a problem to begin with."

Oh thank God, he's keeping quiet. I want to exhale in relief, but I can't. It still feels like I'm not getting enough air.

"Of course there is!" Claire shouts, her voice full of emotion. "Dr. Roberts, you must see that."

The image before my eyes begins to blur, but I can still make out Ethan opening his mouth.

"That's enough!" Dr. Roberts's hair seems to tremble with rage—at least I think it does, because he's suddenly just as blurry, even though he's much closer to me than Ethan is. "Dr. Walters, thank you for your input," he says, turning to Claire. Then he locks eyes with Ethan. "Dr. Stone, I couldn't care less what may or may not be going on between you and Ms. Wells."

I blink in surprise. Did the hospital director just give Ethan and me the green light, or are my ears playing tricks on me now too?

"You know what you have to do," Dr. Roberts adds, fixing Ethan with a pointed stare.

I have no idea what he's talking about, but Ethan lowers his gaze. Something in his expression sears itself into my heart, which suddenly begins to pound so hard it feels like drums are beating in my chest.

"What exactly is he supposed to do?" Claire asks sharply.

Dr. Roberts gives Ethan a prompting nod, but he shakes his head, which causes the hospital director to turn his attention to me.

"Fine, then I'll do it myself," he says. A strained sigh escapes his lips. "Sonora Wells. You're fired."

What? I gasp, yet I can't breathe.

He didn't really just say that. Did he?

"But… I…"

"Of course the little employee has to go, not the great big boss." That was Claire—or at least I think it was—because my panic is so overwhelming that I can no longer be sure whose voice I'm hearing.

"I…" Even on my second attempt to form a coherent sentence, I fail miserably.

"No, Dr. Wells is not leaving," I thankfully hear Ethan protest on my behalf, causing Dr. Roberts to flush red with anger.

"She's not even a doctor, for God's sake—when will you finally get that through your head!" he shouts so loudly that his words hurt my ears.

Not a doctor?

Me?

What's going on here? Why would he think that?

"That's not true. I can show you certificates that prove it." In the middle of the sentence, a sharp pain shoots through my chest. A burning sensation, hot as fire, spreads out. It takes my breath away. Dizziness overwhelms me.

Dr. Roberts raised a warning finger. "Ms. Wells, don't make this any worse than it already is. Forging documents is outrageous enough but lying after you've already been caught—that's beyond the pale."

Beyond the pale, the words echo inside me.

Forgery.

I don't know what that means anymore—my head can't make sense of anything. With a clumsy motion, I clutch my chest, right where the burning intensifies with every breath.

Oh God, I'm about to suffocate.

"Dr. Wells has certificates, she just said so. This is all a huge misunderstanding."

The dark voice grows more and more distorted.

"Uaauauauau"

Excuse me? What is he babbling about?

I lift my eyelids, which suddenly feel as heavy as lead, and see Dr. Roberts's distorted face. His lips are moving. "Uaauauauau," he says—again those strange words no one can understand—and suddenly it feels like my chest is going to explode. My knees give out.

"Uaaua!" a man's voice calls out, perhaps in concern.

Ethan? Was that Ethan?

Someone rushes toward me, but I don't know who it is. My field of vision seems to be shrinking.

Something dark flutters before my eyes.

Like the wings of a raven.

Strange. How did a bird suddenly get into Ethan's office? And why is it now sweeping its wings over my eyes?

The last bit of light disappears, I fall, not knowing where to, deeper and deeper, until time and space lose all meaning.

Chapter Forty-Seven

ETHAN

"Call the emergency team!" I drop to my knees beside Sonora and reach for her wrist.

Irregular heartbeat. Her lips are turning blue—she's not getting enough oxygen.

"I need a resuscitation bag!" I shout, starting mouth-to-mouth until Claire kneels beside me and places the mask over Sonora's face.

Behind me, Dr. Roberts calls for the emergency team. Carefully, I lift Sonora's left eyelid and shine the flashlight into her eye.

"Pupil reaction is normal." Whatever caused her to lose consciousness, a neurological reason seems unlikely. "It's the heart."

"Most likely." Claire, rhythmically compressing the resuscitation bag with both hands, nods toward the stethoscope in her lab coat pocket.

I pull it out, hastily plug the earpieces into my ears, and push up Sonora's hospital gown. With my eyes closed, I listen to the sounds of her heart.

Pa pong, pa pong.

The rhythm is irregular.

Why?

I squint my eyes, blocking out everything around me. Even the emergency team that bursts into my office at that moment.

Pa – first heart sound component. Contraction of the muscle with a filled ventricle.

Pong – second heart sound component. The aortic and pulmonary valves close.

There's something there, but what?

Carefully, I shift the stethoscope's chest piece further to the right.

There!

"Possibly a flow murmur," I inform Claire, while mentally running through every possible explanation for Sonora's symptoms.

Fainting. Decreased respiratory rate. Irregular heartbeat. There could be many causes.

"What's going on with you, Sonora?" I murmur tensely. Out of the corner of my eye, I see someone inserting an IV line into her arm.

I turn back to Sonora's heart, unable to shake the feeling that I've missed something, so I listen again more closely. It takes five cycles before I can isolate it: the flow murmur is in the pulmonary area.

An excessive amount of blood is flowing into Sonora's pulmonary artery. There's a hole in her heart. "Suspected ASD!" I inform my colleagues.

A cold shiver runs down my spine.

"What? Sonora's heart has a hole in it?" Claire asks, breathless.

Yes, that fits. It's possible her mom even used drugs

during pregnancy that could have caused the defect. Such a heart condition often goes undetected for a long time, and the extreme stress she experienced over the past few minutes pushed her over the edge. All her secrets, everything she's fought for her entire life, just slipped away from her—she's probably never faced a crisis like this before.

"Intense emotional stress can affect the autonomic nervous system and lead to an increase in heart rate and blood pressure. In patients with ASD, that can trigger an acute episode." Sonora must have noticed symptoms her whole life: shortness of breath, dizziness, swollen legs, fatigue. She probably never thought much of it.

"Oh no, I didn't mean to. Putting her under that kind of pressure, that…" Claire stammers, guilt-ridden. "What was I thinking…"

I place my hand on Claire's arm to reassure her. "Of course that wasn't intentional, don't worry—no one would ever suspect that."

A surprised expression washes over her face. "We should do an echocardiogram to confirm the suspicion," she stammers.

Claire is right. Imaging would be important not only to confirm the heart defect but also to assess its severity and any potential complications during surgery. But does Sonora even have enough time for the examination?

"What's the oxygen saturation?" I ask the emergency team.

"Ninety-two percent."

That will have to be enough.

I nod to Claire, seeing that she's desperate to do something, feeling guilty about Sonora's condition. I know that feeling—and no one knows better than I do what helps against it.

"Would you take care of that? I'll make sure an OR is prepped," I say, hoping to give her a little peace of mind.

For a split second, her gaze lingers on me. "Gladly," she replies with a brief smile.

While she instructs the aides to lift Sonora onto a stretcher, I stand up and turn to my desk, where Dr. Roberts already has the phone receiver in his hand.

"Prep an emergency OR, alert the on-call team," he instructs someone on the other end of the line. "Dr. Stone and Dr. Walters are coming in with an ASD in…" He looks at me questioningly.

"Twenty minutes," I estimate, because I'm sure Claire will do everything in her power to get Sonora into surgery quickly.

He nods with a serious expression. "Twenty minutes," he then says into the phone and places the receiver back on the hook.

"I need to get ready," I say and rush out of the office.

On the way to the operating rooms, my heart pounds in my throat, my temples throb unpleasantly, and my thoughts are so jumbled I can't make sense of them.

There are too many problems, too many secrets that have been revealed, too much worry about Sonora's future. I reach into my jacket for the blood samples, pull them out, and with trembling fingers, peel off the labels. Then I toss them into the biohazard container as I pass by—at least one of my problems is taken care of.

What remains is the chaos in my head.

And the fear.

Fear that in just a few minutes, I'll be operating on Sonora's heart. Her life will be in my hands—and I can't even focus for three seconds at a time, let alone stop myself from repeatedly losing control of my emotional state as I walk down the hallway.

I run my hands through my hair, take a deep breath, and loosen my tie knot.

Waves crashing.

"Exhale," I whisper to myself, but I can't.

Sonora is losing her job. Because of me. If I hadn't fought so fiercely against cutting the surgical position, Dr. Roberts would never have thought to take a closer look at Sonora.

It's my fault. I ruined her.

Salt on my tongue.

And now she might lose her life.

Because of me. Because my feelings have too strong a hold on me.

"Stop," I tell myself. "Focus on the procedure." I pull myself together. "Open the chest, prepare the heart, connect the heart-lung machine."

Sand between my toes.

What then?

I clench my fists. "Identify the anatomy of the heart defect." In my mind, an image of Sonora's heart appears.

It lies before me, completely motionless. I examine it, checking the atrial walls.

A piercing scream.

The image blurs before my eyes.

My God, this can't be happening.

Sonora's life depends on me getting myself under control and finding my focus now. I'm the heart specialist in this hospital—if I handed the operation over to someone else and something happened to Sonora, I would never forgive myself.

I caused her condition. I have to make it right.

Breathless, I rush into the scrub room of the emergency OR, shut the door behind me, and press my fist to my forehead. "From the top."

Open the chest, prepare the heart, connect the heart-lung machine.

Ethan! The waves are perfect.

Identify anatomy of the heart defect.

Come on, Ethan. Surf with me.

Complete repairs. I can vaguely see everything in front of me, far too indistinct. Now I'm taking Sonora off the heart-lung machine.

But her heart isn't beating.

You should have saved me.

Fuck.

Why isn't it working?

What am I supposed to do?

How do I get it to beat?

I don't know.

Damn it, why don't I know?

Beep.

I snap my eyes open and brace myself against the sink. The memory of Liam should give me strength, but it does the opposite. It only makes everything worse.

It scares the hell out of me. Damn it, Sonora's life is on the line and I'm nothing but panic! A tortured sound escapes my mouth, and I bury my face in my hands.

I'm definitely in no condition to operate.

Claire has to perform the procedure.

The door opens behind me, and I flinch. It's Claire, striding purposefully toward the sink. "You were right—hole-like opening between the left and right atrium, just under thirteen millimeters. The images should already be available on the OR monitors." She turns on the faucet and looks at me searchingly. "Why haven't you changed yet?"

Come on, Ethan, ask her to do the surgery.

"I…" Damn it, I'm just standing here like a clueless schoolboy during an exam.

"Is something wrong?" Suddenly, her expression softens with concern.

"Everything is fine," I say quickly.

Claire fixes me with an intense stare. "You're afraid."

She can't possibly know that.

"Dr. Perfect isn't afraid." Without taking her eyes off me, she walks toward me. "You have feelings for Sonora."

Just moments ago, I swore to Dr. Roberts that there was nothing going on between Sonora and me. We should have told the truth a long time ago instead of getting ourselves deeper and deeper into this mess.

"She actually means something to you. No—not something, a great deal."

More than that. And that's exactly why I can't show any weakness now. "Haven't you already done enough damage to yourself with your slanderous accusations?" I ask, trying to sound stern. "I strongly advise you to stand down now, Dr. Walters."

She shakes her head. "Fine. If you truly don't have feelings for her, then performing surgery on her shouldn't be a problem for you, should it?" she asks sharply, and I know she'll be watching my every move in the OR—every worried glance, every quickened breath.

I have to deliver, or Sonora and I will be exposed.

"Not at all, and I honestly have no idea how you could even come to such a conclusion." I flash her a slick smile and hate myself for it. "Now, if you'll excuse me, I forgot my surgical cap."

Before she can say anything, I run to the door. I don't have time to think any longer.

I have to change clothes, scrub in, save a life, protect a secret—and there's only one way that can work.

My pills.

I need them.

Just this one last time.

They'll help me get through the procedure. With them, I can perform the operation, and I know that as long as I dose them correctly, there's no danger.

I reach into my pants pocket for the tin, but I don't find it.

Of course not—I don't have it with me anymore. It felt good to leave the tin at home, liberating, but now that knowledge makes everything even more horrifying.

I can't operate without my pills. It's not possible. And the fact that I have to operate is unavoidable.

The surgical ward doesn't stock amphetamines—our patients don't need them.

The medication storage room.

That's where I need to go—they have what I need.

Just one last time.

There's no other way, I know that. Still, on the way down to the ground floor, a wave of nausea hits me. By the time I push open the door to the medication center, I can barely stand it.

Even so, I have no choice. I never wanted to lose a life, but Sonora's is different.

It means more than any before. It means everything.

Liam's death was my fault, and it haunts me to this day. I have to save Sonora's life—if I don't, I'll die with her.

As a senior physician, I have no trouble getting what I need from the medication storage, and ten minutes later I'm back in the washroom. With only a single tablet, because I know taking it poses no risk—neither to Sonora nor to me. Taking it simply means I can focus better on my task.

I place the tablet in the palm of my hand, and suddenly, doubt washes over me.

You promised Sonora, I hear my own voice whisper inside me.

I stare at the pill, my breathing shallow.

Sonora will understand. She'll know I have to do this, that it's an emergency—one that will never happen again.

You're just as much a junkie as she is. That's what Sonora said to me, and even now, her words echo inside me.

Is she right?

Am I? Am I addicted?

The thought terrifies me.

Still, that doesn't change the bind I'm in. So I swallow the pill and pray to a god I stopped believing in long ago that it kicks in in time.

Chapter Forty-Eight

SONORA

The raven's wings wrap around my body. They envelop me. They're pleasantly warm.

Darkness.

"Sonnygirl," says a woman's voice. "What are you doing here?"

"Mom?" I blink, but everything stays dark.

Someone touches my arm, and the spot turns cold. "You don't belong here."

Here where? With her? Where even is this place?

In heaven?

Or more like in hell?

Suddenly, the dark wings lift from my eyes and I see Mom, crouched on her mattress. Her hair is a mess, her cheeks sunken, and that dazed look in her eyes.

She's using.

Again.

"You don't belong here," she repeats wearily.

Her words cut into my chest like a scalpel. "No, I don't."

Where she is, I don't want to be. Haven't wanted to for a long time.

"Then look away." Her accusing expression hits me. "That's what you're best at, isn't it?"

I shake my head with my lips pressed tightly together. Strangely, her features sharpen, her hair looks fuller, and a faint blush colors her cheeks. It's as if she's transforming before me—from a junkie into a healthy woman.

The woman who was sometimes my mom—even if only for a few weeks, before she relapsed again.

"This is what you want to see, isn't it?" she asks, reaching her hand out to me. "And this." Her manicured fingers grasp mine, and with her free arm, she makes a sweeping gesture—and suddenly, we're standing in the middle of our dream house.

It looks exactly the way we imagined it. There's the kitchen, a pot of basil sitting next to the stove. The thin curtains lift in the breeze drifting through the open windows. Sunlight floods the room.

There is warmth. And hope.

Tears burned in my eyes, and my heartbeat stopped for a moment. "What's happening here?"

"Do you like it?" she asked instead of answering me.

I nodded silently.

This was the life I had always wanted to live. And she, standing in front of me like this, was the mom I had always wanted to have.

"All of this could have come true." Mom's voice grew brittle. "The two of us, Sonnygirl, we could have made it real."

"No, I'm the one making it real." I had been doing that since my seventeenth birthday. Since she left and I left that damn trailer park—and my past—behind. I had shed that life like an ugly rag no one should ever see me in.

Mom shook her head. "You really believe that, don't you?"

What else? "You don't know me. I've been someone else for a long time now—someone different from the girl who left back then," I replied.

Like in slow motion, the house around us blurred and transformed into our filthy trailer.

"No!" I shout. "Take it back!"

"You'll never have it," my mom says, and she sounds like she actually pities me for it.

The termination notice, it dawns on me.

Suddenly, my heart starts pounding in panic. She's right—I'll never have it. I lost my job. I have a loan I can't pay back. Rent I can't afford. Friends who were never really friends, since I lied to them from the start. My God, I even used their college transcripts as templates for my forgeries!

"This is your fault!" I scream at her. "It all started with you and your damn drugs."

"Yes, I made mistakes." Her expression turns serious now. "But that doesn't justify all the mistakes you're making." She takes her hand off my arm. "Stop running away. Face the truth."

Face the truth? Like Ethan did all his life and nearly broke because of it?

Mom snorts in disdain. "Ethan," she says, as if she can read my mind.

Now she's got something against him too? "What about him?"

"You're going to lose him." Her words echo inside me as we look at each other. "You're going to lose him just like you lost me."

I won't! I cross my arms over my chest and shake my head vehemently.

"Because you still haven't understood that it didn't all start with me and my damn drugs," she continues relentlessly.

"That's a lie." She needs to stop—this is long past, it doesn't matter anymore. I press my hands over my ears and turn away, but even there, her face is waiting for me.

"Yes, I gave you a rough start, but now you're an adult. Now you make your own decisions and choose who you are," she says.

"Bullshit," I shoot back. "You're insane—your fucking drugs turned you into a monster."

Now she raises her arms in a calming gesture. "As you wish."

Exactly. As I wish. That's how my life works. "Ethan and I will make it," I say firmly, even though I have no idea what lies ahead for us. But one thing is certain: I won't lose him. Not ever.

At last, she steps aside, her silhouette blurs, and the raven returns.

"You will lose him," I hear Mom say one last time in a faint voice before the bird wraps its wings around me, envelops me in its warmth, and pulls me back into the darkness.

Chapter Forty-Nine

ETHAN

Twenty-five minutes have passed since I took the pill. I barely made it through the start of the operation, but now it's finally kicking in. My thoughts are razor-sharp, energy surges through my body. I'm in my element.

"Begin dissecting the ascending aorta for connection to the heart-lung machine," I say.

The monitoring machine beeps.

"Oxygen saturation 91, blood pressure systolic 85, diastolic 67, heart rate 120," the assistant reports.

So the saturation is still dropping. I glance at Claire meaningfully. "We need to hurry."

She nods and reaches for the scalpel. "I'll handle the preparation. In the meantime, you can study the ultrasound image."

That would be a good idea—after all, I should get a sense of what to expect during the procedure. I'd do that with any other patient, but with Sonora, I just can't manage it.

I can look at the image during the surgery as well.

“Thank you for the offer, Dr. Walters, but I’m nearly done,” I press out, even though the aorta hasn’t even been remotely prepared.

My colleague gives me a probing look. “Of course,” she says, then turns to the assistant. “Prepare the cannulas.”

With a deep breath, I reach out moments later, and the assistant places the first cannula into my hand. My fingers tremble slightly as I grasp it.

There’s no reason to be nervous, Ethan, you’ve performed far more complex procedures, I silently remind myself, but even with the pill, it’s hard to stay calm.

Someone clears their throat. “Should I maybe…?” Claire asks.

“I said I’ve got this,” I snap at her a bit too sharply.

Damn it, I should have better control over myself.

Carefully, I place one cannula after another, while cold sweat forms on my forehead. I ignore it, just like I ignore my pulse, which keeps speeding up.

“Connect them,” I ask Claire, whereupon she attaches the cannulas to the tubes of the heart-lung machine and switches the device on.

Next, we will…

What was that again?

“Should I inject the cardioplegic solution?” Claire asks. Worry lines form on her forehead.

Of course. We have to inject the solution to induce artificial cardiac arrest.

My gaze falls on Sonora’s pounding heart.

If we stop it now, it might never beat again. The thought overwhelms me, narrowing my field of vision, making my muscles tremble.

I could lose her. Might never wake up beside her again, taste her lips, hear her infectious laughter.

"Dr. Stone?"

No idea who's speaking. I nod as if I'm fully focused, but in truth, I'm anything but, as I now realize.

My emotions are controlling me, though it should be the other way around—earlier, I snapped at Claire unfairly.

I'm sweating—so much that I can feel the drops crawling down my temples.

My heart is racing—so intensely that it's starting to stab in my chest.

"Vitals are deteriorating. Oxygen saturation at 90, blood pressure systolic 82, diastolic 63, heart rate 125," the assistant says.

Fuck.

"Should I inject the solution now?" Claire asks again, this time more forcefully.

I should be the one doing this, but I don't feel ready. What if I position the syringe incorrectly? What if my hand trembles before I insert it into the muscle tissue? What if I make a mistake?

Words like uncontrolled cardiac activity, myocardial injury, and prolonged ischemia time swirl through my mind. Can I take that risk?

Is performing this procedure myself—and thereby keeping our secret—worth the risk?

The monitoring machine lets out an alarm. "Oxygen saturation has dropped below 90," a woman's voice calls out. "Condition critical."

"Dr. Stone, we have to act." Claire fixes her gaze on me. *What are you doing?* she asks silently. "Now!"

Yes. Act. Now.

Once again, I lower my eyelids to Sonora's heart, my own racing wildly.

Waves crashing.

I can't do this.

Sand between my toes.

It'll feel like giving up. Like ending the fight I've waged so relentlessly and passionately all my life—and with it, losing my chance at forgiveness.

I'll break my promise to Liam, and with that, lose him for good.

A piercing scream.

But what if that already happened long ago, and there's nothing I can do to change it? No matter how many lives I save, Liam's will always be lost.

But Sonora's life isn't.

And nothing should stop me.

Not my fault.

Not my ego.

I will save her. I'm ready to pay the price, no matter how high it is.

"Inject the solution," I say to Claire, who then takes the prepared syringe handed to her.

A few seconds later, Sonora's heart stops beating.

"We're ready. You can open the heart." Claire nods at me expectantly, and an assistant hands me the scalpel.

I reach for it—and hand it to Claire. "Would you take over?" I ask her, because I know it's the right thing to do.

Now is not the time to be perfect. It's the time to admit the truth to myself. That I have far too strong feelings for this woman lying on the table before us. That I shouldn't be the one operating on her. That I'm not the doctor she needs right now.

Claire catches my gaze. I can see she doesn't understand any of what's happening.

"Please," I say quietly, letting her see in my eyes how deeply fear for Sonora has taken hold of me. I don't care what she does with that information—I just want Sonora to receive the best possible care.

With a knowing nod, Claire finally takes the scalpel from me. "Are you sure?"

I have never been more certain of anything. "You're a fantastic doctor, Dr. Walters. I know Sonora is in the best hands with you."

Her eyes fill with tears, which she quickly blinks away. Something shifts in her gaze—it becomes soft and understanding.

She clears her throat. "Would you guide me?"

There is so much hope and sincerity in her request, but there is also something else.

I believe it is forgiveness, and as crazy as it seems, in that moment, for the first time in my life, I manage to forgive myself—just a little.

"Let's begin with opening the heart," I reply with a grateful nod, signaling for her to continue the operation.

Chapter Fifty

SONORA

Dark wings, everywhere.

Light filters through the feathers. A tiny beam that grows wider and wider.

A flutter.

Blurry white.

"Hey." Someone squeezes my hand.

I want to pull it away, but I'm not sure if I manage. "Go away, Mom." My words sound strangely distorted. "Get lost," I add, just to be sure.

"It's me, Ethan."

A comforting warmth surrounds me.

Everything is fine.

"Ethan," I sigh. *See, Mom, I'm not losing him*, I think to myself and lift the corners of my mouth into a smile.

"Try to open your eyes," he asks me, and I lift my heavy eyelids.

"Hi," I say to his handsome face hovering above me. His eyes look darker than usual, his forehead glistens.

Now he kisses my cheek.

His lips are hot, as if he has a fever.

"How are you feeling?" he asks gently, stroking my cheek with affection.

"Why me? You're the one with the fever," I reply, confused.

He laughs. It's a beautiful, warm, heartfelt laugh. "You just came out of surgery," he explains, and as he tells me what happened in the last few hours and that I'm going to make a full recovery, the memories slowly start to return.

Claire, who discovered Ethan's blood samples.

The hallway rushing past me as I race after her toward Ethan's office.

Dr. Roberts with a stern expression.

Oh no.

"I've been found out." Yes, that's what happened. Ethan's boss discovered that I faked my application documents, but that's not even the worst part. Alarmed, I try to sit up in bed, but immediately collapse back down. "We've been found out!"

It's over, the game is done, and I've lost—completely. No, worse than that: I'm ruined.

Not only did I lose my job. The heart surgery must have cost a fortune.

"I don't have health insurance." The words leave my mouth in a flat, lifeless tone.

"I'll handle it, we'll find a way, everything's going to be okay," I hear Ethan say, his voice filled with at least as much worry as I feel inside.

I look at him, desperate for help.

He's sweating.

Why is he sweating so much?

"Also, I'm going to talk to Dr. Roberts. I'll convince him not to fire you," he bursts out. "The fact that he even reviewed your application materials is my fault. I'll fix this."

A strange, nervous tremor runs through his whole body. *What's going on with him?* I squint my eyes.

Wait a second.

That's not darkness in his eyes—those are dilated pupils. Despite the lingering effects of my anesthesia, I understand what that means. Not least because it's not the only clue.

You're going to lose him, Mom whispers knowingly inside me. I have no idea where her voice suddenly comes from, but it doesn't matter.

Damn it. Ethan took way more than his withdrawal plan allows.

I wanted to believe he had it under control, gave him a chance, even covered for him.

And he did it again.

While a whirlpool of emotions drags me into the abyss, Ethan rushes to the door. "Don't worry, you won't lose your job—I won't let that happen," he says before disappearing outside.

I turn my head, see him close the door—and at the same time, a completely different door opens inside me, behind which lurks the one memory I need the least right now.

Still, it hits me with full force.

"Sonnygirl, come on, don't be so dramatic." Mom flails her hands through the air.

"Not so dramatic?" Shit, she can't be serious. I hold up the little paper bag, gasping for air, but I get so little that I start to feel dizzy. "You're using again, for god's sake!" And she's doing it in secret, thinking I won't find out. That might have worked when I was eight and didn't understand what was wrong with her. But I'm almost seventeen—why does she think she can still lie to me?

She waves it off casually. "Just now and then, don't worry, I've got it under control."

"Like the last five times you tried to get clean?" A heavy weariness washes over me, and my shoulders slump forward. "You need professional help."

"I can do it again, sweetheart, but only with you—not with some stranger who doesn't understand me."

She pulls me into her arms with affection, then places one hand on mine and the other on her breastbone, right where the butterfly tattoos are—the ones we both got three weeks ago after her rehab.

A symbol that things are finally looking up for us, that we're sticking together, and that she'll never fall again.

"This," she says, tapping the spot with the tattoo, "is proof that I can do it."

"Do you?" Tears burn in my eyes, even though I shouldn't have any left in me.

She pushes out her lower lip. "Don't you believe in me anymore?" she asks, only making everything worse.

I look at her for a while. I recognize the first signs that she needs a hit. The nervous trembling of her fingers, the greedy glance at the packet in my hand. And I realize there's only one right answer to her question.

"Of course I believe in you," I say anyway, because I just can't help it. I want to help her, be there for her. We've made it through so much together—we'll make it through this too. "Come on, let's do this together. Let's start right now, before things spiral out of control."

"Tomorrow," she replies quickly and reaches for the paper packet in my hand, but I close my fist around it. "Come on, Sonnygirl. Don't be like that with me—you want Mommy to be okay, don't you?"

Now the tears spill from the corners of my eyes, and with them, the last bit of hope drains from my body.

"You're never going to change." It wasn't a question—it was a statement. And I know it's true.

Shocked, she runs her fingers through her tangled hair. "If you don't believe in me, then get out of here. You've been freeloading off me long enough anyway." She grabs my backpack, and as she shoves clothes into it at random, I suddenly feel absolutely nothing.

No sadness, no fear, no hope.

When she presses the backpack against my chest, I shake my head silently, refusing to take it.

When she holds out her palm to me with an expectant look, I place the damn packet into it.

And as I sink onto the narrow bench beside the kitchenette at the sound of the lighter clicking, I search within myself for the hope I so desperately need.

Tomorrow we'll start all over again. Go through it all once more.

The begging, the trembling, the scratching at her arms.

The yelling, the vomiting, the sweating.

And this time she's going to make it—she has to.

Like a storm, the memory sweeps through me and leaves nothing but chaos behind. I never stopped being there for my mom, never stopped believing in her. And still, she killed herself with that shit.

It'll end the same way with Ethan.

Not even twenty-four hours after he swore to me he had it under control, he did it again.

The pills are going to ruin him.

I have to leave him before he drags me down with him, just like Mom did. I can't go through that again.

Stop running away. Face the truth, I hear Mom whisper, even though it's none of her business.

My chest tightens. I don't want to do it, I don't want to see the shards I've so carefully swept under the rug of my life.

But there they are.

In my mind's eye.

And in them, I see myself. The curly-haired girl from

the gutter with the broken shoes. The girl who never wanted to admit how sick her mom really was. The woman who gave in again and again, downplayed problems, and blindly hoped for the best.

I see a woman who pretends to be strong but is really just always running away. A woman who already lost someone because she couldn't face painful truths.

I should have stayed strong, forced her into therapy, endured her hatred. If I'd had the courage back then, maybe everything would've turned out differently.

The thought weighs heavily on my chest. It sits there now, along with the knowledge that Ethan, like Mom, won't escape his vicious cycle. Not unless I leave him no choice but to face the truth—by reporting his addiction to the chief physician, the way I should have from the very beginning.

It might be the thing that finally wakes him up. It could save his life. But he wouldn't just lose his job—he'd lose his medical license, and with it, everything he ever cared about.

He would never forgive me for that.

Now I really can't breathe anymore.

You're going to lose him, Mom whispers gravely, and this time, I don't fight her words.

"Yeah," I say flatly, my eyes fixed on the door he just walked through, because I know it's true. "No matter what I do, I'm going to lose Ethan."

Tears well up in my eyes, tracing cold, damp paths down my cheeks before falling from my jaw like they're tumbling off a cliff into nothingness.

I'd rather jump into the darkness with you than stand in the sunlight without you. Those were Ethan's words, back when neither of us knew we'd never have either.

And suddenly, it's no longer about whether I can keep my job or save our love from falling apart.

Because both are completely impossible.

There's only one thing I can still do right: I can save Ethan's life—and that's exactly what I'm going to do. Even if it means we'll each have to leap into our own darkness. Because that one fate we searched for together, the one that would shine for both of us—it doesn't exist.

Chapter Fifty-One

ETHAN

I stop in front of Dr. Roberts' office door and take a deep breath. All night, I searched in vain for a solution to Sonora's problem.

The certificates are forged. That's a fact I can't deny. But even more than that, I can't expose the truth and betray Sonora in the process. I promised her I'd keep the secret of her past. If I break that promise, she'll hate me forever—even if it means she gets her job back.

The woman who brought all the light and so much love back into my heart, who means the world to me—she would slip through my fingers.

I lift my eyelids and stare at the grain of the light wooden door.

All my life, I've wanted nothing but the truth, no matter how painful it was. I wanted it to torment me, to consume me, so it could make me a better man.

But losing Sonora won't just torment me. It will destroy me. And yet, at the same time, it would secure her job and give her the chance to achieve what she's dreamed of her entire life: to no longer be the girl from the gutter.

In the midst of my thoughts, the door to Dr. Roberts' office suddenly swings open and my boss stands in front of me.

"Ethan," he says, startled, eyeing me for a moment. "I was just about to come see you. Come in."

I step into his office, still completely clueless about how I'm supposed to save Sonora's job.

Tell the truth and lose her?

Or come up with a lie that might be enough, pay for her surgery, and keep being with her in secret?

A lie to cover a lie, just to keep lying.

Damn it, what have I become?

"How is Sonora Wells?" my boss asks, gesturing toward the round conference table beside an overgrown houseplant.

Relieved to start the conversation with an easy topic, I sink into one of the chairs and tell him about Sonora's successful surgery.

"Good." His smile lasts only a fraction of a second. "Even though it may seem inappropriate given the situation, we'll still have to let her go."

I shake my head. "Look, I don't know exactly what's going on with her credentials," I say, trying to keep my tone neutral. "But I do know she's a fantastic surgeon, and this hospital can't afford to lose her."

He forms a triangle with his hands. "That's irrelevant—we have to cut a position regardless."

"We don't have to. Let me speak to the board. I'll present a plan…"

"You really never give up, do you? Fine, have it your way." He raises his hands as if surrendering. "If you manage to eliminate the position, we'll look for a replacement for Sonora Wells," he continues.

Damn it. That gets me what I've always demanded: a full team. But it also leaves me with hardly any solid reasons not to fire Sonora.

"But I want Dr. Wells on my team," I hear myself say in desperation. "She's integrated herself extremely well, fits in perfectly, and is exceptionally talented." Those are valid arguments—perfect ones, even—but from the look on my boss's face, I can tell they don't matter to him.

"There's something going on here." He leans forward now, locking eyes with me. "I'll ask one last time: When you swore yesterday that there was nothing between you and this woman—did you lie to me?"

I did. And just like before, I'm on the verge of telling him the truth about Sonora and me.

Sweat forms on my forehead, my heart is racing—just like my thoughts.

"What's really going on here, Ethan?" my boss asks, this time more gently, almost with pity.

I want to tell him, get everything off my chest, be free of these secrets. "I…"

Before I can finish my sentence, the office door suddenly opens and in walks…

…Sonora!

Chapter Fifty-Two

SONORA

My pulse races as Ethan and I lock eyes. There is so much love in his gaze, so much warmth. More than anything, I want him to look at me like that for the next hundred years, but at the same time, I know he never will again after this conversation.

You're doing this for Ethan. He's the only thing that matters, I remind myself. Then I turn to the nurse who has helped me into the wheelchair and brought me here along with my IV bag. "Thank you. I can manage on my own from here."

Out of the corner of my eye, I see her leave the office while I focus on Ethan once more.

Feigning confusion, he furrows his brow. "Dr. Wells, what are you doing here?"

Yesterday, when I was still confined to bed, my plan had seemed feasible. But now it feels like a noose is tightening around my neck.

Dr. Roberts approaches me. "If this is about your job, I'm afraid I have to…"

"I'm here for a different reason," I interrupt him, trying

to tear my gaze away from Ethan, but I can't. I feel our connection far too intensely. Before I met him, I was always on my own, and that was fine. But without him, I'll be alone in a way I've never known before. As if only half of me remains.

"Well?" The hospital director raises his eyebrows.

I swallow hard. "It's about…" My voice falters. I clear my throat and see a mix of confusion and fear in Ethan's eyes. I see that he wants nothing more than to come to me and hold me. Because he realizes just how dangerously close I am to the edge of a cliff.

"…about Dr. Wells and me," he finishes my sentence suddenly, as if trying to take the burden from me, assuming I no longer want to carry it. Now he steps closer, stands right beside me, and places his hand on my shoulder. "It's true, we have feelings for each other."

Dr. Roberts places his index fingers at his temples. "Heavens, and I didn't want to believe it."

I'd love to leave it at that. I'm fired anyway—there's nothing standing in the way of a relationship with Ethan. We could walk out of this office right now and be happy together. I don't know how I'd pay off my debts, but at least he could go on with his life.

His life, which he so recklessly puts at risk.

I can't let that happen.

"There's more," I say, and instantly feel my own words knock the breath from my lungs.

In a few seconds, I'm going to destroy everything. My life will be in even more ruins than it already is. But Ethan is worth the sacrifice.

"So you're pregnant. Great." Dr. Roberts snorts and runs his hands through his hair. "At least now everything makes sense," he says, fixing his gaze on Ethan. "You were used, Ethan, don't you see that? This fraud"—he points accusingly at me—"first faked her application to get this job, then pretended to be in love with you and got herself pregnant as a precaution so we couldn't fire her once she got exposed."

I've been accused of many things in my life, and I've learned to hide the parts of myself that make people judge me. I've learned to let it bounce off me, but now I feel like little Sonora from the trailer park all over again.

"That's a ridiculous accusation that has absolutely nothing to do with the facts," I hear Ethan say, far too emotionally.

As if this weren't already disastrous enough, the two of them now launch into a heated argument.

"Enough! I'm not pregnant!" I shout loudly, and Ethan gently squeezes my shoulder in response.

As if to show me that no matter what I say, no matter what I do, and no matter how big the problem is—he'll be there for me. For me, the woman who's about to betray him.

I can't do this. There has to be another way. But how will Ethan ever realize he needs to break his vicious cycle if I keep covering for him?

I look up at Ethan, who's still standing close by my side. "This is about something completely different," I say.

He nods at me. You've got this, he lets me know silently. For a split second, I wonder what he means by that, but then it becomes clear.

And I know it's the answer. I know how I can open Ethan's eyes without betraying him. How I can save him without losing him.

I have to prove to him that it's possible. That anyone can escape the prison they once locked themselves into—no matter how many times they've failed trying.

Even I can do it.

For him.

Maybe deep down I always knew the rug I'd swept my past under might one day lift in the winds of fate. That it would happen here, of all places—in Halifax Harbor Hospital—I never would have believed.

And yet, that's exactly what's going to happen.

"Yes, my credentials are forged." My voice trembles, but I look Dr. Roberts straight in the eye. "But if you're willing to hear my story, I hope you'll understand why I did it."

I gesture to the chair beside him. With a suspicious expression, he crosses his arms. "Well, this should be interesting."

Despite my fear that this could go horribly wrong, I do it: I lift the rug, drag out the ugly details, tell him everything.

Everything no one was ever supposed to know about me.

Everything I'm so deeply ashamed of.

Everything I usually downplay.

One by one, I lay my shitty cards on the table, let him see that I never had a chance of winning the game of my life, and hope he understands that bluffing was my only option. How else could I have made it this far?

"I've made a lot of mistakes in my life," I finally finish my monologue, looking into the eyes of a now noticeably pale Dr. Roberts. "I've lied more times than I can count, but one thing is true: I am a doctor. And I would have earned the degree I led you to believe I had—if I'd had the money to officially study at Dalhousie University."

Clearly confused, he shakes his head. Ethan strokes my shoulder. I reach for his hand, intertwine my fingers with his, and lower my gaze.

"I was at Dalhousie and I did attend the lectures." The other students thought I was studying with them—June, Olive, Nyla, and Autumn. To this day, they still believe it, because I made sure of it, by any means necessary. "The only thing I did at the community college was take the exams."

As I hear my story come from my own mouth, something happens that I never expected:

I feel pity.

Exactly the kind of pity I never wanted from anyone. For the fact that I barely had a chance to escape the gutter from the very beginning, and also for the fact that I held on to the belief for so long that I could make it. That I was blind and deaf and mute, and never stopped clinging to that future Mom and I dreamed of together, as if it were my lifeline, while I was the one conjuring the storm myself.

Not for a single second did I want to imagine that I might fail. And yet now, my life is going down in flames.

"Wow," I hear Dr. Roberts say quietly. "That's…"

I don't dare open my eyes. I don't want to see in Dr. Roberts' face what I already feel so painfully: that I've failed at life. I can't bear his pity, his disapproval.

"Yeah, I know." My voice breaks.

Silence spreads between the three of us, and I wait for the boss to finally pass judgment—but it never comes.

"I'm sorry," I say, because all I want is for this to be over, but again, no one responds. Confused, I look up and see something I don't understand.

For so long, I did everything I could to hide the girl from the gutter. Because I couldn't have borne the way people would have looked at me. As if poverty were all I was. As if I had no goals, no hopes, no dreams.

I wanted to be more and have more than that.

So much more.

But now that the truth is out, I don't see a trace of pity on Dr. Roberts' face.

Instead, there's contemplation.

Now the boss rises from his chair and walks toward me. "Most people with your background would be where their parents ended up," he says, burying his hands in his pockets. "What you've made of yourself is incredible."

Of course it is—who could ever claim otherwise, I would've replied casually just four weeks ago, striking an exaggerated pose as if his words didn't touch me in the slightest. "Thank you," I whisper today, moved, with a shy smile and a pounding heart.

Then I look at Ethan—after all, I didn't tell my story for myself, but for him. To prove to him that anyone can own up to their mistakes—and that it's never too late to do so.

Our eyes meet, and for the first time since I've known him, he has tears in his eyes.

Chapter Fifty-Three

ETHAN

Sonora's words moved me deeply, along with the courage and strength with which she just spoke so openly about something she had tried for so long to keep hidden at all costs.

It marks the end of a game of hide-and-seek she believed she needed to play in order to let her own fate shine in a way that could illuminate even the darkest shadows. To find happiness someday, once her memories had finally faded.

But the truth is, her past should never fade. Everything that happened in her life, every mistake she made, and every decision she took—it's all a part of her. It's what makes her this incredible person who now looks at me with so much hope in her eyes.

Waves crashing.

Sonora denied her past in order to look toward a better future, while I was so fixated on my own past that I never asked myself what that meant for my future.

Sand between my toes.

For years, my mission to save as many lives as possible—and in doing so, to one day overcome Liam's death and my own guilt—felt like the only right path. I helped patients and, in doing so, gave myself at least a fleeting sense of the forgiveness I so desperately longed for. What I never saw was the price I paid for it.

I sacrificed myself.

Everything I was. Everything I had. And if I keep going the way I have these past years—everything I could still have.

I catch Sonora's gaze and can finally admit what I've suspected for quite some time thanks to her: That day on the beach, I made a terrible mistake, but nothing I do can ever undo it. It doesn't matter how many lives I save—there's no changing the past.

All I have is the future, which I've never cared about. The future I'm about to destroy.

A piercing scream.

I can still stop it.

My gaze rests on Sonora. "I'm addicted to amphetamines," I say loudly and clearly enough that Dr. Roberts undoubtedly hears it.

Relief spreads across Sonora's features.

At the same time, I hear my boss gasp. "What the hell is this now?"

"For years, the only reason I've functioned so perfectly is because of the pills." Saying it out loud feels unbelievable—and even more unbelievable is the hopeful look Sonora gives me now. "I promised you I'd stop," I say to her. "But I broke that promise."

"I already know that," she replies, her voice hoarse.

"I panicked," I explain to her. "You collapsed right in front of me, you needed surgery, and I wanted to be there for you."

In the background, I hear Dr. Roberts stammer something like "not this too" in disbelief.

"It was a mistake, a damn mistake in a moment when my emotions overwhelmed me," I admit. "I was so scared for you."

She bites her lower lip. I sink to my knees in front of her and lift her chin with my index finger until she looks at me again. I couldn't care less that my boss is standing behind me. I want him to hear every word I say.

"I wanted to be strong—for you and for us. After all, not operating on you would've been the final proof Claire needed to expose us once and for all." I look at her intently. "But I couldn't do it."

Confusion spreads across her face. "What do you mean?"

Gently, I take both her hands. "I didn't operate on you, Sonora. Because I knew I wasn't capable of it." I let my thumbs glide over her palms. "But I only realized that after I reached for the pills in a panic."

"You didn't operate on me?" she asks, and I can see she's struggling to make sense of it.

She can't believe that Dr. Perfect gave up control—for her sake.

I nod. "Claire saved your life."

"You handed command over to Claire, of all people?"

"I did." Fully aware that with what she had let us both know through that gesture, she could have ruined us. "After all, it was nothing less than the love of my life."

Tears well up in her eyes, and I sense that she understands how much she means to me. But that's not all.

"Taking the pills was a mistake." I take a deep breath for the one truth I never wanted to see myself. "I always thought I had it under control, because I'd taken the pills for years without incident and always functioned perfectly. But I'm still addicted to them. To the safety they give me. To the perfection they allow me."

I was never perfect—even with the pills, I wasn't. I was a fraud who lied not only to others, but to myself. We both were.

"So this is… this is…" Dr. Roberts seems to be searching for words, but he doesn't need to find them, because I already carry the right ones within me. I know exactly what I need to do to save Sonora, our love, and myself.

I give Sonora one last meaningful look, then turn to my boss.

I smile at him. "Sonora is staying, and I won't need to beg the board for it."

Waves crashing.

The roar of the ocean builds inside me. I hear the screams, taste the salt, feel the sand between my toes.

All the things I had so eagerly welcomed for so long, all the things I had loved to torment myself with, want to take hold of me. But as I form the words in my mind that I'm about to speak, the sound of the waves begins to fade.

The screams fade away.

I can barely taste the salt on my tongue anymore.

"I quit," I say, and wait for the silence.

One last wave.

It's almost time.

I intertwine my fingers more tightly with Sonora's. She squeezes my hands, and deep inside, I feel how my heart—shattered by fate years ago—is finally ready to heal.

My eyelids close.
There it is.
Silence.
I exhale, relieved.

Chapter Fifty-Four

SONORA

Five weeks later

For the first time since my heart surgery, I slip back into my white coat, clip the pager to the waistband of my scrubs, and close the locker door.

The plaque Ethan gave me to mark my new beginning at Halifax Harbor Hospital gleams in the sunlight streaming in. I run my index finger across the metallic surface.

Dr. Sonora Wells. Trailer girl. Lifesaver. Light.

A smile steals across my lips, the kind I know will stay with me forever. The fact that I still have my job is thanks to Ethan, and it's Dr. Roberts' doing that the clinic fund, created specifically for patients in need, covered the cost of my surgery.

All my life, I thought I would go down in flames if my past ever came to light. I never wanted to be the girl from the gutter, the one who isn't worth supporting, acknowledging, or loving—at any cost.

Five weeks ago, I was exactly that girl—and I received

more love, recognition, and support than ever before. It's strange how convinced we sometimes are that we're doing the right thing, even as we're heading straight toward a cliff.

"Welcome back!"

I look up and spot Claire. Her cheeks are flushed bright red, and her chin-length hair is wildly tousled as she hurries toward me.

The moment she reaches me, she pulls me into her arms. "I was such an idiot. I'm so incredibly sorry for accusing you unfairly."

She didn't—her suspicion about Ethan and me was absolutely right. I'd love to tell her right now, but she's going to find out soon enough anyway.

"I was so angry and hurt, and I didn't realize how far I'd gone," she continues pleadingly. "Can you forgive me?"

"Aren't we all sometimes angry and hurt and don't realize we've gone too far?" I ask gently, sinking into her embrace. And once again, I can't help but smile, because I can't remember the last time I was hugged so often in such a short amount of time as I have been in the past five weeks.

After all the truths came to light in Dr. Roberts's office, I immediately knew what had to happen next.

Olive, June, Nyla, and Autumn had to know too.

None of them reacted the way I'd imagined for years. None pushed me away—on the contrary, we're closer than ever, and instead of the Vegas trip, we had a picnic on the beach with a Joshua Friedberg concert playing on the radio.

"Thanks, that means a lot to me." Claire lets go of me and nodded toward the door. "Dr. Stone has called a meeting."

I raise an eyebrow. "What happened to Dr. Perfect?"

"Somehow he's changed since your surgery. He's…

become more human. No idea why, maybe it's just a tactic," she says with a shrug.

At the moment, no one on the ward knows that Ethan resigned five weeks ago and is only staying until a replacement is found.

As I smile to myself, something behind me catches Claire's attention. "Trailer girl?"

"That's right," I reply, feeling almost a little proud of it. "Grew up without a dad and with a drug-addicted mom in Spryfield."

She nods absentmindedly. "There's more to you than meets the eye."

Much more. I link my arm through hers. "Come on, we don't want to be late, do we?"

She rolls her eyes. "Heaven forbid, we wouldn't want to get fired!"

"No one's getting fired." With those words, I pull her with me out of the locker room. Not even I got fired, even though the clinic would've had every reason to. "I even heard the board tried to force Dr. Stone to cut staff, but he found another solution."

"Dr. Stone made sure no one had to be fired?" Claire asks, clearly struggling to process the thought.

I wink at her. "Maybe he's more human than you think."

"Hm," she murmurs absentmindedly. "It's actually starting to make some kind of sense."

It's only a few more steps to the doctors' lounge. "Maybe he does deserve a second chance."

She hums thoughtfully again as we walk in. The room is packed—every staff member, from surgeons to cleaning personnel, is here. Lively conversations and muted laughter fill the air. Claire and I weave our way through to where

Jake is leaning against the wall. The two exchange wistful glances but keep their distance.

Now Ethan enters the lounge and makes his way through the crowd toward the window. In a T-shirt and jeans, with three-day stubble and a relaxed expression, he draws surprised murmurs. As he passes, he gives me a smile, and I return a conspiratorial one. When he finally stops and turns around, the staff falls silent.

"In my inaugural speech, I told you I was excited to turn this surgical department into a flagship unit with all of you," he says after a brief greeting.

A nurse rolls his eyes toward the ceiling, and Claire lets out a sigh. "Oh, come on, not this speech again," she mutters.

"To make that happen, I wanted to see top performance from everyone here," Ethan continues, letting his gaze sweep across the room. "Mistakes were something I couldn't and wouldn't tolerate."

Suddenly, everything falls completely silent. I can almost physically feel the team's fear. They're wondering what they did wrong this time, worrying about their jobs.

Ethan smiles openly. "You're all doing an excellent job." He pauses, clearly wanting his words to sink in. "And that was already the case before I started working here."

"So he is human after all?" Claire whispers to me, and I just flash her a mischievous grin.

With his hands buried in the pockets of his pants, Ethan begins pacing in front of the staff. "I wanted to do just as good a job as all of you, wanted to be infallible—for the department and for our patients."

Claire nudges me with a questioning look. I nod toward Ethan, thinking she shouldn't miss what he's about to say.

"But I'm not. On the contrary, I've done harm—to you,

to myself, and therefore to our patients." A murmur ripples through the room. "The last thing this department needs is a control-obsessed, perfectionist senior physician who trusts no one and ends up suffocating everyone here," he says firmly.

Some employees exchange confused glances, others seem to struggle to keep their mouths closed.

"Wow." Claire looks so stunned that I can't help but grin. "Is this actually happening?"

I lean toward her. "Told you—our Dr. Perfect is just a regular guy."

"Five weeks ago, I handed in my resignation to Dr. Roberts," Ethan continues, unfazed by the excited murmuring among the staff, and now Claire's expression completely falls apart.

"Oh. My. God." She claps her hands over her mouth.

"About time," Jake murmurs to Claire.

But instead of nodding, Claire shakes her head, and I sense that it's no longer about getting rid of him for her. That maybe it never was. That all she ever wanted was a boss who's human—just like her.

Now he fixes his gaze on Claire. "I'd like to formally apologize to Dr. Walters. For my selfish behavior, for giving her so little space and trust as my deputy."

Claire inhales sharply and blinks noticeably hard. "No," she says—at first so quietly that only Jake and I hear it. Then she repeats it louder. "I'd like to apologize to you. For not giving you a chance from the very beginning."

Ethan walks up to us. He stops directly in front of Claire. "You had understandable reasons for that." He smiles warmly, his gaze shifting between Claire and Jake. "I hope this isn't coming too late."

Ethan hands Claire a sheet of paper. She lowers her eyelids, and I, too, glance at the text.

Halifax Harbor Hospital – Hospital Regulations, I read. My eyes move downward and find a crossed-out passage.

The relationship rule.

"You…," Claire stammers in disbelief and passes the sheet on to Jake.

Ethan nods. "That rule was completely ridiculous. It was like arresting an innocent person just because you think they might commit a crime someday." He gives her a conspiratorial wink, as if his words hold a deeper meaning. "At least that's what someone once told me."

"Oh really? She must've been a damn clever woman." A bright laugh escapes Claire's lips, then her expression softens. "Thank you."

"It was long overdue," Ethan replies, pulling a phone from his pocket and holding it up for everyone to see.

It's the on-call attending physician's phone, the one he insisted on being reachable through twenty-four hours a day, seven days a week.

"Just like this was long overdue," he adds, handing Claire the ward phone.

"What? … Wait… Um." Her gaze flicks back and forth between the phone and Ethan. "You want me to…?"

"It would be an honor if you would lead this department from now on." Letting go was never his strength, but I can see in his expression that this isn't hard for him at all.

Silence spreads through the doctors' lounge, the team's attention fixed on Claire, who presses her lips into a wistful smile.

Her eyes locked on Ethan, she exhales, then reaches for the phone with trembling fingers.

I don't know what the two of them are thinking right

now, in this moment when Ethan lets go of the phone—and with it, the last tie to his old life—but I hope it's the same thing I'm thinking: that we must never stop believing that even from the blows fate deals us, something good can still emerge. That this thought can be a light in the darkness, whenever we can't see our way forward.

I think so. Because that's exactly what I see in Ethan's eyes now, as his gaze shifts from Claire to me. And the feeling grows even stronger when he walks toward me, brushes a strand of hair from my face, and gently lets his fingers glide across my cheek.

Murmurs spread through the room—maybe there's laughter, maybe even whistles. Claire might be saying something, I don't know, and it doesn't matter at all.

I wrap my arms around his neck, rise onto my tiptoes, and do what I've been yearning to do longer than I've been willing to admit to myself.

I kiss him. Right here in Halifax Harbor Hospital, in front of the entire team, I kiss him until I can't breathe.

"The meeting is over." Claire sounds distant, even though she's standing right next to us. "Back to work, we've got a lot to do."

I feel Ethan's mouth curl into a smile against my lips. "Those are the exact words I used to end my inaugural speech."

Whatever happened over the past few weeks didn't just change Ethan and me—it changed Claire too.

I pull away from him. "And now?" I ask softly. "Are you going to become a pro surfer after all?"

He shakes his head. "Much better..."

Epilogue

SONORA

Three months later

Ethan beams at me. "Ready?"

I can barely breathe, but I nod. "Let's do this."

He reaches out his hand to me, I take it, and together we step through the door leading into the largest lecture hall at Dalhousie University. The sight of the auditorium completely takes my breath away. Every single one of the four hundred seats is filled; some students are even sitting on the steps, others leaning against the wall behind the rows. Claire and Jake are up there too. He's holding her in his arms, her head resting on his shoulder.

In the front row, I spot June, Autumn, Olive, and Nyla, each of them wearing a wide grin.

Ethan steps up to the lectern and greets his students. "The woman beside me, Dr. Sonora Wells, will teach you more in the next thirty minutes than I will in the coming years," he says.

With a warm feeling in my chest, I watch him. Even

though I've already attended several of his lectures and seen how fantastic he is in his new role as a university professor, I still can't suppress the proud grin on my face today.

He's found his passion, because with what he's doing now, he's essentially saving more lives than ever before. All these students, listening to him intently as he announces the most important lesson of their lives, will be trained by him to become outstanding doctors. They'll carry his knowledge out into the world and do more good than he ever could have on his own.

"Ladies and gentlemen, please welcome: Dr. Sonora Wells." With a broad smile, he steps aside and signals that the space in front of the microphone is mine.

My roommates applaud as I step behind the lectern. Ethan's students eye me with a mix of curiosity and skepticism.

When Ethan asked me if I would speak here today in front of his students, I first thought he was joking.

"What could I possibly tell them that you couldn't convey a thousand times better?" I asked him.

"No one knows better than you how to make fate shine," was his reply, and not only did I immediately understand what he meant, I also knew I absolutely had to do it.

"Hello, I'm happy to be here," I say into the microphone now, glancing over at Ethan.

His expression is blissful, so open and full of love.

I turn to my audience. A few students whisper to each other, some are playing with their phones, but I begin anyway.

"When I was a kid, my mom and I had a dream. We wanted to live in a house with pretty curtains that fluttered in the summer breeze, windows made of real glass, and a bed of our own for each of us."

I can see confusion on the faces of the students who've been listening to me.

"There was even a house we liked. We went there often and imagined what it would be like if we could buy it." In my mind, I'm standing once again with Mom at 523 Greenwood Ave, holding her hand, feeling her warmth. "It was nice, pretending with her that it might be possible. But the truth is, we both knew it would never be ours."

"Why not?" calls the blonde in the Gucci sweater and horn-rimmed glasses from the third row.

I look her in the eyes. "Because all we could afford was a few potatoes and Mom's drugs."

Suddenly, the lecture hall falls completely silent. The blonde stares at me, shocked. I hear a few students gasp. And that doesn't change for the next twenty minutes, as I tell my story.

"Life dealt me a shitty hand," I conclude at last.

I look over at June, who smiles at me warmly. At Nyla, who gives me a look of respect. At Olive, who blinks rapidly, and at Autumn, who beams at me.

The blonde in the third row raises her hand. I nod to her.

"And still you wanted to become a doctor?" she asks. "Weren't you afraid you'd fail?"

All at once, I feel Ethan's hand on my back. His warmth surrounds me, gives me strength. "Every single day," I reply, admitting something I hadn't even dared to admit to myself until now. "But you know what?"

"What?" She seems to hold her breath.

"We're all bound to our fates and fear, in the midst of this darkness, that we'll never find our way." I let my gaze wander meaningfully, and in every face I look at, I see the same thing: agreement.

They all know what I'm talking about because they've lived it themselves—even the blonde in the Gucci sweater who, at first glance, looks like she's living the perfect life.

"But what matters in the end isn't what happened to us," I say with gravity. "It's how we deal with it. What we make of it."

My roommates suddenly all have tears in their eyes, and I see how each of them is lost in her own thoughts—her own story and the wounds it has left behind.

"As if it were that easy," someone calls out from the back row.

"I never said it was easy," I say into the microphone. "But it's possible—and the proof is standing right in front of you today."

That's exactly why I wanted to be here today and tell my story. To show all those who doubt themselves, who are afraid they're not enough, who'd rather hide than step into the light, that anything is possible.

If a girl from the gutter, who spent her whole life lying to everyone and was completely alone, can find happiness and love, then so can they.

"Thank you for letting me share my story with you." I look out at the auditorium, invitingly. "Now, go out into the world and let your destiny shine."

With those words, I step back from the podium—there's nothing more to say. I glance at Ethan, see so much love and pride in his face, and know that all the happiness I feel right now, I owe to him.

Suddenly, I hear someone clapping. The initially hesitant applause grows louder, and moments later, the lecture hall erupts into thunderous applause.

Embarrassed, I lower my gaze to the floor.

Ethan wraps his arm around me. "They're clapping for

you," he says, gently guiding my head so I'm looking back at the audience.

It's insane. Completely surreal.

Now they're even rising from their seats, raising their hands above their heads, clapping even more fervently. Whistles and cheers ring out.

I let my gaze sweep across the auditorium, unable to believe this is really happening.

They're celebrating me.

Me, the girl from the trailer park.

Caught up in my emotional turmoil, I hardly notice Ethan pulling away from me. I only register it when he joins the applauding crowd. He's now standing right next to my roommates, and together with Olive, Nyla, June, and Autumn, he gives a slight bow. I can't help but rush toward him. He opens his arms, catches me, and spins me around.

The still-applauding students blur past my eyes like splashes of color, and behind them, the sun shines dazzlingly bright through the windows. Gradually, the colors and light melt into one another until my eyes overflow.

Ethan lowers me gently to the ground. Just like back on the roof of the Halifax Harbor Hospital, he kisses the tears from my cheeks—but something is different today. Because I'm certain that, for the first time in my life, they taste sweet.

Afterword

I admit, this time I bent the truth a little…

Because there's something in Sonora's story that doesn't align with real-life hospital practice. Maybe you even noticed it. It's not realistic for Sonora, Ethan, and Claire to perform such a wide variety of surgeries. Normally, surgeons are specialized— a brain surgeon wouldn't operate on the heart, and a trauma surgeon would treat bone fractures but not remove gallbladders.

However, I made an exception for your reading pleasure. I tried to make the medical aspects of the story as varied as possible, and I hope you'll forgive me for taking a few liberties in the name of drama.

But that wasn't the only challenge with this book.

There was something that gave me sleepless nights— Sonora's heart surgery and the fact that all the stories in the Halifax Harbor Hospital series take place at the same time. I didn't want this operation to be spoiled in June's, Autumn's, Nyla's, or Olive's books, but at the same time, it would've been unrealistic for such a major event to pass unnoticed by her friends. I was close to scrapping Sonora's heart issue altogether when the saving idea came to me: Sonora's story is the longest of the five books. The stories of the other four doctors end before Sonora's surgery. So if you were wondering while reading why this pivotal moment in Sonora's life doesn't appear in the other books in the series—now you know ;).

The fact that two doctors meet here also meant I had to include more technical terms in the dialogue. After all, surgeons don't explain medical terminology to each other, do they? For those who'd like to look up the terms, you'll find a glossary on the following pages this time.

But now it's time to say thank you. Without the people who have stood unwaveringly by my side for years, none of this would mean anything. A thousand thanks to my family, to the tireless book professionals, test readers, bloggers, and release helpers—now so many that I can no longer name each one individually. I'm at a loss for words to express how deeply grateful I am.

But most of all, I want to thank *you*—for buying, reading, and maybe even loving this book.

Glossary

Acute appendicitis: a sudden inflammation of the appendix, often accompanied by abdominal pain, nausea, and fever.

Acute abdomen: a sudden onset of severe abdominal pain that may indicate a serious condition within the abdominal cavity.

Acute pancreatitis: a sudden inflammation of the pancreas, often involving severe upper abdominal pain, nausea, and fever.

Adderall: a combination of amphetamine and dextroamphetamine. It's commonly prescribed to treat ADHD.

Addison's disease: a rare condition in which the adrenal glands produce too little of essential hormones (e.g., cortisol).

Aneurysm: a bulge or weakening in the wall of a blood

vessel. It may go unnoticed but can cause life-threatening bleeding if it ruptures.

Aorta: the largest artery in the body. It carries oxygen-rich blood from the heart to the entire body and branches into smaller vessels to supply organs and tissues.

Aortic aneurysm: an enlargement or bulging of the aorta (main artery) caused by a weakness in the vessel wall.

Aortic replacement: a surgical procedure in which a damaged section of the main artery (aorta) is replaced with an artificial or biological prosthesis.

Aortic valve: a heart valve located between the left ventricle (heart chamber) and the aorta.

Aortic root: the section at the beginning of the aorta that is directly connected to the left ventricle (heart chamber) of the heart.

Aortic wall: the wall of the aorta, the largest artery in the body, which carries blood from the heart to the rest of the body.

Ascending aorta: the upward section of the main artery (aorta) that transports blood from the heart to the body.

ASD: Atrial septal defect. A congenital defect characterized by a hole in the wall between the atria.
Atrial walls: the walls of the two upper chambers of the heart.

Autonomic nervous system: A part of the nervous system that automatically regulates body functions we do not consciously control, such as heartbeat, breathing, digestion, and blood pressure.

Bilateral hernioplasty: a surgical procedure used to treat inguinal hernias on both sides of the body.

Bile ducts: a network of tubes that transport bile from the liver to the gallbladder and eventually into the small intestine.

Butylscopolamine: a medication used to relieve cramp-like abdominal pain and gastrointestinal discomfort.

Cholecystitis: an inflammation of the gallbladder, often caused by gallstones.

Chronic: a term used to describe a disease or health condition that persists over a long period or recurs repeatedly.

CT scan: Computed tomography. A medical imaging procedure that uses X-rays taken from multiple angles to create detailed cross-sectional images (slices) of organs and tissues.

Dehydration: a condition in which the body lacks enough fluid to function properly.

Diastolic blood pressure: the lower value in a blood pressure reading, measuring the pressure in the arteries when the heart is resting between beats.

Dislocated shoulder: a condition in which the upper arm

bone (humerus) has slipped out of its normal position in the shoulder joint.

Distal humerus fracture: a break in the lower part of the upper arm bone (humerus), near the elbow.

DNA replication: the process by which a cell creates an exact copy of its entire genetic material (DNA).

ECG: Electrocardiogram. A procedure used to measure the electrical activity of the heart.

Electrolytes: Minerals in the body that carry an electric charge and are essential for normal bodily functions.

Enzyme: A protein that accelerates or enables chemical reactions in the body.

Epigastrium: The upper part of the abdomen, located directly below the breastbone.

Epilepsy: A neurological disorder characterized by uncontrolled electrical discharges in the brain.

Fentanyl: A powerful synthetic painkiller that belongs to the group of opioids.

Fluoroscopic guidance: an imaging technique that uses real-time X-rays to visualize internal structures of the body.

Fracture: a break or crack in a bone, which can result from injury, excessive strain, or an illness.

Gallstones: solid deposits that form in the gallbladder and consist of components found in bile.

Heart rate: the number of heartbeats per minute.

Heart attack: a condition in which part of the heart muscle dies because it is no longer adequately supplied with oxygen due to a blocked or narrowed coronary artery.

Heart-lung machine: a medical device that takes over the functions of the heart and lungs during heart surgery.

Heart sound component: The heart sounds heard during auscultation of the heart with a stethoscope consist of several components. The first heart sound (S1) and the second heart sound (S2) are the main components that reflect the cardiac cycle.

Hodgkin's lymphoma: a form of cancer that affects the lymphatic system, including the lymph nodes and lymphatic tissue in the body.

Inferior pancreaticoduodenal artery: an artery that supplies blood to the lower part of the pancreas and the duodenum.

Intravenous: the administration of fluids, medications, or nutrients directly into a vein.

Intracranial hemorrhage: bleeding in the brain, which occurs either within the brain tissue or in the area between the meninges.

Irreversible: a condition or change that cannot be undone or cured.

Ischemia time: the period during which a tissue or organ does not receive sufficient oxygen and nutrients due to disrupted or interrupted blood supply.

Laparoscopic instruments: specialized tools used in laparoscopy (also known as "keyhole surgery").

Leukemia: a group of cancers affecting the blood-forming system, characterized by the excessive production of abnormal white blood cells.

Myocarditis: an inflammation of the heart muscle, which can be caused by an infection—often viral—or by other factors such as autoimmune diseases or medications.

Myocardial injuries: injuries to the heart muscle (myocardium).

Oxygen saturation: indicates the percentage of hemoglobin in the blood that is bound to oxygen. Hemoglobin is a protein in red blood cells that transports oxygen from the lungs to the tissues.

Perforated gallbladder: a condition in which the gallbladder develops a hole or tear, allowing bile to leak into the abdominal cavity.

Perforated gastric ulcer: a stomach ulcer that becomes so deep it creates a hole in the wall of the stomach or duodenum.

Peritonitis: an inflammation of the peritoneum, the thin membrane that covers the internal abdominal organs.

Pulmonary valve: a heart valve located between the right ventricle and the pulmonary artery.

Renal cyst: a fluid-filled sac or pouch that forms in the kidney.

Stroke: occurs when the blood supply to a part of the brain is suddenly interrupted. This causes brain cells to be deprived of oxygen and nutrients, which can lead to cell death.

Systolic blood pressure: the higher value in a blood pressure reading, measuring the pressure in the arteries when the heart contracts and pumps blood into the arteries.

Tachycardia: an abnormally rapid heart rate, typically exceeding 100 beats per minute.

Ulnar nerve: a nerve that runs along the arm and primarily supplies the muscles of the forearm and hand.

Vital signs: important measurements that indicate a patient's state of health and are regularly monitored to assess life and health status.

Next in the Halifax Harbor Hospital Series

vinci-books.com/MiracleGlow

Some wounds heal. Others make you fall.

I've spent years hiding behind a smile at Halifax Harbor Hospital, pouring my heart into my patients. Then I meet Tay, a guarded father whose pain mirrors my own. Drawn together despite every reason not to, we must risk everything… or lose love forever.

Turn the page for a free preview…

Miracle Glow: Prologue

AUTUMN

Sometimes you meet someone who puts the broken pieces of you back together, only to lose them again. Sometimes miracles glow in our hearts, only to ultimately yield to the darkness. What remains is the realization that it was never a miracle—just a fleeting moment we desperately mistook for one.

Until this morning, I still wanted to believe that Tay and I had a future, but now there's no hope left.

I turn to him and see in his eyes that he has already known it for a long time too. A mix of despair, longing, and pain is reflected in his expression. He cups my face in his hands, and I do the same to him. We hold on to each other, even though we both know we've already lost one another.

"I'm so sorry," he repeats tonelessly. The wind carries his words away, far out to sea.

How could this have happened?

How is it possible that the only man in this world who makes me feel whole, the man who loves me despite everything that isn't perfect about me, the man who made me believe in miracles again—how is it possible that this man is slipping away from me?

His thumbs gently stroke my cheeks. "In a few years, we might get another chance."

Years? That's hundreds of weeks in which we won't be close to each other even once. Thousands of days I'll have to fall asleep and wake up without him.

"You'd be willing to wait that long?" I look deep into his eyes.

His expression turns serious. "I would wait for you until the end of time."

"So would I." My lips curl into a wistful smile. My heart doesn't know whether to break from sadness or burst from love. This moment is bittersweet, and yet it is and remains a goodbye.

"Kiss me," he pleads longingly. "Kiss me one last time."

Miracle Glow: Chapter One

AUTUMN

One and a half weeks earlier

The problem with wounds isn't the pain, but the fact that they leave scars when they heal. They're like letters, words, and lines of an ugly story that life burns deep into our skin without asking for permission. Doctors don't feel responsible for how we deal with them, how we manage to move on, how we find our way back to a happy life. They declare us "healthy," discharge us to a place they call "home," and rush off to fix the next patient.

It's time to change that, and today I'm taking the first step.

"Dr. Autumn Hall?"

The female voice startles me. I push my red hair just far enough out of my face to see the tall woman with the asymmetrical bob and teddy bear earrings. In the breast pocket of her lab coat is a pen with an oversized pink tassel.

Dr. Abby Parker—the woman I hope will soon be my boss.

I jump up from my chair. "Nice to meet you."

She waves me into her office. "Come in, come in, have a seat. Would you like something to drink? Water or coffee? We're out of milk, unfortunately, but you can have sugar if you'd like."

A bit overwhelmed by her boundless energy, I slide into the chair she offers me. "No, thank you, I'm fine."

"But it's going to take a little while, you should know that. You'll have to answer some questions—I want to find out everything about you." She whirls through the simply furnished office, past the bookshelf where a teddy bear crouches in the corner wearing a surgical mask, eyeing me with its dark button eyes. "You know what? I'll just get you a glass of water."

And just like that, she's gone. Dazed, I look around. My gaze lands on a copy of People Magazine on her desk. Tay Lawson beams from the cover.

Everything about him is perfect. The jawline, the dark eyes, the lips, the teeth. His broad shoulders, the chest muscles peeking out from the V-neck of his shirt, the muscular arms—even his fingers are perfect. Every single one of them.

I catch myself imagining how flawless every millimeter of his body must be. A painful tightness spreads in my chest. To distract myself, I read the headline.

Hollywood star takes a break while renovating his Los Angeles mansion.

I flip open the magazine, studying the pictures of his dream villa in the Hollywood Hills, as well as shots of him and his stunningly attractive wife on the red carpet. He's in a suit, she in a low-cut dress, both glowing with happiness. The next page is filled with photos of him lounging casually on a designer chair, apparently answering the questions printed alongside in the interview.

People Magazine: Your holiday starts tomorrow. You'll need it—after all, your last film was a total flop. How much did that hurt?

Tay Lawson (smiling wryly): Not in the slightest.

Once again, I look at one of the photos. He really doesn't look unhappy or wounded.

People Magazine: That's hard to believe, especially since it's obvious how much heart and soul you poured into that role.

Oh yes, I saw the movie. The pain of the male protagonist was so palpable, so real.

Tay Lawson (laughs): I'm just an excellent actor.

He certainly is. Unbelievable that it was all just acting—what a talent!

People Magazine: But the fact that you have no chance at an Oscar nomination for this role must be devastating for you. And now your biggest rival, Scott Pears, has been nominated. He's already snatched the award from you once before—you must be frustrated.

Tay Lawson (smiles): He's a great actor who deserves the Oscar.

And he's got a big heart, too.

Out of nowhere, Dr. Parker sets a glass of water in front of me. "Are you a fan?" She nods toward the open magazine. "He's pretty hot, isn't he? I certainly wouldn't kick him out of bed. And you?"

I quickly close the magazine. "I like his movies," I reply evasively to her more than inappropriate question.

She sighs, as if I've ruined her fun. "All right then, let's get started—we've got no time to waste, right?" With a flourish, she walks around the desk. No sooner has she sat down than she props her head in her hands and raises her perfectly arched brows. "So, why pediatrics? What is it about working with the little rascals that fascinates you enough to choose this specialty?"

Those are the questions I want to hear. The ones that, unlike those in People Magazine, truly matter to me.

"Sick children need special protection, and as a doctor, I can give them that." Instinctively, I think back to the time when I was a patient myself. So many years have passed, yet I still feel the same loneliness that was always with me despite the bustle. I feel the fear, taste the bitterness of unspoken questions, hear the medical terms doctors and nurses used to discuss my progress as if I weren't even there. "I want to be there for them, want to make sure that—no matter why we're treating them—they can smile." Openly and honestly. Because they're happy, not to please someone else.

Dr. Parker laughs. "Wow, that was very dramatic, Dr. Hall. You've rehearsed that well, but I must admit it sounded very convincing."

Of course it did, because it's nothing but the truth. I let her see that now with my expression. "Pediatrics is also a fascinating field," I continue, straightening my back. "Pediatric medicine is a broad discipline that encompasses many different aspects of medicine. This interdisciplinarity is a challenge I'm eager to take on."

Her expression brightens as she taps her chin with her index finger. "All right then, show me what you've got. How would you treat a child with pneumonia?"

Over the next seventy minutes, Dr. Parker grills me more intensely than any of my professors ever did at Dalhousie University, but I answer each of her questions with the utmost professionalism. I give it my all, because this job is the best possible next step toward my goal.

"And finally: Where do you see yourself in ten years?" she asks me at last.

In my own children's clinic, where not only wounds are

healed, but the little ones also learn to live with the scars that will forever be a part of them.

In exactly the place I would have needed back then to avoid becoming the monster I am today.

"Wherever I can best help sick children," I reply vaguely —after all, today is about the job as a pediatric specialist.

She studies me a little longer than necessary. "And that's here at Halifax Harbor Hospital," she says suddenly. "Welcome to the team, Dr. Hall."

I got the job? Wow, that was fast.

A little firework explodes in my chest, and I reach out my hand to her. "Wonderful, I'm looking forward to working with you."

"Likewise." She signals for me to stand up from my chair. "Now, do the following: go down to HR and sign your employment contract. We'll see each other tomorrow at seven o'clock on the ward, bright and early."

I'll have to get used to her waterfall-like way of speaking, but that's no problem. I got the job—that's all that matters.

"Wait, take this with you." She now pulls the pen with the pink tassel from the breast pocket of her coat and hands it to me. "Everyone here has one, it's important. The kids like it, and you want the little ones to smile—this is perfect for that."

Yes, I do want that, but not because I have a funny pen that distracts them from their worries, but because they have none—or at least fewer. Still, I take the pen; it seems important to her.

I thank her and head to the HR office. On the way, I text the good news first to my mom, then to Sonora, who's starting her job as a surgeon at Halifax Harbor with a night shift tomorrow and is currently painting the living room of our newly founded shared apartment. Mom sends me a hug emoji back, Sonora a high five.

It takes a whole hour before I've signed the papers and received an initial orientation. When I finally get home and open the door to the apartment, I'm greeted not only by an adventurous mix of pizza and fresh paint smells but also by exuberant laughter. Are all four of my roommates already here?

"You're seriously the only person who doesn't eat takeout pizza with their fingers," I hear Nyla, who starts in the ER tomorrow, say amusedly, and I smile to myself because I know she can only mean one of us: Olive, our always-perfect glamour lady with a cleanliness obsession.

"Order is essential. You'll all thank me soon enough when I make sure this apartment doesn't descend into chaos," Olive replies right on cue.

"Hello?" I call out, making my way through the towers of moving boxes.

"Hey there," June calls back—she had her job interview in the diagnostics department today.

I walk down the hallway and find Nyla, Olive, and June in what will be our future living room, where Sonora has clearly done a stellar job painting. The dusty pink is fantastic, and once all the paint splatters are scraped off the floor, the plastic sheeting removed, and the furniture in place, this will be a great spot for the five of us to unwind after work at Halifax Harbor Hospital.

As I step into the room, I pull my employment contract out of my pocket. "Got it!" I shout, prompting cheers all around.

Nyla claps so enthusiastically that her oversized earrings

swing back and forth. Warmth floods her elfin features, and her big, doe-like eyes sparkle. June sets her slice of pizza aside to applaud as well. With her high ponytail, blue eyes, and small nose, she looks like a Barbie doll. Olive, whose Marlene Dietrich-style trousers make her look more like a glossy magazine cover model than an ICU doctor, nods at me approvingly.

Immediately, I feel my cheeks flush with joy. "Is there any Margherita?" I ask, eyeing the pizza boxes stacked on top of a pile of moving crates.

"What do you think?" June gestures for me to help myself.

As I reach for a slice, the fifth member of our group enters the living room—our surgeon Sonora, pressing both hands against her stomach. Wet strands of hair cling to her dark curls. "I think I've had enough pizza for today," she groans, joining us.

Smiling, I settle into a cross-legged position on the floor and take a bite of my pizza. Nyla studies the food selection like she's making a life-or-death decision. Olive pushes aside the clear plastic cover on the sofa and pats down the cushion before sitting.

I watch the scene thoughtfully. We're all doctors, we all studied together, and now we're all starting a new chapter at Halifax Harbor Hospital. Still, the question of whether it was the right move to leave home and move in with the girls keeps nagging at me. Even though Mom's response to the news that I got the job gave no reason for concern, I'll call her after dinner. I need to be sure she's okay, that she can manage without me.

"You know what?" June, who has since let down her ponytail, lets her gaze wander around the group.

"Waf?" I ask with my mouth full.

A warm smile creeps across June's face. "I think this is going to be amazing," she says, voicing exactly what I am hoping for.

About the Author

Belinda Benna is an award-winning author whose moving romance novels are filled with emotion, allowing you to lose yourself between the lines and find yourself at the same time.

Experience stories that will make you cry, laugh, and fall in love—each with a message that will stay with you for a long time.

www.ingramcontent.com/pod-product-compliance
Lightning Source LLC
La Vergne TN
LVHW030916080826
845145LV00013B/2915

9781036727369